# The Thief's Daughter

# The Thief's Daughter

## Victoria Cornwall

*Where heroes are like chocolate – irresistible!*

Published 2017 by Choc Lit Limited

Penrose House, Crawley Drive, Camberley, Surrey GU15 2AB, UK

www.choc-lit.com

A CIP catalogue record for this book is available
from the British Library

ISBN 978-1-78189-397-5

Printed and bound by Clays Ltd

*A loving, supportive family provides a firm
foundation on which to build the rest of our lives.*

*I would like to dedicate* The Thief's Daughter
*to my parents for the unwavering love, support
and guidance they have given me.*

# Acknowledgements

There are many people who have supported me through the writing process and along the journey to publication. I have been enthusiastically questioned by friends, family and acquaintances and received many words of encouragement and praise. Their remarks may have been made in passing, but their interest in my writing was more precious to me than they will ever know.

I would particularly like to thank my daughter, Jade. One summer, over a Cornish cream tea, she patiently listened to the storyline of my first novel and instantly became my most enthusiastic and helpful supporter. Thank you, Jade. Your opinion, and the interest you have shown in my work ever since, are greatly appreciated.

I would also like to thank the Romantic Novelists' Association. Their New Writers' Scheme assessor advised me to submit *The Thief's Daughter* to a publisher and gave me the push I needed.

Finally, I would like to thank Choc Lit and the Choc Lit tasting panel, who believed in my novel and recommended it for publication. You have turned me into a traditionally published author and made my dream come true. Yet, at this very important moment when I have a chance to thank you, I cannot find the right words to truly express my gratitude and joy. So I will just say 'thank you' from the bottom of my heart to: Sheila S, Victoria G, Alma H, Sarah C, Lizzy D, Jenny K, Ester V, Rosie F, Kathleen A, Stacey R and Jo O.

# Prologue

*1765, Cornwall*

As quietly as she could, Jenna slowly released the breath she was holding; instinctively her body sucked in another. Her eyes widened in fear at the sound of her soft gasp. Did he hear her? She prayed he did not.

She could hear the man's boots pacing the floorboards in the adjoining room. His boots are muddy, she thought, hearing the grit on his soles scoring the wood beneath. Frightened, she remained silent and hidden, not breaking her cover even when she heard her mother and father begin their cursing. It did no good, more boots arrived and her parents were forced away.

Jenna hugged her knees to make herself smaller. She stared at her little toes, as she felt the vibration from his footsteps through her feet. The vibration grew as the boots came into the room and she tried to shrink even smaller. She fought to control her silent, shallow breaths, while the rest of her body froze with fear. She was cocooned in her hiding place, scared of being found, yet inside her heart hammered loudly as if daring to be heard. She hoped she would wake up and discover it was all just a bad dream. And she was safe. And her brothers and parents were too. But it was happening and the fear she felt was real. Her head began to throb and tingle as she listened to the grit scratch the floorboards with each step. Mother will be angry when she finds out he is ruining her floor, thought Jenna. Such a silly thought, considering the circumstances.

The man shouted and more boots entered the room.

He had found what he was looking for: her brother, Paul. A scuffle broke out between them, more cursing, more shouting and more mud on mother's floor. It sounded like Paul was putting up a fight. It did not surprise her; he always said he would if the man came to get him. A valiant attempt, but Jenna knew that his resistance would do no good. Only moments before they had taken David and he was the strongest of all her brothers. This morning everything had been normal, now she had lost two of them and everything had changed. And she might be next.

For a moment there was silence, but even so, Jenna dared not move. She would wait until her mother came to get her, just as her parents had told her to do. The sound of a man's boots returned to the room again. She strained to listen for the noise of the grit. She could not hear it. Had it worked loose or was it her father?

The footsteps stopped before her. The silence that followed felt heavy and her legs began to tremble, causing the pile of clothes that covered her to shake too. The slight tremor was enough to give her away. A large, thick-fingered hand reached underneath and grabbed her bare foot, pulling her roughly out into the daylight and causing her dress to ride up behind her head and expose her knees. She lay stiff and motionless at his feet, like a submissive dog, waiting to be slayed. 'Hide from the thief-taker,' her parents had told her, 'for if he finds you, he will take you away.'

The man looked down on her. His dirty beard covered his lips and hid any expression of a smile he may have had at finding a four-year-old child at his feet. He reached down and grabbed her clothing. His fist twisted in the cloth of her dress as he lifted her off the floor. Her face came level with his. As her bare, grimy feet dangled in the air, she dared to look into his face and saw there was no smile.

'Do I scare you, child?' he asked her menacingly. 'Do I make you want to weep?' He gave her a little shake, making her body sway in the air. His breath smelt of rotten eggs and she could see her frightened face reflected in his bloodshot eyes. Struck dumb with fear, she was unable to answer him. 'Remember what it is like to be caught by a man such as me.' He looked down at her thin body dressed in rags. 'Your family has bad blood running through them and you will turn out the same if you don't mind your ways. If you don't, we will seek you out and hunt you down.' He held her closer until she could feel his breath on her face. 'Remember, child, we will watch you as you grow, and one day a thief-taker will come calling and he will take you away.'

Satisfied with his warning, he opened his fist and Jenna dropped to the floor like a stone, where she lay twisted on the wooden floor, too scared to move and too frightened to weep. Time seemed to stretch and play a peculiar game, for Jenna had gained a grave worldliness that she had not possessed only minutes before. A strange, solemn numbness engulfed her like a shield and the feeling remained until she finally felt the vibration of the floor against her cheek and heard his boots walk away.

Jenna remained silent and still for some time, until another child's hand slipped into hers and broke the fear that had frozen her. She clutched it and turned, burying her face into their grasped hands. Silas was the only brother she had left. His hand gave her comfort and finally she allowed herself to weep.

# Chapter One

A crowd of people was gathering at the crossroads. The mood was jovial and the expectation was high. Hoping to take advantage of the potential trade, hawkers hastily set up their stalls to display their wares, while barefoot urchins played chase games through the throng of waiting people. As pleasantries were exchanged between neighbours and spontaneous laughter broke forth, a foreigner to these parts would be forgiven for thinking a travelling theatre had arrived to entertain the folk of Cambryn. That assumption would not be unwise, until one learnt the local name for the site or saw the old, well-used gibbet in the place of a stage.

The site was on the outskirts of the small market town and was aptly named Deadman's End. The gibbet overshadowed a point where three tracks met, acting as a warning to any who passed that way and considered breaking the law. It had been used for hanging criminals for as long as anyone could remember, its macabre use becoming part of the normal fabric of countryside life. Stealing property, even just a loaf of bread to ward off starvation, was considered particularly heinous by the property-owning lawmakers of the land. Today, in this hour, it was a poacher's time to die.

Jack Penhale watched from the shadows as he leaned against the remnants of a medieval boundary wall further up the hill. He usually avoided hangings as it was not a form of punishment he could detach himself from. The dead man's dance, the jerking and twisting for several minutes as he died, Jack found grotesque to watch. Yet he understood why the crowd sought some fun here today. Forms of entertainment to take them away from their hardships and poverty were in short supply, and to relish in a criminal's demise distanced them from their own wrongdoings. He did not blame the crowd for their voyeurism; it was the same in every town where hangings were held. Hanging and entertainment were sleazy bedfellows and he could not see it changing in the foreseeable future. For a man who disliked hanging, Jack would have liked two other men to die by Mr Gibbet today: Amos and Job Blake, known locally as simply the Blake brothers.

Amos and Job were built of solid muscle and sinew, had long, scraggy beards and a notorious reputation for thuggery. In recent years they had added smuggling to their crimes. Yet despite their involvement being common knowledge in the area, no man was willing to bear witness to their crimes for fear of retribution. Jack would have liked to see them brought to trial, but with no one courageous enough to speak against them, there was little hope of this happening and that frustrated Jack greatly. To onlookers Jack looked relaxed, almost disinterested, as he bit into his meat pie, but unlike the crowd below him, he was not happy.

There was a shout from the crowd. The cart carrying the poacher had been spotted lumbering its way along the bumpy track. Expectant faces craned their necks to get a better view, while others jeered at the shackled prisoner in the cart. Jack did not know the poacher, but it appeared he was not a popular man. Although poaching was a hanging offence, judges usually showed leniency and sentenced them to long gaol sentences. Not in this case, it seemed. This man, with brutish fists and a face more worn than his thirty years, had a history, and he was to pay on the end of a rope. No wailing relatives accompanied him. No tankard of ale was offered by a landlord en route. No mercy was to be shown. Yet the poacher did not show any fear. To the contrary, he swore and spat back at the crowd, almost relishing in his own demise. His lack of fear and remorse buoyed the crowd even more, and their insults grew.

Jack's attention was taken by a shadowy movement beside him, and for the first time he noticed a small boy with sunken eyes watching him. His feet were bare, his skin grimy and the ragged clothes he wore were too small for his skinny frame. Malnourishment made him look younger than he probably was, and Jack felt sorry for him. He knew from experience what it was like to have no money coming into the home and the pain of a hungry belly. Although his circumstances had changed, the county remained littered with children who were no more than bones draped in dirty cloth. Jack tossed him the remainder of his pie.

'Go home,' he said kindly to the boy as he watched the eager hands catch the food in mid-air. 'This is no place for a child.' Without taking his eyes off the dark stranger, the boy bit into the pie before running away.

Jack turned his attention back to the entertainment below him. The cart was now positioned below the gibbet, and a man of God was reciting some carefully chosen words. The poacher had finally quietened, his bravado deserting him at the sight of the rope. The crowd surged forward to get a better view before falling silent to listen to the final prayer. Jack noticed the poacher was not praying, instead his eyes darted around the crowd as if he was looking for someone. The hangman stood beside him, waiting for silence and holding the white hangman's hood in his hands. Next to him, Jack believed, was a surgeon's assistant with a warrant in his hand. It appeared some good would come from the poacher's life after all, as his dead body was to be claimed for dissection.

The poacher stopped searching the crowd and Jack, his interest piqued, tried to see who he was looking at, but the crowd was too thick and he could not make out who his target was. The preacher had stopped talking and the white hood was quickly pulled over the man's head. Jack saw the poacher smile before his face was hidden. He would never see the world again, thought Jack, yet whomever he had spied in the crowd had given him some comfort.

The rope was hastily placed over his head and around his neck. Fear had returned and his body went rigid as he resisted the guard's hands guiding him towards the edge of the cart. He began to shake. No time must be wasted now. A signal was given for the cart to move forward. The horse whinnied and strained at its harness. The cartwheels began to turn. There was no drop to kill the man outright. The slack in the rope was small and as the floor of the cart withdrew from his feet, he was forced to take another step forward towards the edge. The poacher hesitated, resisted, stumbled and stepped into the air. The dead man's dance had begun.

Suddenly there was jostling in the crowd. A youth broke free and ran towards the gibbet. Before anyone could stop him, he climbed the cart, took aim and leapt into the air. He grabbed the jigging body with both arms. The rope, and his extra weight, succeeded in breaking the poacher's neck. His death was instantaneous and his body grew still.

Jack pushed himself away from the wall and braced himself. An unhealthy silence had descended and the atmosphere became tense. The crowd's entertainment had come to an abrupt end because of the boy's actions, as the dead man would dance no more. The boy continued to hold on tightly to ensure his job was well done. His own feet hung precariously in the air, his face hidden tight in the poacher's body. An angry roar erupted from the gathering, pulling the boy from his focus. He let go, dropped to the ground and took off as fast as he could.

From the top of the hill, Jack watched as the boy tried to get away, but it soon became clear he was in danger. The crowd's jovial mood had indeed changed, and they wanted the boy punished. Several men tried to grab him as he ran past, a woman hit his shoulder as he darted by. A tankard was thrown through the air in his direction, but it missed its target as the boy was too fast for the drunkard's aim. Word travelled to cut off his means of escape and the crowd worked as one and closed in on him until his body disappeared under a pile of moving rags. Jack's eyes narrowed in concern; he was too far away to be of any immediate assistance, but his thoughts were too involved to walk away.

Jack could not help but admire the boy's attempts to escape. He showed determination and courage to grant the man's dying wish. He would have known that it would anger those who had travelled to watch, yet he had done it all the same. He had shown true friendship, or family loyalty, at a time when he was needed most. He must have cared for the lout very much.

He was about to set off down the hill when he spied the boy's small frame scramble in the dirt as he crawled out from between someone's legs, and ran towards the hill where Jack stood. Those few precious seconds before he was noticed gave him the advantage he so badly needed. A gap grew between the angry crowd and the boy, leaving only the fittest few to follow him. From his vantage point, Jack could see the boy's speed was diminishing. He was tiring and his remaining pursuers, young men, were gaining on him. He would not be able to outrun so many and he would soon be caught. Jack had no doubt that he would suffer the beating of his life. His concern for the lad grew. He was just a young boy on the verge of manhood and he did not deserve such hatred. The boy was almost upon him, he was stumbling, his breathing heavy, his face concealed by his overly large and battered tricorn hat. Jack grabbed his collar and pulled him aside.

'Quick, boy, over the wall,' he ordered, bending and making a stirrup with his hands. The boy hesitated. 'Quick,' said Jack again, without looking up. 'They will catch you.'

Needing no more encouragement, the boy placed his boot into his open hands and Jack lifted him up. The boy stretched upwards, his fingers grasping the top bricks of the wall. Lacking in strength, he struggled to pull himself upwards. Jack pushed the boot he held higher. 'Quick, boy. They are coming,' he urged.

The small foot, encased in a woman's boot, left his hand. Jack grabbed the ankle as he registered what he had just seen. The boy looked down in confusion and, for the first time, Jack could see his face.

Fear-filled eyes returned his gaze, her brows furrowed in concern. She looked nervously up to see the men approaching, then down at him again. His grip tightened.

Then the strangest thing happened and Jack was momentarily struck dumb. While the crowd continued to shout obscenities and bay for her blood in the distance, the woman's fear appeared to leave her face. Calmly, she looked directly back at him, with a kindness in her eyes that fear had previously concealed, and she smiled. It was a sweet smile, an inviting smile that was filled with temptation and secrets that had no business to be used at such a time or place. While his gaze lingered on her soft lips, his grip on her ankle loosened. Unnoticed, she gently eased her leg away.

A loud shout from someone brought him back to his senses. He blinked and tried to speak, but she had already gone and taken her smile with her, leaving his outstretched hands holding nothing but air. With one smile she had bewitched and disarmed him, leaving him with questions that filled his head and a need to know more about her. The men arrived and jostled him from behind.

'Have you seen the boy?' a breathless man gasped. 'He ran this way.'

Jack turned in his direction. 'I have not seen a boy run this way,' he said solemnly.

'Are you sure?' asked another.

Jack straightened his shoulders. 'I swear on my life that I have seen no boy run this way.'

Satisfied, they ran on, leaving Jack alone. It was time to go, he thought, as he had other things that needed his attention. He must not be diverted by one chance meeting with a woman he would never meet again. He had come here today to ensure he would not forget what he had failed to do: make Amos and Job Blake answer for their crimes. The poacher and his friend had nothing to do with him. Yet as he collected his horse and made his way home, the woman's face lingered in his mind, long after he resolved to forget about her. He had started the day not a happy man, but now, he realised, his mood had subtly changed. He smiled to himself as he looked down at his muddy palms. The change in his state of mind, he believed, happened when a woman's boot was placed in his open hands.

# Chapter Two

Jenna walked briskly along the narrow road searching for the address she had been given. She asked for directions several times, and although everyone claimed to know the location of the debtors' prison, their explanations of how to get there were at best confusing, at worst inaccurate. The warren of narrow streets, and the astonishment expressed by many of the people she asked that she did not know its location, added to her embarrassment and eventual reluctance to ask for further help.

She finally found it by accident when she came upon a single door in a long brick wall, with heavy hinges and a barred window. A badly painted sign was nailed to the wall beside it, but as Jenna could not read, it was no help at all. Thankfully, two sparsely clothed children, who were squatting on the ground underneath it, confirmed she had found what she was looking for. Jenna reached into the basket of food she was carrying and broke off a piece of bread to give to them.

'Thank you,' she said, holding it out to them. Wary, sunken eyes looked up at her. 'Take it,' she urged. 'It is a gift for your help.'

The eldest child tentatively took it from her and, as if fearful Jenna would take it back, quickly grasped the younger child's hand and made good their escape. Jenna watched until the boy and girl disappeared from her view, before turning her attention back to the plain-looking door.

The people of Goverek called it 'The Hole in the Wall'. The nickname suited it well as its nondescript entrance swallowed up those whose creditors had taken action against them. Men and women, sometimes whole families, disappeared behind its thick wooden door. Without a means to pay or earn a living, there was every chance that they may not emerge again for many years. Their only hope was to rely on the goodwill of family or friends to get them out, and as Jenna's brother had very few friends or family left in the area, the burden lay with her.

She knocked and a gruff voice answered within. After explaining who it was she hoped to visit, the keeper opened the door and held out his hand. Jenna placed a penny in his grimy palm, then silently followed him into the dark, narrow passageway beyond.

The air in the open passage smelt foul. The stony walls were damp and the absence of sunlight allowed green algae to grow rampantly in the shadows. Water trickling down the high walls and the sound of a rodent shuffling away in the distance accompanied their echoing footsteps. Jenna was thankful when the passageway ended and opened up into a narrow yard with irregular buildings sited haphazardly around it. Jenna looked up at the three-storey buildings, which must cast a chilling shadow over the yard for most of the day. The building on the right appeared the best maintained.

'Is my brother in that one?' she asked hopefully.

The keeper spat on the floor before answering, 'Debtors who have family willing to pay for better food and rooms are housed on the Master's side.' He gave her a sidelong glance. 'Debtors who have no one to help them are housed on the left – the common side.' The keeper nodded to one of the buildings on the left. 'Your brother's in there.'

Jenna looked at it and her heart sank. The building, with its lopsided roof and walls, appeared to defy gravity. If it did not fall down on its own accord within the next year, thought Jenna, it ought to be demolished to prevent a tragedy occurring.

The predicament her brother was in suddenly became real to her and she shivered. This was her first visit and payment. Unfortunately, she had no more money to give to help improve her brother's comfort. The basket she held, which she hoped would supplement his meagre rations, now seemed inadequate.

This morning she had visited her brother's home in the hope he would help her. Instead of a welcome from his thin little wife and children, she discovered them gone and another family moving in. It was only then that she learnt of his imprisonment. The man she hoped would help her, it seemed, needed help himself.

Jenna entered the building that the keeper had indicated. She was aware that places such as this were run by the prisoners themselves, with the expected undercurrent of internal hierarchy, rules, noisy squabbles and discourse, but she was still ill-prepared for what she saw.

The smell hit her first. It was a mixture of body odour, musky damp and stale air that seemed to cling to the back of her throat like a leech. For a moment she could not see, but gradually her eyes became accustomed to the dimly lit room. Twenty, maybe thirty inhabitants began to appear before her like ghosts. The noise was louder than she expected, as tempers were quick to flare and arguments appeared to require little provocation.

The room itself was large and sparse of furniture, with a grey slate floor that held in the cold. A single, barred window allowed a hefty draught into the room, but did little to rid the place of its smell. Jenna looked up and saw the ceiling was stained by damp, decorating the planks of wood with veins of mould and fungi that moved with the vibrations of the inhabitants above. In the far corner was a rickety wooden ladder in the place of a flight of stairs. It did not look strong enough to support the weight of one climber let alone all those who lived here.

Jenna tried not to show the horror she was feeling as she instinctively clutched her basket tighter and looked around her. Despite its great size, the degree of overcrowding, insanitary conditions and lack of provisions helped make it a noisy and squalid place to live. Men, women and children were crowded in together, some sitting in groups while others preferred their own company and huddled in a corner for warmth. Although the quality of their clothing varied, their skin shared the same sickly pallor brought on by lack of sunlight and poor nourishment, while their eyes held little hope at all. When an argument broke out beside her between two of the prisoners she almost turned and fled, but her brother saw her first and took her aside by her arm. Holding her tight, he led her to two wooden chairs and a wobbly table and gave her a hug.

'It's good to see you, Sister,' he said, squeezing her so tightly she could almost not breathe.

'Oh, Silas. This place is awful,' said Jenna. 'How are you?' She searched Silas's face for the answer. His shoulder length hair had always been scruffy, but she could tell he had lost weight from the shadows on his cheeks. He was also in need of a shave and a good wash. Something he would not get in here. 'How long have you been here?' she pressed.

'Two weeks, maybe three.' He smiled and Jenna recognised the Silas she knew. 'It is better now you are here,' he reassured her. 'Do I smell food?'

Jenna showed him her basket, which he immediately took to look through. Satisfied with its contents he gave her another lopsided grin.

'Stay here,' he told her as he picked up the basket.

Jenna tried to protest, but she was too late, he had already disappeared into the shadows at the far end of the room. She sat down and waited. Although she dared not move, her eyes remained watchful at the strange assortment of people around her. Only her hands placed on her lap hinted at her fear as she nervously rubbed the nail of one thumb with a single finger. Suddenly, she saw her brother weaving through the other inmates as he approached with an empty basket in his hand.

'Are Nell and the children here?' she asked him as he sat down opposite her and gave her the basket.

He nodded. 'I expected you sooner.'

A woman began shouting in the corner, drawing Jenna's attention. She watched, filled with concern, as the woman was hustled away by her family.

'How did you end up in here?' asked Jenna, turning back to her brother.

Silas rubbed his face with his hand. 'I owed a bit of money, here and there, and they wanted it back before I was ready to pay. They paid a bloody thief-taker to catch me, Jenna.'

Silas hated thief-takers. It was a visceral hate that had been passed down by their parents and had stayed with him and festered. Thief-takers were hired by the victims of crime to capture the perpetrator and bring them to justice. They were ordinary folk, with no special training or uniform to distinguish them, and by their very nature difficult to spot amongst the crowd. A successful thief-taker was cunning, mingled with both sides of the law, until it was time for him to catch the culprit.

Unfortunately, some thief-takers' main motivation was a financial rather than a moral one and the men who had taken it upon themselves to bring law and order to a community were often corrupt themselves. Many extorted protection money from the criminals they were supposed to catch, while others were known to claim they had witnessed a crime, accuse and arrest an innocent bystander and collect a fee for their troubles. Unlike Silas, Jenna did not hate thief-takers, but she was wary and fearful of them, and could not forget that if they had not been so good at their job, many of her family would still be around.

'I didn't know you were in here,' said Jenna. 'I only found out when I went to your house this morning.'

'Henry's parents have told you to leave, I suppose,' said Silas.

Jenna nodded. She had never liked her late husband's parents. Now that he was dead they felt no responsibility for her and wanted her gone.

'Did Henry suffer?' Silas asked.

Jenna shook her head.

'Pity. He deserved to suffer.' Silas looked up at his younger sister and narrowed his eyes. 'Oh, Jenna, tell me you did not help him on his way.'

'He asked me to. It was his dying wish. How could I refuse a dying wish?'

'The crowd may have turned nasty.'

Jenna thought of the dark stranger who had helped her escape. For a heartbeat his handsome face filled her thoughts.

'I was in no danger,' she replied absently.

'You owed him nothing,' Silas grumbled. 'Hanging was too good for the likes of him.' He leant forward so no one else could hear. 'When I saw what he did to you it near broke my heart. No one treats a Cartwright the way he treated you. Too handy with his fists, he was. I would have put a stop to it sooner if I had known.'

Jenna looked about her nervously. 'Sooner?' she whispered, leaning forward too. 'What do you mean sooner?'

Silas's eyes looked about the room aware that there were too many ears and tongues willing to talk for the price of a coin. Satisfied no one was listening, he whispered, 'Some folk may say it was bad luck that Henry went poaching the same night four gamekeepers were in the area.' He smiled, showing his blackened teeth. 'Some folk may say that it was lucky that I did not go with him.'

Jenna's eyes widened. 'You were meant to be there?'

Silas nodded. 'But I don't believe in luck, Jenna. Henry got what he had coming to him, and it worked out better than I had planned. I thought he would get time in gaol, but hanging was even better. You are free now, Jenna.' He stopped smiling. 'He would have killed you in the end if I had not done something. I had to protect you, like I always have.' Silas grinned and patted her hand. 'It is over for you. Are you not as glad as I?'

What could she say? There were many nights Jenna had lain awake praying for her marriage to end. She married in haste and far too young, believing that marriage would mean a new life for her. She was mistaken. Life with Henry was far worse than her life as a Cartwright.

Having the Cartwright name was the catalyst for her disastrous marriage. In truth, her lineage was a burden to her, as her parents hawked stolen goods for a living and her older siblings were no better. Two of her brothers, Paul and David, had been taken to Bodmin Gaol years before and had never been heard of again. Another, Mark, ran away to sea when she was a child in the hope of finding a better life. Her parents too had disappeared one day, never to return. The Cartwright reputation for lawbreaking followed her everywhere. Jenna had given up trying to recall how many jobs she had lost when it became known who her family were. She was viewed as one of them – untrustworthy and to be avoided.

So at the age of sixteen she had married Henry Kestle, with the naive belief that her life would be better when she no longer bore the surname of her parents. How wrong she was. His morals were no better and by the end of the first week she knew what it was like to be punched in the face. She spent many nights wishing he was dead. Now, God forgive her, he was. Thanks to her brother, Silas. Yet even though she had grown to hate Henry, she could not refuse his request to hasten his life at his hanging. She had taken a great risk and was almost caught, but for the help of a dark-haired stranger standing at the top of the hill.

'Well, Jenna? Are you not as glad as I that he is dead?'

'No one should be glad someone is dead, Silas, but I am glad to be free of him.'

Silas sat back in his chair, looking pleased with himself.

'Now that he is gone you already look healthier.'

'And you look paler,' said Jenna. 'It is not healthy for you and the children to be here. I will find another job and help pay your debt. Michaelmas is next week and the Mop Fayre is in town. Someone will hire me.' Silas looked uncomfortable as he rubbed his neck. She saw his discomfort. 'It is time for me to help you,' she reassured him. 'I will come again with more food and soon you will be home again.'

'You were always such a good girl,' he said pensively. 'I don't understand where you get your high morals from. Father always wondered if you were a changeling.' Jenna took the empty basket off the table and held it tightly against her. 'He couldn't understand why you were different from the rest of us. No matter how many times he taught you how to pick pockets, you would refuse to do it on the street. "There is something wrong with that girl," he would say to Mother.' Jenna lowered her eyes, waiting for him to ask her as he surely would. 'Mother would say, "She will come around. She has our blood in her veins." Will you come around, Sister? Acknowledge our blood and lift a few gentlemen's purses, like Father taught you? It will pay my debts sooner.'

Jenna looked up. 'It is tainted blood that runs through me and it's cursed me all my life. I will go to the Mop Fayre and give you my wage. I will do all I can to get you out, but I will not break the law.'

'You helped a man to die.'

'He was being put to death by the law of the land. I only eased his suffering, which is not a crime. If I am guilty of anything it was spoiling the crowd's entertainment.'

Silas nodded slowly. 'Changeling or not, you mean the world to me. I'm glad Henry's dead and I'm glad I had a part in it.' There was food waiting for him in the shadows and he had a mind to get back to it. 'It is time you left,' he said. Heavy-hearted, he stood, and so did Jenna. The room remained noisy and crowded yet it felt as though they were alone.

'I'm glad Henry's dead too,' she said quietly. 'I agreed to his dying wish but, I have to confess, I did not do it for him.'

Silas frowned and caught her arm as she turned to go. 'So why did you do it?' he asked, intrigued.

Jenna lifted her chin and looked him in the eye. 'I wanted to make sure he died.'

She watched Silas's eyes widen at the revelation. It was time to tell Silas the truth, even if she was not proud of it herself.

'I did not love him, Silas, so I had no desire to shorten

his suffering or grant him his wish. I hung onto his legs because,' she swallowed the bitter taste in her mouth, 'I wanted to make sure he would not escape. I wanted to make sure he was dead and would never hit me again.'

She saw hope in her brother's eyes and knew what he was thinking. He saw the defiant child she had once been when she stood up to her father's coercions. Only in reality the child was gone and she was no innocent – Henry had seen to that. Now he was dead and she was free to live again, scarred and bruised inwardly, but hopeful for the future.

Jenna lowered her eyes, ashamed at what her brother saw. She should not feel such joy at a man's death, particularly if the man was her husband. Suddenly, the foul stench and squalid conditions seemed to crowd in on her. She needed fresh air to cleanse her of the words she had just spoken.

'Forget what I have just said,' she said hurriedly under her breath as she picked up her basket. She attempted to feign an air of confidence. 'I promise I will do my best to get you out of here, Silas.' She looked around at the other inmates, who she could now see were no different to herself, but for their debts. She gave her brother what she hoped was a reassuring smile. 'Goodbye, Brother. I will visit you again soon.'

'I will look forward to it,' he said as she turned away and tried to walk calmly from the room.

Jenna crossed the cobbled courtyard towards the alleyway and freedom. All around her she could hear the sobs and cries of the inmates emanating out through the glassless windows and thick stone walls. The smell of unwashed bodies and damp slowly receded, but refused to go away completely. Outside the prison walls Jenna rested the back of her head against the damp wall and breathed in deeply. The taste of the stench remained in her throat and her brother's face remained behind her lids, but at least the sun now touched her skin and she knew what she must do.

Silas's face brightened as he watched his sister leave. During her brutal marriage she had wilted like a flower in a drought. The plucky Jenna of old had disappeared for a time, but the hangman's rope had finally freed her from the man she had grown to fear. Her parting words showed him that the old Jenna had returned, with a strength and attitude that could be used to his advantage. With Jenna's help, perhaps there was a chance that he could be freed from the hell he found himself in. Hole in the Wall was his prison, but Jenna was his means of escape.

# Chapter Three

Jenna smelt the succulent aroma of the pig roast as it wafted towards her. It mocked her senses, making her empty stomach rumble in protest. Nearby, laughter broke out at a puppet show, while traders bartered over their wares in the market square. Jenna ignored it all as she had more important things on her mind. This was not the first time she had been to the Mop Fayre at Goverek, but it would be the first time she waited to be hired.

Held at the end of the harvest, a Mop Fayre provided a means for agricultural workers and domestic servants to be looked over by prospective employers. The initial period for hire was one week. This enabled workers to return the following week and be rehired if the placement turned out to be unsatisfactory. If all parties were happy with the arrangement, the period lengthened to a year.

Jenna held her mop in her right hand and looked down the line of men and women on either side of her. Each person held a tool to represent their trade and from her cursory glance, she could see that she had competition. Four other women held mops too, while the men held an assortment of trade implements – one pitchfork, two blacksmith irons and one scythe. Jenna looked ahead and held her mop more tightly. She had no home, money or food in her belly and her brother's debts to pay. At her feet lay a bag containing all that she owned as she had finally left the home of her parents-in-law and did not plan to return. Everything depended on her giving the impression that she was healthy and willing to work hard. She had not eaten all day and spent almost all of her money to buy a ticket so she could take part in the hiring process. Jenna was desperate, but she was determined not to let it show on her face.

Although Jack was not a frequent visitor to the Tolbridge Inn, he sensed the tense atmosphere as soon as he entered it. Unlike many drinking houses, this one was unusually sparse of customers, and those that were present soberly stared into their ale and talked in whispers. Beads of perspiration glinted on the landlord's forehead and he appeared preoccupied as Jack asked for a tankard of ale. As he poured the drink he nervously looked over his shoulder at his wife and grown daughter. They stood stiffly, side by side, in the narrow passageway leading to the cellar stairs. They appeared to be waiting for something and were as nervous as the landlord, with their arms interlinked to provide comfort to one another. Something was not right and Jack wanted to learn more.

After tossing a coin on the counter, he sat down at a table that allowed him a good view of the women. He saw an unspoken message pass between husband and wife and suspected what it might be. Shortly afterwards, the sound of heavy, booted footsteps on the cellar stairs confirmed Jack's suspicions – the premises was being searched for smuggled goods.

Jack watched from the shadows as four preventative men emerged from the darkness of the cellars. To the relief of the women they had found nothing illicit, but Jack noticed the landlord sigh deeply as he wiped perspiration from his face with his sleeve. He shows the relief of a guilty man, thought Jack, as he nursed his ale.

'We have found nothing this time, but we will return,' the leading officer warned the landlord as he walked past him. Some customers looked up to watch him leave, but instead he chose to address the room. 'I am Captain Henley, Head of the Land Guard. My riding officers make up the preventative force that patrols the coastline in this region. I am determined to reduce the smuggling trade in the area. Does anyone here have any information that would help us?'

Someone got up and left the room, ignoring his request, whilst the few customers who had bothered to look up turned their faces away. The Captain frowned.

'If you will not speak to me, speak to Tilbury here.' One of his men stepped forward, but the customers who had chosen to remain kept their heads bowed. The captain snorted; he would get no help here. He signalled to Tilbury with a jerk of his head. 'Gather the others and leave. We will find nothing here as I suspect they have been warned we were coming.'

As he was leaving he noticed Jack for the first time. He hesitated, but Jack looked through him as he lifted his tankard and took a long drink. The captain shook his head in frustration and led the rest of his men out into the daylight.

As soon as they were gone the atmosphere changed. Laughter broke out and whispers returned to normal conversation. More customers entered and the landlord, who had been mute before, welcomed them in as if nothing was amiss. His banter ensured his customers' attention; his relief that the danger was gone was evident to all who had seen him before. Only Jack noticed his wife and daughter lift their skirts to reveal two kegs of brandy hidden beneath their petticoats.

The smuggling trade had grown over the years, helped by the government's high taxes on imported goods such as tea, cloth, wine and spirits. Only the rich were able to afford such luxuries. However, the demand for such imports remained and the free traders stepped in to dodge the taxes and make a profit.

Jack believed there were few people in Cornwall who had not made use of, or profited from, illicit contraband. He did not begrudge them their luxuries or a means to earn money to feed their families. Britain had fought many expensive wars in recent years and the burden of debt was crippling. The long talons of poverty, and the suffering it brought, could be felt and seen everywhere in the county. If the free trade meant that a child had a full belly as a result of the money his father earned as a free trader, so be it, but unfortunately Jack knew from experience that smuggling had a darker underbelly. It fed on fear and controlled by torture, and while many enjoyed and profited from the trade, there were others whose involvement was brought about by coercion from violent gangs. Gangs like the one led by the Blake brothers, who he would like to see hanged at Deadman's End.

Jack called for another drink. The landlord heard him. Smiling, he came over carrying a warm jug of ale.

'They have gone away empty-handed today,' Jack observed, attempting to engage him in conversation.

The landlord's smile faded and refused to be drawn. Silently, both men watched the ale pouring into the tankard.

Jack tried again. 'I hear smuggling is a profitable trade. I may have some money to invest. Who do I need to see?'

The landlord stopped pouring. 'That will be another halfpenny,' he said, ignoring his question. Jack took out some money, placed it on the table and pushed it towards him. The landlord reached forward for it, but Jack stopped him with his hand.

'They found nothing here,' whispered the landlord

gravely, looking nervously about him before adding, 'and you will learn nothing from me.'

Jack released him and smiled. 'I'm sorry. I thought you could help me. Forgive me, I was mistaken.'

The landlord narrowed his eyes and straightened. 'You are not from these parts,' he said.

'I'm from Zennor way.'

'An isolated place.'

'Isolation has its advantages.'

'So they say.'

Jack realised he needed to tread more softly to gain this man's trust, for the landlord had much to lose.

He took a drink and nodded in appreciation of its flavour. 'A few months ago I took over the tenancy of the Captain's Cottage and have since rented a few fields nearby.' The landlord said nothing, although Jack noticed that he did not leave. He saw this as a good sign. 'I have a mind to start a smallholding and farm the land.' Jack did not like to be untruthful, but he needed the community to feel they had nothing to fear from the stranger in their midst. Pretending to be a farmer was the best cover he could think of. At least he knew what he was talking about. 'The land on the cliff is too exposed for farming, but some of the fields sweep down to the valley and are south facing. They have rich soil and would grow a crop or two. I think I will be able to make a living in time.'

The landlord's face softened. 'An empty house soon decays over the winter,' said the landlord. 'It needs a living soul to warm its belly with a fire. You sound like you know about farming?'

'I do. My father was a farmer.'

The landlord smiled. 'Then perhaps you are not such a stranger after all. Cornwall is littered with farmers and fishermen. Have a trade in either and you will be accepted wherever you settle.'

'But I will need to earn the odd penny from elsewhere until it is up and running.' Jack noticed the smile slip away from the landlord's face once again. He must be more patient, he told himself, and not press further. He smiled. 'There is a strong community in these parts,' he said, changing the subject yet again. 'I saw the hanging a week or so back. Quite a crowd left their homes to watch.'

'The poacher?'

'Yes, did you know him?'

The landlord nodded. 'He drank in here some days. Henry Kestle was his name.'

'A boy hung from his legs to quicken his death.'

The landlord frowned. 'A boy? He had no son.'

'Perhaps someone paid him.'

'He was not well liked. There are many who are glad to see him gone.'

'Did he have family?' Jack asked, surprised to find himself fishing for information that had nothing to do with smuggling or the Blake brothers.

'He had a wife called Jenna. She is a pretty, quiet little thing, with long brown hair. She may have paid someone.'

Jack nodded, satisfied.

'Yes, she may well have paid someone,' he said, not wishing to give away her deception.

Their conversation was interrupted by a heated argument at a table nearby and the landlord was forced to leave Jack and attempt to calm the frayed tempers. Jack, leaving the rest of his ale untouched, sat back to watch the farce that was developing between a disgruntled man, his wife and her unsuspecting lover.

The woman's temper would not be easily calmed. She

stood squarely between the two men arguing and told the landlord to shut up before he had a chance to speak. Her stance was mutinous, her black, greasy hair lay flat to her head and her ample bosom heaved against the grimy neckline of her dress. She is a catch indeed, thought Jack with a smile, as he watched the men fight over her.

'Spendin' my money, then sneakin' off to see 'im!' shouted her husband as he pointed at the thin man on the other side of his wife. 'I can't stand the sight of ya – both of ya!'

Her lover was taller and older than his rival, but did not carry the lines of worry as heavily. The men's eyes locked over the woman's head, as they clenched their fists in an act of bravado.

'Nor I, you old fool,' shouted back his wife. 'I can't stick another ten years of your moanin' and snorin'.'

Her husband's face reddened with rage as he made to grab her, but was held back by those who had gathered to watch. Angrily, he shook them off, but was soaked in ale, thanks to his wife.

A roar escaped him as he lunged for her again. People scattered as he fell upon her with open arms, but she was ready for him. Clutching one another in a crude wrestling hold, they fell onto a table, before ungainly rolling off the other side and landing with a grunt on the unforgiving slate floor. Eager hands dragged them apart and held them fast, as husband and wife aimed wild kicks at each other. The lover stood between them to try and ease the tension, but it only fuelled the husband's anger more. While he writhed and swore, his wife broke free of the drinkers who held her and, taking advantage of his captivity, tried to hit him with her flailing fist. Inadvertently she hit her lover and a new shouting match began. Before long all three were trading insults as a cheering crowd looked on.

The landlord had had enough.

'Stop!' he shouted. 'Stop or I will throw you all out! I'll have no more fighting!' Surprisingly, like naughty children muted by their guilt, the three culprits stopped. The landlord pushed his way through the crowd and looked at the husband.

'You come here every evening moaning about your wife and wishing you never married her.' He turned to the woman. 'And you are always telling my wife how much you hate him. This cannot go on.'

The husband shook off his captors. ''Tis true. We 'ate each other and no one is 'appy.' He pointed to the other man. 'You can 'ave 'er!'

There was a short silence while tempers simmered and cut lips and noses were dabbed.

'But I wan' it done proper,' the husband insisted, having no reason to trust either of them. 'I don't want 'er comin' back to me and tryin' to lay 'er 'ands on my money. It's been a livin' 'ell puttin' up with 'er. 'E's right, it cannot go on and I want the marriage ended.'

'It's what I want too, you big lout,' said his wife angrily, linking her arm with her lover's.

'Sell her to him,' a voice suggested from the back of the crowd who had gathered around them. The husband considered the proposal then nodded.

'All right, but I want witnesses. I want proof that the deed 'as been done.'

Keen that another fight would not break out, the landlord made a suggestion. 'There is a Mop Fayre in town. You could buy a vendor's ticket that will provide proof of sale. It's being held at the market square so there will be plenty of witnesses. The Mop Fayre will provide you with all the evidence you will need.'

The husband, satisfied with the suggestion, took off his belt and tied it to his wife's wrist. 'Come with me,' he said, leading her out of the inn. 'You are about to be sold to ya lover – God 'elp 'im.'

The trio left, followed by several customers who had a mind to watch. Jack had heard of wives being sold to end an unhappy marriage, but he had never witnessed it. He thought for a moment as to his next course of action as the inn began to empty around him. He had gained little information from the innkeeper regarding the smuggling trade in the area, although he was more forthcoming about the poacher's widow.

Frustratingly, the woman had continued to tease his mind since the hanging and he found himself often wondering what her story was. At least now he knew she was the wife of the poacher and that the battered tricorn hat, which was too big for her head, hid long brown hair underneath. The colour, he imagined, would be dark and go well with her almond shaped eyes. The name, Jenna, matched her well. It was a shame it was such a pretty name and rolled off the tongue so gently, as it was just one more thing that would make it difficult to forget her.

He pushed his ale away from him. He rarely drank more than a tankard, as too much drink loosened a man's tongue. In his line of work he had to remain vigilant, and women, or too much drink, could land a man in trouble. It did not matter that it might taste as good as the ale at Tolbridge Inn or look as good as a woman called Jenna Kestle, both were best avoided in great quantities.

Jack decided that there was nothing to keep him at the inn and, looking for a diversion from his thoughts, he followed the trio and the other customers out into the sunshine. The Mop Fayre was not the usual place to obtain a wife, he thought, but it seemed today that it was and he wanted to be there to see it.

Jenna had stood in line for almost an hour. One at a time she bent her knees to soothe her aching muscles. Standing still was not natural for her, and her legs were starting to rebel at the forced confinement. She had begun the day hopeful, but with each passing minute her hope was dwindling. There were only two hours of light left and the crowd was already beginning to disperse. She was almost hired twice, but one recognised her as a Cartwright and the other took a disliking to her.

'You will cause trouble with your doe-like eyes,' said the woman through narrow lips, as she looked down her nose at Jenna. Ignoring Jenna's pleas that she would not, the woman passed her by in order to hire the next person. Jenna's desperation and stubborn streak impelled her to stay and her hopes rose again when a large woman with a florid complexion climbed the makeshift stage and waddled towards her on arthritic legs.

Jenna's attention was so taken by the potential employer that at first she did not see the two men, one of whom was leading a woman by the wrist, come into the square. The noise from the crowd behind them, as they encouraged others to follow too, was a large enough spectacle to finally take both the women's attention and the hiring process was momentarily interrupted.

'I 'ave 'ere in my 'and a ticket to sell,' shouted one of the men. 'In my other, I 'ave a wife. Who wants to bid for 'er?'

A bid was dutifully offered by the second man and a cheer went up. A jovial atmosphere had descended in the square at the entertainment on view.

Jenna had not seen a wife sale before, although she had

heard tales of it. She knew from her own experience that a wife had few rights. Her money and her property became her husband's and she, in turn, became his property too. Her own marriage had been so unhappy and brutal that if Henry had agreed to end their marriage by selling her off, she would have been grateful to have been sold. Now he was dead. The distance between this unhappy period of her life and today allowed her the luxury of watching the spectacle unfold without feeling the despair she had endured during her own unhappy marriage. For the first time that day, she forgot how desperate she was to be hired.

The husband, smiling, was about to accept the bid when another was shouted from the crowd. The trio had not expected a stranger to bid and a heated argument broke out as the husband considered it and then accepted it. His wife and her lover were livid, their anger only apparent by their clenched fists and scarlet faces. The husband smiled as her lover was forced to increase his bid. By the third round of bidding her lover's determination to buy her was waning. A quarrel broke out and as they argued Jenna's eyes wandered over the crowd.

A variety of faces were turned to watch the sale. Men, women and children craned their necks for a better view, eager to see what was happening. Only one man, who stood on the edge of the crowd and casually leaned against a cart, had no interest in the farce. From his stance and jet-black hair, Jenna instantly recognised him as the man who had helped her escape. There was no mistaking him, as there were few men with such well-balanced features that held strength and kindness in equal measures. He was looking at her intently through narrowed eyes and she wondered if he recognised her, too. Heat rushed to her face, making her feel exposed and a little panicked. Furtively, she moved her mop in front of her face hoping to block his view. The last thing she needed while she was trying to be hired was him asking questions.

Keeping her eyes lowered, she heard the wife sale progress as the men agreed a price of two shillings and a quart of beer, and the lover emerged victorious. The crowd erupted about Jenna, but she dared not look up in case the stranger was still looking at her. Instead she remained rooted to the spot hoping that he would soon be on his way.

The wife sale completed, the woman and her lover walked through the crowd, their noses tilted upwards, their arm interlinked and both with a slight swagger to their step. The crowd was delighted at the unplanned entertainment and even broke into a spontaneous applause when the pair granted them a joint bow before finally exiting the square. The fayre slowly returned to normal and Jenna took the opportunity to furtively glance up. She saw him moving through the thinning crowd, and then she lost sight of him. He is gone, she thought, relieved, but she should have known better. His earlier attention had indicated an interest in her, and when she heard a man's boots climb onto the left side of the stage, she did not need to look to know it was him.

The woman with the florid complexion ordered Jenna to show her hands. Obediently Jenna held one out, whilst trying to keep the mop head in the right position to obstruct the stranger's view of her face. When the man's well-shaped hand suddenly closed around the handle of her mop and brushed against hers, a wave of unfamiliar sensations swept over her. They caught the breath in her throat and slowed her mind to that of a drunkard, leaving her little choice but to allow him to take it. With her mop in his hand, the dark-haired stranger watched in silence as the woman examined her.

The larger woman looked at her now free hand. Satisfied, she ordered Jenna to open her mouth and show her teeth, before checking for lice in her clothes and hair. Jenna closed her eyes in shame at being examined like livestock. The man continued to say nothing, even when he handed the mop back to her when the examination was complete. His brows furrowed deep in thought, and for the briefest of moments she wondered if he was considering hiring her. However, when the woman offered a price he remained silent and when the ribbon was pinned onto Jenna's dress to confirm that she was hired, he turned and walked away.

Jenna frowned as she watched him leave. His presence had unnerved her, but strangely, now that he was leaving, she felt disappointed that he had not bothered to barter for her. Had he come onto the stage to hire her, but on closer inspection thought better of it? The truth was, the handsome stranger had rejected her, and rejection is never a pleasant feeling to have.

From a short distance away, Jack watched the woman lead Jenna Kestle away. He had been shocked to see her again and found himself marvelling at life's habit of tossing coincidences in one's path. Moments before he caught sight of her he had been thinking about her, and then she was there, standing on a makeshift stage waiting to be hired.

At first he put it down to mistaken identity, or worse his imagination playing tricks on him, but the longer he watched her, the more he was convinced it was *her*.

The woman's hair, previously hidden below a battered tricorn, was in fact long. Today, it was neatly plaited and lay over one shoulder. The last time he saw her, her feminine shape was hidden under boy's clothing. Now it captivated his attention and drew him towards the stage, while a devil on his shoulder whispered in his ear and encouraged him to hire her. Jack almost succumbed, but thankfully saw sense and walked away. He knew that having an extra pair of ears beneath his roof was far too dangerous. It was best he kept his distance until he had completed what he had come here to do.

He watched her body sway to the movement of the cart as her new employer took her away from him. For a brief moment he felt a strange sense of loss for a woman he knew so little about. True, she had never been far from his thoughts. The last time he had seen her she was being chased by a crowd. It was only natural that he would feel concern for her welfare, he thought. He need not have worried as he remembered their hands briefly touching. Although her hand felt tense, during her examination she had a tilt to her chin, which showed determination – a trait he recognised in himself. He knew in that moment that he need not be concerned for her, for he saw that she was of strong character which would bode well for her future.

This newly acquired knowledge freed him from feeling concern for her and he found himself laughing a little too loudly at his earlier foolishness. The cart was long gone before Jack finally straightened his hat and turned away to head back to the Tolbridge Inn. He had further business to attend to, but, thankfully, he now had a clear head to do it with.

# Chapter Four

The wooden spoon caught Jenna on the brow, bringing tears to her eyes which would remain unshed. It was the last straw and helped her to make the decision to leave. She pushed past Mabel Hobba and went to the empty room she shared with two other servants. Her employer followed with surprising speed, considering her lazy and slovenly ways. Ignoring the tirade of abuse that spilled from her wet lips, Jenna silently packed her meagre belongings. It did not take long. To ensure she had left nothing behind, Jenna lifted and tossed aside the moth-eaten blankets that masqueraded as her mattress and bed linen. Dust and cake crumbs billowed about them in a cloud as Mabel continued to shout at her.

The job was a disaster and Jenna would tolerate no more. One week was long enough to put up with her employer's behaviour. Mabel was a bully and her son a gluttonous, spoilt child who took great joy in manipulating the people around him for his own entertainment. New servants were great fodder for his twisted games, which wreaked havoc amongst the staff and sent his mother reaching for her beating spoon.

The final incident occurred as a result of a cake going missing. Jenna knew who had taken it and despite the evidence found to the contrary, it was not her. In the early hours of the morning she saw the culprit eating it as she scrubbed the floor in the adjoining room. She also watched him place a handful of crumbs in his palm before leaving. Jenna said nothing, preferring to keep out of trouble, but when Mabel accused her of stealing the food she found herself in the midst of it all.

Despite Jenna's denial, and telling her employer that the real culprit was her own son, the scattered crumbs on her bed pointed to her as the guilty party. Her son smiled as he watched his mother lift her wooden spoon to 'beat the evil' out of Jenna. Jenna dodged the first blow but the second had caught her with such force it momentarily stunned her. She had spent the last two years being beaten by Henry, she would not put up with it again. If she ran all the way, she thought, she might just get to the second Mop Fayre before it closed.

By the time Jenna arrived, stalls were starting to be packed away and people were beginning to disperse. Dishevelled from running the two miles to the fayre, and with a swelling on her left brow, which was already beginning to discolour, Jenna knew that she did not look like a reliable employee. However the hiring fayre would not be held again for another year, so she had little choice in the matter. She bought her ticket and took her place on the stage, trying not to shiver in the chilly October breeze. She realised she had no tool to represent her trade and, to add to her misery, the black clouds in the sky reminded her she had nothing to keep her dry should it rain. Thoughts of her brother's debt, and her own homelessness, bolstered her determination to find a new job. Straightening her shoulders she waited on the empty stage, a lone figure, hoping for someone to notice her.

Despite his best efforts to engage the landlord of the Tolbridge Inn in conversation, Jack had discovered no new information on the smuggling organisation that traded in the area. The landlord was friendly enough, and would talk for hours on anything and everything – everything except the source of his French brandy and kegs of strong ale. Jack knew a lot already. It was *who* financed it that took his interest, but if he could not get the landlord to talk of the commonly known factors, he would not be able to discover the less known ones. For seven days he had visited the inn. One whole week, and he was no further forward for his efforts. It had also been a week since the fayre and he wondered if it would be there again today. His interest piqued, he pushed his chair back and decided to go for a little walk.

The square was quieter than he expected and for the first time he realised how late in the day it was. There were still a few stalls set up, but the items for sale were meagre and of poor quality as the best of the stock had already been sold. Jack gave them a cursory glance, but it was not the stallholders that interested him, but the makeshift stage on the edge of the square and the person on it.

He hadn't expected to see her again. He had believed she would be a hard worker and her new employer would have no need to be rid of her. Yet there she stood, all alone in the darkening light. Jack wandered around the square, pretending to take an interest in the few stalls that remained by picking up the odd trinket on display, but all the time covertly glancing in her direction. Eventually, against his better judgement, he made his way towards the stage. Unsure as to what he hoped to achieve, he hesitated. She had not seen him yet, which was just as well. Jack did not usually suffer from bouts of indecision and for her to see him dither would be a humiliation. This thought helped him to make up his mind, but as he turned to leave for home a man walked by him and climbed the creaking steps of the stage.

Jack recognised him instantly as a regular drinker in the Tolbridge Inn. He also knew that the landlady and her daughter gave him the nickname 'Handy'. After seeing his many lecherous advances to the women, he knew the name did not come from his skills in trade. When he heard Handy begin to discuss hiring her, Jack felt compelled to intervene.

Handy left Jenna to collect a ribbon from the organiser and seal the contract. Feeling duty-bound to warn her before she accepted it, Jack walked towards her.

'Do not accept him,' he whispered next to her ear.

She jumped. Her attention had been taken by the prospective employer, so hearing Jack's voice so close came as a shock. She quickly turned her head towards him before he had a chance to withdraw. Fleetingly her lips grazed his cheek. Still feeling the feather-like sensation on his skin, he quickly straightened.

Perplexed, she frowned at him. 'Why not?' It was the first time he had heard her speak. Her tone was not at all unpleasant, although perhaps a little angry.

'His hands are quicker than his wit and he is best avoided.'

She raised an eyebrow at him. 'I don't know of any man whose wit is quicker than his hands.'

He would have found her retort funny, had she not been directing it so strongly at him. He wanted to put her straight.

'Well, you have now.'

'Then you must have very slow hands for you do not present as a man of wit. Do you dither often?'

Jack pressed his lips into a thin line to prevent a smile. It seemed that she had seen him after all.

'You have a sharp tongue,' he replied.

'Why is it that if a man makes a retort he is admired and respected for his cleverness, yet if a woman says something her tongue is considered sharp?'

He ignored her question. 'What happened to your face?' he asked, seeing the swelling on her brow for the first time.

'Are you considering hiring me?' she replied. Jack shook his head. 'Then it is of no concern of yours.'

Handy returned with a broad smile on his lips and a ribbon in his short-fingered hand. Jack realised he was running out of time to persuade her, so he must try another tack.

'Sir,' Jack addressed him. 'I suggest you do not hire this woman.'

Jenna's eyes grew wide as she looked at him.

Handy frowned. 'Why not, sir?' he asked, holding the ribbon in mid-air.

What could he say?

'She has the pox, sir.' He watched Jenna's mouth drop open in surprise.

The ribbon fluttered in Handy's wavering hand. 'What makes you say this?' he asked, his voice edged with concern.

Jack looked accusingly at her shocked face. 'I know this, sir,' he said decisively, 'for she has given it to me.' The man looked doubtful. 'It is true,' Jack insisted. 'The lesions are suppurating as we speak.' Handy's face mirrored his discomfort. Without saying a word he handed the ribbon to Jack and left the stage. Jenna was furious.

'Sir, I must be hired!'

'I am sure you will be, but not by that man. Unprotected, you will spend every waking hour trying to avoid his wandering hands. You are best out of it, madam.'

'I can look after myself, sir. I did not ask for your assistance.'

'No, but you needed it all the same. If he did not have designs upon you, being afflicted with the pox should not have mattered to him.'

'It would if he wanted to run a healthy household. He wanted to hire me to care for his children.'

'He has no children. He lives alone.'

Jenna's confidence appeared to wane a little but she remained stubborn. 'You seem to know a lot about his circumstances, or perhaps you embroider them to suit your own ends.'

'I make it my business to know,' Jack retorted.

She raised her eyebrow. 'And what is your business, sir?'

Jack pressed his lips closed. He had said too much. It was time he was gone. Without saying more he turned and left the stage.

'You are going to leave me?' she shouted after him, dismayed. He dared not turn around but continued to walk away.

Jack did not go far and when it started to rain he sheltered in the mock Greek portico of the town hall. A steady stream of water poured from the front corner of his tricorn as he moodily watched Jenna from a distance. Stubbornly, she remained on the stage, waiting to be hired. The heavy downpour continued on, drenching her garments and hair until they both clung to her like a second skin, yet she refused to be defeated.

Jack glanced around the empty square and saw the organiser seeking shelter in the adjacent doorway. Cursing, Jack lifted his collar against the driving rain and went to him. Without speaking he grabbed a ribbon from him and headed for the stage.

'Madam, you are hired for one day,' he said, angrily pinning the ribbon to her dress.

'I'm available for hire for one year, not one day.'

'It is one day or not at all,' Jack replied, pulling out his purse and searching for some coins. 'Five pennies,' he said, taking her hand and forcing them into her palm. Her hand felt cold in his and he saw that her body was trembling despite her best efforts to conceal it. 'Now go home and get some food in your belly before you catch a fever,' he ordered.

'What is your name?'

'Penhale. Jack Penhale, now go home.'

'Penhale, you say? No, I owe you a day's work,' Jenna insisted picking up her bag.

'You owe me nothing. I have hired you and you do as I say. I say go home.' Jack turned abruptly and walked angrily away. Despite his own good intention to protect her from the lecher, he had now fallen into the trap of feeling responsible for her. From his experience, payment could remove such an irritation and now he could return home with his conscience clear. It was only when he collected his horse and mounted its creaking, leather saddle, did he realise Jenna had followed him.

'I owe you a day's work,' she argued. 'This ribbon is proof of our contract. I will not have it said I took money for nothing.'

He almost relented. She looked cold. She was drenched. She looked desperate. What harm would one day bring? At the end he would have a tidy house, a warm meal and tomorrow she would be on her way. He looked at her wet body – too risky, he decided. After four and twenty hours he would find it harder to send her on her way. Silently, he turned his horse and encouraged it to walk home.

The rain finally stopped and the familiar smell of damp horse filled his nostrils. In the fading light, only the squelch of his horse's hooves in the rain soaked earth broke the silence of the early evening. He felt quite alone so there was no reason for him to turn and look behind him, but for an innate instinct to remain vigilant for footpads. At first he mistook her for a shadow of the hedge that lined the narrow road, but then the shadow moved with a rhythm of a person on foot and he realised he was mistaken. He could see that the figure wore a dress and carried a bag, and although he could not see her features, he knew it must be her. He swore and resumed his journey. She would soon tire, he thought, and return to the comfort of Goverek town.

Confident she would give up, as any sane person would, he did not look again for almost three minutes. He congratulated himself that he waited that long, having counted out the time to prevent himself turning sooner. He intended counting to five, but could wait no more. Although she was further away, the long straight track provided him a good line of sight and he saw that she continued to follow. Her steps appeared more laboured and she swapped the hand that carried the bag as if her arm ached. His heart told him to ride to her, his head told him to continue on. Cursing, he did the latter.

The gradient of the road rose and fell as Jack slowly followed the contours of the Cornish countryside. He turned around to look behind him again. The brow of the hill obstructed his line of sight and the road was empty. He soothed his horse to be quiet and he strained to listen. The eerie silence concerned him. Although there was some distance between them, he thought he might still hear her footfalls. All was quiet, except for a bat haphazardly flying through the air. He should be pleased, as it appeared she had turned for home just as he had told her. Yet he had a growing concern that all was not well and that she may have fallen victim to a footpad herself. He stopped his horse and was about to turn it around when her figure appeared on the horizon. A little slower, a little more swaying in her rhythm, but it was her all the same. He smiled at her obstinacy as he turned his horse around and rode towards her.

'I told you to go home,' he said not unkindly as he looked down on her. She was a little out of breath and had dropped her bag on the ground in relief at his arrival.

'And I told you I owe you a day's work.'

'I admire your work ethic.'

'Then hire me for a year.'

'Why would I trust a woman who likes to dress as a boy?' he asked. Her lack of surprise at his question told him that she had recognised him too.

'You can trust me,' she insisted.

'I have heard those words before. I rarely believe them.'

'There are many who would take your money and call you a fool for your soft heart. I did not. I have walked miles on an empty belly and chilled to the bone so I would not be in debt to you. If my actions do not show good character, I do not know how to convince you otherwise.'

He considered her reply. She waited patiently, looking hungry and cold.

'How does five pounds sound for a year's work?' He saw her eyes brighten for the first time.

'If I am to be your housekeeper I expect twelve.'

'I live in no grand house and have no other servants. Six is fit for a year's wage.'

'But I will keep house for you.'

'I will turn and leave you be,' he threatened.

'And return to a house that has no fire or food in the larder.'

He smiled in the darkness. It was as if she had already seen it.

'My last offer is eight,' said Jack, reaching down. Jenna nodded her acceptance. 'I believe I may have offered twelve if you had insisted,' he teased.

'And I would have taken five if pressed,' she replied. She picked up her bag and handed it up to him, then held out her hand. He pulled her up behind him on the horse.

'You know how to dent a man's pride,' he countered.

'It is not the only thing that I know how to dent if your hands do prove to be quicker than your wit. But I have confidence in you, sir, for you do have a sharp wit which bodes well for the future.'

Jack felt her arms wrap around his waist.

'In such dire circumstances I am surprised you haggled your price considering I may not have stopped at all.'

'I knew you would not leave me alone as you did not press your horse to go faster than an elderly mare's walk.'

'I hope I have not hired trouble this day,' he muttered, but this time she did not answer. He felt the warmth of her head lying heavy against his back. It was not an unpleasant feeling and he found himself smiling inwardly. She is not as strong as she pretends to be, Jack thought to himself as he brought her cold hands further around his waist. Holding them tightly against his stomach with one hand, so she would not fall off as she slept, he turned his young gelding in the road and headed for home.

# Chapter Five

Jenna opened her eyes and looked around her. Her room was clearly visible in the early morning sunshine and now appeared serviceable and quite ordinary. This was very different from when she arrived last night, when every shadow in the room had appeared threatening and sinister.

She had fallen asleep on the ride, but remembered waking in her new employer's arms as he carried her to the door. She recalled that his body had smelt of damp horse and leather, whilst his breath held a hint of sweet malt as he spoke. He had placed her on her feet as he opened the door and she had suddenly felt cold without his warm body around her. The strength of the wind, and the deep rumble of the sea in the distance, told her they were near the coast, yet the starless sky did not allow her to see the exterior of the house she was entering.

Inside she was no wiser. Every room was cloaked in darkness, except for the dim, fragile light of a flickering candle as they passed from room to room. The corners remained hidden in the shadows and ordinary objects took on strange shapes and a sinister air. It was sparse, small and lacked any evidence of comfort or permanency. It was as if it were a place to stay and no more, not a home to retreat to or a place to build memories.

After seeing Jack Penhale's home, she felt she knew no more of the man who employed her. The enormity and vulnerability of her current position, alone with a stranger, suddenly struck her, but if she was in doubt about her decision, her employer was not. In a matter-of-fact way, he told her he would be out for most of the following day and gave her some money to fill the larder while he was gone. After showing her where she would sleep, he bid her a good night and she did not hear from him again.

This morning the sound of his leaving woke her. She stretched and smiled as she realised she was now quite alone. For the first time since her hurried marriage more than two years before, she felt at peace and safe. She was free from her husband's beatings, free from his parents' insults and free from Hobba's wooden spoon. Jenna allowed herself one more delicious stretch in bed and then eased her feet out from beneath the sheets to the cold wooden floor below.

Jack's small cottage was indeed sited near the coast. Although the wind had eased, the roar of the sea remained and its presence provided a permanent moving backdrop to his home. She spent the first day cleaning the cottage and buying supplies from the small neighbouring village of Lanros. When Jack returned he had a warm meal waiting and a fire lit. He appeared surprised at the subtle change an airing and an early fire could make to the comfort of a house, but he seemed content when he settled himself before the fire after he finished his meal.

The first evening she left him to his own thoughts, but as the week progressed, the awkwardness of sharing a home with someone she did not know well lessened, and she began to relax.

Jenna learned that the cottage was called the Captain's Cottage, as it was built by a sea captain for his wife. It was said that she would sit at the window and watch for his ship to appear on the horizon, waiting for its return to port after yet another long and arduous journey. One day the ship did not return and the sea captain's wife could bear to live there no more. When asked, Jack was evasive about how he came to possess it or how long he had lived there, but did tell her he planned to farm the land. Jenna knew better than to press her employer and did not question him further. In fact, it suited her not to pry as although they talked of many things, both were reluctant to share their history with the other.

Jack spent two days a week working on the land. He mended gates, fixed barns and trimmed hedges, which pleased the tenants of the neighbouring farms. Jenna knew that Cornish folk did not like to see land neglected and were glad that the new tenant of the Captain's Cottage was taking an interest in it. However, Jenna knew he spent the other five days somewhere other than tending to his land. Where he went was a mystery to her. He would leave early but the times he returned varied. Sometimes he would be hungry, other times he would not and Jenna noticed that if it rained his clothes were only occasionally wet, which suggested that sometimes he was outside a great deal, yet other times indoors. She did not know how he earned his money as he was not gentry, nor did he appear to have regular labourer's hours. If he intended to farm the land, thought Jenna, he would have to buy a plough soon. If he ploughed too late the fields would have to remain fallow for another year. The one time she did ask where he was going, he told her he was looking for farm stock that would be suitable to rear on a coastal farm. He must have found it very difficult, for he never returned with any. The longer she lived with him, the more of a mystery he became to her. So when a visitor came calling several weeks later, Jenna's interest was stirred.

Jack arrived home earlier than expected and in the company of a well-spoken gentleman dressed in well-made clothes. Taken by surprise at the appearance of a guest, Jenna took his hat and coat, fumbling a little as she did so.

'My friend is hungry, Jenna. Please bring us a tray,' Jack said as he took off his own hat and coat. She looked at him in horror. She knew what Jack and Mrs Hobba ate. She knew what Henry, his parents and her own parents would eat, but she had no idea what a gentleman would consider suitable to eat mid-afternoon.

Jack saw her dilemma and came to her aid. 'Bread and mutton will suffice, and perhaps some port.' He showed the man into the adjacent room and just as he shut the door, Jack gave her a reassuring smile. The sudden, intimate curve of his lips caught her off guard, and left her staring blindly at the closed wooden door, before she came to her senses and turned stiffly away.

Jenna entered the room some minutes later with a tray laden with food and port. She was aware that Jack's visitor looked at her thoughtfully as, with great care, she laid out the plates.

'How are you finding it here?'

She looked up, only to find it was not her he was addressing.

'It will suffice,' Jack replied.

'It is a windy place to live.'

'Only in winter.'

The conversation appeared stilted and trivial, so when Jenna left it was only natural that she should press her ear up against the door to learn more about her new employer and his only visitor. It was as she suspected, the conversation flowed much easier when she was out of the room.

'Friend, I offered you a housekeeper but you refused.'

'I did not plan to have one, but circumstances changed.'

'A comely wench, perhaps it is not only housekeeping duties she undertakes. Bedchambers are cold places in winter without a woman to hold.'

Jenna, indignant at the insult, snorted with contempt – although the idea of lying with Jack was not an unpleasant one. In fact, her heart began to race at the very thought of it.

'She is my housekeeper, no more.' Silence followed. Fearful she was missing out, Jenna pressed her ear harder against the door. 'I suspect her legs are bowed beneath her skirts,' Jack continued, 'and she has a problem with wind.' The door opened and Jack's smile broadened as he saw Jenna's bowed head and hunched shoulders. Her face flushed with the colour of guilt. She had been caught.

'Eavesdroppers hear no good about themselves,' he told her.

'How did you know I was listening?'

'Because it is something I would have done in your position.' Jack held out some coins. 'I would like to talk in private,' he said more seriously. 'Go to Lanros and treat yourself.'

Confused, Jenna frowned.

'To what?' she asked.

Jack shrugged; he did not appear used to women asking him what they should buy.

'Do you like sweetmeats?' he asked.

'I don't know. I have never eaten one.'

'Well, treat yourself to some and then you will know.'

Jenna's fingers closed over the coins in her palm. Silas once asked her to steal a box of sweetmeats when she was a child. She did not want to, so she took a long time looking at the stall. Her brother finally gave up waiting for her and Jenna left without stealing anything, just as she hoped. Thanks to Jack, she was now able to buy a box. As she collected her shawl, she had the sudden urge for him to think well of her. She could not explain it, but for some reason it mattered greatly.

She turned to him. 'I don't have bowed legs or suffer from wind. I wanted you to know that.'

The corner of his lip lifted slightly. 'I know,' he said quietly, before shutting the door.

Jack watched her from the window as she walked towards Lanros. The wind twisted her long hair and buffeted her dress about her legs. She had a spring in her step, like a child who had been given a treat. He wondered what sort of childhood she had had for her to feel such pleasure at being treated.

He turned to his friend. 'She has gone, Enoch. We can talk now.'

He found Sir Enoch Pickering staring at him, deep in thought. Jack knew him well enough to know that Enoch would soon voice what was on his mind. Instead of pressing him, Jack selected two glasses and began to pour them each some port.

They had worked together on many occasions as Enoch had commissioned Jack's services several times in recent years. It was at Enoch's request he was in this part of Cornwall now. They both wanted to bring an end to the smuggling trade and while Jack was the one to get his hands dirty, Enoch watched silently from the sidelines. However, at the end of each mission he always paid Jack well for his thief-taking services and often referred his rich friends to him. The arrest of the odd debtor or poacher for Enoch's affluent friends helped Jack put food on the table in lean times. Lean times such as now, when no one was willing to share what they knew. Jack respected Enoch and his vision regarding the smuggling trade, however he wasn't sure he wanted to hear what was on his mind now.

'It is dangerous to have another person here,' said Enoch. 'Do you know much about her?'

Jack paused before answering. 'She is a widow,' he said, carefully replacing the bottle of port. 'Her husband was called Henry Kestle. He was hanged at Goverek gibbet for poaching a few weeks ago.'

'His name sounds familiar. I believe he offered information to Captain Henley a while back, but disappeared shortly afterwards.'

'He knew about the smuggling trade around here?'

'We will never know. Although, I would be willing to wager there are few men who do not know something about it. Strange that he was hanged. I know that poaching is a hanging offence, but leniency is usually shown.'

'I understand he was a troublemaker. Perhaps the judge felt it was time that he paid with his life.'

'And now you have his widow under your roof. You are taking a risk, Jack.'

'In what way?' Jack offered his friend a glass of port.

'She may be involved in the smuggling trade. She may be a spy.'

A deep furrow marked Jack's brow. 'Jenna has given me no reason for concern. I will not turn her out now.' He heard Enoch suck air through his teeth. 'But I will remain vigilant, Enoch.'

'Are you sure that your bed is not crying out for warmth and damaging your judgement in such matters?'

'November has a habit of bringing a chill to the bed, but a warming pan will suffice for now.' The other man laughed into his port, but Jack was not so jovial. 'Captain Henley almost gave me away in the Tolbridge Inn.'

'I will speak to him.'

'I have spent the last few weeks mixing with the local folk here. I do not need the head of the land guard being loose with his tongue.'

'He is struggling. It seems everyone in Cornwall is connected in some way. He does not have enough men to enforce the prevention of contraband. He has one man to guard each four-mile stretch. At the moment, if he discovers a landing site, he can call upon the dragoons for help, but it is only a matter of time before they are sent to America to help quell the rebellion there.'

'Enough young lives have already been wasted in that unjust war.'

'Every war has a side that believes it is unjust. Henley's task is difficult now and will be impossible once they leave.'

'Smuggling is only profitable because of the high taxes the government places on imported goods. If the taxes are lowered there would be no profit to be made.'

'War is expensive and needs to be paid for. We need the money from the taxes to pay for our wars.'

'Yet the government is unable to collect it because imports are smuggled into the country under the cover of night.'

Enoch nodded in agreement, tore off some bread and took a bite.

'When the majority of the population lives in poverty,' Jack continued, 'it is little wonder that men in need of money cannot resist such a window of opportunity.'

'I do not always agree with the members of parliament who make rules for the majority,' said Enoch. 'Unfortunately not all have the skills to see the world through another class's eyes. I can offer advice but my job is to assist, not to persuade them to change policies. I have only asked for your help because the major traders in tea and brandy are losing huge sums each year due to the smuggling trade in England.' He waved a chunk of bread at Jack. 'And Cornwall harbours the worst culprits, with its numerous hidden coves and miles of coastline. But now I discover that you are beginning to sound like you condone the free traders.'

'I don't condone the trade, but I understand what drives it. One needs to understand the enemy if one is to find its weakness.'

His friend narrowed his eyes. 'And what of your weakness, Jack?'

'I have no weaknesses that I am aware of.'

'That is where you are wrong, my friend. All men have a weakness. The question is does yours come in the form of a comely figure and dark brown eyes? I grant you that it is a pleasant weakness to look upon, but it is just as dangerous as any other.'

'She is recently widowed. I do not make a habit of taking grieving women to bed.' Jack suddenly smiled to ease the tension. 'Consider my employment of Jenna Kestle as part of my plan to infiltrate the community.'

'I can see you jest, but I am serious. Perhaps she has also seen your weakness. Perhaps your enemy is closer than you think.'

Jack tore off some bread and quietly chewed it. 'I will watch her, but apart from her husband being a rogue she has done nothing for me to doubt her good intentions. True, she was persistent that I should employ her, but it was only after I chased away the only person who was going to hire her.'

'And what made you do that?'

Jack looked at the freshly baked bread Jenna had made. He could not deny that she was an attractive, beautiful woman. Would he have been so concerned for her welfare if she was an old hag with a foul tongue? He had to acknowledge that he probably would not have been. 'I think it had something to do with her comely figure and dark brown eyes,' he conceded. 'You are right, Enoch, I should remain wary. This game we are playing is too dangerous to lose.'

Jenna sat on the grass and looked down on the beach below her. Deciding to walk along the coastline rather than take the stony track from Lanros, she had come across the sandy cove by accident. She had not seen it before, as it was so well hidden from view that unless you looked directly down upon it, it was easy to pass it by. The entrance of the cove was long and lined with jagged rocks. The sandy beach had a gentle gradient and a wide track, which led directly out to the countryside. Protected from the wind, the water within the cove was unusually calm and although Jenna knew nothing of smuggling, even to an inexperienced eye the cove looked an ideal place to land contraband.

Jenna opened her box of sweetmeats and selected one of the sugar-coated delicacies in her fingers and took her first bite. To her surprise, tears threatened. The delicious taste, and that someone was kind enough to tell her to 'treat' herself, almost overwhelmed her. This moment should be joyful, not filled with regrets for past sorrows, she reprimanded herself as she chewed. It was gone too soon. Determined to make the next mouthful last, she closed her eyes and popped the other half into her mouth, before lying back in the grass, savouring the taste.

Jenna opened her eyes and looked at the blue sky above. She was truly blessed, she thought, to find work in this beautiful place and be employed by a man such as Jack Penhale. Jenna smiled at her good fortune, for she had never met a man quite like Jack before. Although firm and often sombre, he had a gentle quality about him, mixed with sudden flashes of humour that mirrored the twinkle in his dark eyes. Despite his occasional jesting at her expense, for the most part he was respectful and always thoughtful. He would be a reliable provider for his family one day. She wondered if there was a woman in his life at the moment and if he used the hours in the day to call upon her.

A noisy seagull flew across the sky, disturbing her musings and causing her to frown irritably. She closed her eyes to block the disturbance out and Jack's image immediately came to mind. She could see him clearly standing before the fire, looking thoughtfully into the flames as he so often did during the winter evenings. Jenna's frown melted away and the gull was forgotten, as she cast her eyes over his body in a way she would never allow herself to do in reality.

He is a slender man, Jenna observed, yet not too skinny or lacking in strength like many. No, there was a sturdiness and quiet power to Jack Penhale, born from the solid muscle that lay beneath his clothes.

Jenna bit her lip as she watched with her mind's eye Jack undo the buttons from his shirt and let it fall to the ground. The orange glow from the fire caressed and warmed his skin, while casting shadows on the undulations of his chest. Jenna felt the heat too, a strange heat that pooled deep within her. A soft moan escaped her causing Jack to raise his dark brown eyes from the fire and look at her.

In her daydream, neither spoke – or dared to. His steady gaze released a stream of swirling sensations within her, which spiralled down through her body in an uncontrolled, excitable frenzy. She was snared by his gaze and could not move, a hostage to her body's needs – and a hostage to his. He saw it and felt it too, strode determinedly towards her and reached for her—

Jenna woke with a start and sat bolt upright. She looked

guiltily about her, too aware of her heart thumping noisily in her breast and her skin flushed with heat. To her relief, she found she was still quite alone. The dream had been so vivid it was a shock to discover it had not been real at all. She had no right to see Jack Penhale as she had just seen him. Her job was too important to jeopardise with lurid thoughts of her employer. How could she allow herself to be distracted from her brother's plight as if she did not have a care in the world?

She touched her lips with a trembling hand, still feeling the imagined touch of Jack's lips on hers. It was just a dream, she reassured herself, no one need ever know – *he* need never know. She looked up at the blue sky above and, reassuringly, found nothing had changed. The sun was still shining and she still felt blessed.

She looked at the remaining sweetmeats and smiled. She had the sudden urge to share them and bring joy to someone else. Guiltily, she thought of her brother and his family having to endure each day in the debtors' prison. She had denied him the chance of eating sweetmeats as a child, but now, as an adult she could make amends. To see his face brighten when she gave them to him on her next visit would give her far more pleasure than eating them alone. After all, easing Silas's troubles was the most important thing right now. She closed the box and scrambled to her feet. It was time to return, or Jack would be wondering where she was.

Jenna woke in the night to hear Jack moving about downstairs. Hearing the back door shut quietly, she went to the window and saw his dark figure walking away into the night. Something had changed since her return from Lanros. His smiles were gone and he appeared troubled. On several occasions she found him watching her, his brows furrowed as if deep in thought.

Yesterday, he began to question her about her life before he met her and instinctively Jenna's guard went up. Past experience taught her not to mention the Cartwright name, or her family's disregard for the law, so her answers were stilted, evasive and filled with half-truths. She could tell Jack was not fooled. When he chose to leave the questioning, Jenna felt no sense of achievement that she had convinced him, just a sickening feeling she had let him down. The responsibility of her brother's debts, and the fear that she would be dismissed when the truth of her family came out, weighed heavy upon her. As much as she wanted to tell Jack the truth, she did not know him well enough to trust him and her fear of losing her position compelled her to remain careful. If a wedge of distrust had begun to grow on his side, seeing him walk out into the night did not improve her trust of him. Dressing quickly, she went downstairs and followed him out into the darkness.

At first she thought she had lost him. A strong south-easterly breeze whipped her loose hair against her face and she was forced to hold it back in order to see about her. She saw him in the distance against the inky black sky, striding towards the cliff edge. The force of the wind made it easy for her to follow without being heard, as any sounds she made were soon carried away in the opposite direction. She realised he was heading for Porthenys Cove, the inlet she had discovered a few days before. But whereas she had discovered it by chance, Jack knew exactly where he was going.

As he neared the edge, she saw him crouch low. Jenna followed suit, lifting and pulling at her skirts so she would not fall. Eventually she stopped and lay flat on the ground, her chin resting on the wet grass in order to watch Jack in the distance.

For a while nothing happened and Jenna wondered what she hoped to achieve by following him. She had no reason to pry. It was not as if she was his wife and he was leaving the house in the middle of the night to visit another woman. Yet the drive to know was just as strong as if she were his woman. Her stupidity on acting upon it mocked her rational mind, as the wetness of the ground seeped through her dress and stays and chilled her stomach.

A strange noise caught her attention. A gentle flapping, as if someone was shaking a sheet, carried to her on the wind. She turned her face towards the sea to find the source. Moving at speed, and barely visible in the night, Jenna saw what she suspected to be a free trader's lugger. Its angular sails, painted black to avoid detection, flapped in the wind as it manoeuvred past the jutting rocks in the rising gale.

The skill of its captain and crew was unrivalled, as the King's Cutters, which normally patrolled the area, preferred to seek shelter in the local harbours in such weather. Inadvertently they had left the coast clear for a smuggler's drop, which was manned by a crew who did not fear the rising squall.

Frightened, Jenna looked around for Jack. Had he seen it too? Were they in danger of being seen by the smugglers? In horror she watched Jack stand up in the darkness and brace himself against the wind. He had seen the lugger too, she realised, but unlike her, he was not afraid and seemed to expect its arrival. Up until now, she believed him to be a good, kind man, but now, as she looked at his black figure appearing to welcome the lugger's arrival, she began to doubt her first impressions.

She saw Jack look up at the sky and followed his gaze. The rising wind had broken the blanket of cloud in the sky and was now chasing the remnants away. The light of the moon threatened to break through the fleeting gaps and would soon cast a transient light on the area. Jack must have thought that too, for when she looked down again, he had already gone.

Jenna pressed her body into the ground as the first moonbeam travelled across the coast, lighting up the cliff and travelling across the bay. As suddenly as it came it had moved on and she found herself shielded by the darkness of the night again. Jenna should have returned to the cottage then, but the noise of the sails beckoned her forward and fed her curiosity. She wanted to know what was happening on the beach and Jack's involvement in it, so she crawled towards the cliff edge on her belly to get a better view. At the edge, Jenna settled to watch the black shape of the lugger, which was now anchored in the shallow waters offshore. They had taken down the sails and appeared to be waiting for something.

Jenna saw the light from another moonbeam in the distance, travelling up the coastline and across the beach. The illumination lasted longer than the last, lighting up the empty beach, the rolling, white edged waves and the men working on-board the ship. They were fervently dropping bundles of smuggled goods over the side and into the water, one after the other, plopping, splashing, depending on their size. Not far away, heading toward the shore, was a single rowing boat manned by four men. Suddenly, the cove was cast in black shadow once more as the light of the moon was swiftly extinguished by a passing cloud.

Jenna had to wait for several minutes before she had a good view again. By the time the next moonlight passed through, the rowing boat was already returning to the lugger. Jenna suspected they had dropped off something too precious to be hidden underwater until it could be collected. Was that what Jack was waiting for? Jenna shivered. The wet ground was beginning to take its toll. She should go back to the cottage before Jack returned. It was time to go.

Jenna moved away from the edge and used the cover of darkness to make her escape. As she retraced her steps, she thought of Jack and her heart grew heavy with sadness and disappointment. Jack was no better than her brother, her parents or Henry, she thought, for he smuggled goods too and cared not a fig for the law. She should not care, as he was just her employer, yet strangely the discovery tore something inside her and made her want to weep.

The smell was as bad as she remembered, but the building felt colder than before. Winter was knocking on its door and making its arrival felt by the wretched inhabitants inside.

'I have missed you, Sister,' Silas said as he hugged her briefly.

'How are Nell and the children?' asked Jenna as he led her to the same table they had sat at almost two months before.

'Much the same,' he replied, taking an interest in her basket. He began to rummage roughly through it. Fearing the sweetmeats would become broken she slapped his hand away and took them out herself.

Smiling, she opened the box. 'I have brought these,' she said, tilting the box in his direction.

Silas glanced at them. 'Where did you get them?'

'I bought them at Lanros village shop. I live in the Captain's Cottage near the cliff and the village is just a stone's throw away in the valley nearby.'

Silas took a closer look, selected one and popped it into his mouth. To Jenna's disappointment, in two chews it was gone. He screwed up his face in disgust, but reached for another, which soon followed the other.

Disappointed with his reaction, Jenna shut the box.

'You look as if you do not like them,' she grumbled.

'I have eaten it and will eat another if you let me.'

'I want Nell and the children to have one.'

Silas took the box from her and hid it in his shirt. 'I will give it to them later. The children are sleeping and Nell is with them.'

Jenna's eyes narrowed. 'Why are they sleeping in the day?'

'Enough of your questions, Sister. What news do you have of the outside world?'

'Are they ill?'

'They are not,' he replied curtly, looking away and taking an interest in everyone but her.

Jenna realised she would get no further news of them from him. Her time in Goverek was limited as she had arranged to meet Jack within the hour in order to return home. She was determined to make the most of her visit to her brother and she could not spend these precious moments falling out with him.

'I have sent money each week to the keeper. Your food should be of better quality now.'

Silas nodded. 'It is. Where has the money come from to improve our comfort and buy such things?' he asked, patting the box inside his shirt.

'I have a job. I am a live-in housekeeper for a single gentleman. Here are my wages to pay some of your debts. I have been hired for a year.'

'How much?' her brother asked, folding his arms and looking at the purse that lay between them.

'Eight pounds for the year,' Jenna said proudly.

'A princely sum. What other services does he expect you to provide?'

'I shall take the money back if you are to speak to me like that.' Jenna reached for her purse, but her brother snatched it away from her before she could touch it.

'It is my concern for your welfare that makes me say such things,' he grumbled as he looked inside it.

'I can look after myself.'

'As you did when you married Henry.'

Jenna relented. Her brother's orchestration of her husband's arrest had saved her life. Had she still been married to Henry there was no doubt that he would have eventually killed her.

'Let us not fall out, Brother,' Jenna replied softly.

Silas nodded. 'You are right,' he said, pocketing the money. 'Let us talk of other things. So you live near Porthenys Cove?'

'Do you know it?' asked Jenna in surprise.

'Aye, I do.' Silas looked about him to see if anyone was within earshot. Although confident they were not, he still leant towards her and lowered his voice to a whisper.

'A good place to land goods. I have carried a few tubs in my time … and Henry too.'

'I did not know that.'

'It is true. I earned as much as a month's wage in one night. It is a profitable trade.'

'Considering you have never worked for an honest wage in your life, I am surprised you know what you are capable of earning.'

'I get by just fine with the skills I have.'

Jenna looked about her at the squalid conditions inside the prison, but decided not to challenge him.

'If I was not here, I would be keeping an eye on the town hall's weathervane,' he added.

Jenna frowned. 'You are talking in riddles.'

Silas leant still further towards her. 'The weathervane has a cockerel. When news arrives of which beach is to be used for the drop, the cockerel is turned so its beak points to the cove they plan to use. There are not enough preventative officers to watch the entire coastline in this area.' Silas chuckled. 'The free traders are always one step ahead. If the preventative men are seen in one area, the vane is turned to another. The fools are like headless chickens as they run in panic to catch the smugglers. By the time they learn of the landing site, the ship has already gone and the cargo collected.'

'I saw it,' Jenna blurted out.

Her words lit up Silas's eyes in a way that her sweetmeats failed to do.

'Saw what?' He spoke the words as if he almost dared not say them in case he had misunderstood her.

'The free trader's ship.'

'When?'

'Last night.'

'Sails painted black?'

Jenna nodded. The more excitement Silas showed, the more discomfort she felt. She began to withdraw, but Silas grabbed her wrist and pulled her forward.

'I thank you for the money you have brought, but it is not enough. I could earn more if I was out. They sink the goods under the water and inflated bladders are left to mark the spot. The attached feathers make them look like seagulls floating on the surface, but underneath the water are the weighted down goods.'

His sudden excitement at her news seemed almost absurd to her and her discomfort grew with each word he uttered.

He licked his lips. 'The following night they are collected.' He suddenly stopped and looked at her. There was a new glint in his eyes that she had not seen before. 'This could be my salvation,' he said eagerly. Jenna shook her head in denial as she knew what was coming. 'I would go if I could and earn a pretty penny,' Silas continued as Jenna tried to pull her hand away. His hold on her wrist tightened. 'But I can't, sister. I am stuck here.'

'I have given you my wages.'

'It is not enough.'

'How much do you owe?'

'What you would earn in six months.'

Jenna gasped. 'You fool. I should leave you to rot in here for asking me to do this.'

'Four runs and I will be as good as free.'

'Don't ask this of me, Silas.'

'You could dress in your boy's clothing. No man would look too closely as it will be dark and they will be too busy.' Jenna looked away from him but he shook her wrist forcing her attention back to him. 'At the end they will pay you. Just keep your head down so the brim of your hat hides your face. There will be fifty or more men, they will not notice one more.'

'I am not strong enough.'

'Maybe not as a tub carrier, but there will be bacca and silks.'

'I can't do it. It will be breaking the law.'

'You would leave me in here? We share the same blood!'

Jenna shook her head. 'Please, Silas. No,' she pleaded, dropping her eyes beneath his steady gaze as his demand grew in urgency.

'You owe me. I rid you of Henry.' The weight of defeat grew upon her shoulders despite her attempts to resist it.

'If it was not for me you would not be enjoying your fancy sweetmeats.'

'That is unfair,' she retorted, shaking her hand free.

Silas sat back in his chair. 'If you won't do it for me, Jenna,' he said quietly, 'do it for my children. They are not well and they may not last much longer in here.'

'That is cruel. To try and persuade me by using your children.'

'It is the truth. Why do you think I have not brought them out to see you?'

Jenna rubbed her temple to ease the growing pounding in her head. She felt she was losing control of her life with each pressure he placed upon her. She felt sick, as if she were about to fall off a cliff. She tried one last time to deny his request, but she saw it for what it was – a feeble and desperate attempt to grab at something to cling to.

'Please, Silas, don't ask this of me,' she pleaded again.

His voice was firm and unforgiving as he reached for her hand once more. 'I am asking you, Sister. Take my place and run for me tonight. Save my children's lives and set me free.'

As surely as if she felt her body thud against the jutted rocks of Porthenys Cove, she knew that her fate was sealed. She reluctantly nodded as she pulled her hand away from his and buried it deep into her skirts.

Under heavy lids, Jack watched Jenna move about the room. It was a habit of hers, he had come to realise, to have the house tidy and in order before she went to bed. Normally she would sing quietly to herself, but not tonight. Her temperament had changed, and it now matched his.

The first few weeks of her stay had been a pleasant surprise. In a short space of time she had managed to brighten the sparse cottage and make it feel like a home. He found himself looking forward to returning at the end of the day and although he told himself it was the thought of a hot meal and a roaring fire that waited for him, in reality he knew that the real reason was to see her again.

When he discovered her listening at the door, he had found it amusing. It was not unusual for servants to listen to their employer's conversations and later gossip about it with their peers. It was something he may have done if he were in her place and he enjoyed teasing her for eavesdropping. However, time has a way of changing things, and Enoch's warnings shortly after sowed a seed of doubt that had not existed before. Later her evasive answers to his direct questions allowed his doubts to fester. He was used to spying and watching people as part of his work, and now he found himself watching her, doubting the truth of her words and the reason she insisted he hired her.

True, she had been reluctant to be hired by him at first, even hiding behind her mop, but that had all changed when she learnt of his name. From then on she was insistent that she worked for the money he paid her. Anyone else would have taken the money and run, but not Jenna. She was either the pinnacle of saintliness or after something, and neither reason rested well with him. However, how she came to be hired was not the only thing that now concerned him. The past twenty-four hours had added fuel to his sparks of concern.

For months he had been trying to find out how the smugglers communicated and finally he had discovered how they did it. There was no covert messenger but a simple weathercock, which pointed in the direction of the landing place. It was a valuable piece of information, and one that Captain Henley would like to have, but Jack wanted to learn more and knew that secrecy was needed for his success. He wanted to know who financed the trade, as only by stopping the source of the money to buy goods overseas would the smuggling stop. If Jack disclosed about the weathervane, by tomorrow they would use another method and the runs would continue.

Yesterday, he had noticed the weathercock change position. Keen to test if the information he had been given was true, he had set out towards the cove indicated during the night. Just as he had hoped, he saw the free trader's lugger arrive and land the cargo at the bay indicated. Hiding cargo out at sea to be collected later was a new and cunning method, and learning of it was another breakthrough. He returned home exuberant, but the feeling did not last long. Upon opening the door he realised he had been followed, and this new discovery concerned him greatly. He had no doubt that the person was Jenna, as a trail of wet footprints led from his own front door, up the wooden stairs to the only other bedroom in the house – hers. Her earlier eavesdropping lost its innocence. The footprints proved she had spied on him again and he was no longer amused by it. Discovering her furtive behaviour hurt him more than he cared to admit and sleep eluded him for the remainder of the night.

Jack threaded his fingers into a steeple, as his elbows rested on the arms of his wooden chair. He continued to watch her as she washed the dishes, his focus on her bottom as it moved with each rub of the plate. A pleasant view for any man, but Jack's mind was too entrenched in his thoughts to soften towards her.

The news that her late husband, the man she loved enough to risk the wrath of an expectant crowd, had taken part in the trade was unsettling enough, but what he learnt today was far worse and gave her a more sinister motive for being under his roof. His brows pinched together as he remembered the events of the day in each minute detail, while his eyes remained unwavering and followed her every move.

This morning she'd asked him if she could accompany him to Goverek. It was not an unusual request, but this time he found himself questioning her reason for the journey. She told him that she had a friend she wished to visit, yet when questioned further she evaded giving him a name.

When he saw her pack the sweetmeats he had paid for, this *friend* took on an even greater significance. Disliking the distrustful man he had turned into, he had followed her to the debtors' prison, waited outside until she emerged with an empty basket. It was only natural for him to pay the keeper to find out who she had visited.

He was surprised to feel a sense of relief when he found out that it was a brother, and not a lover, as he had not been aware of harbouring such concerns. However, when he heard that her brother was called Silas Cartwright, his blood ran cold. He knew the man well, for he was the reason Silas was in there.

So the motive for her insistence to be employed by him was now clear. It was for revenge of some sort. Perhaps, at first, her initial intent was to be hired by anyone, but after learning his name, no one else would do. He had been a conceited fool to think it was him, as a person, she wanted. It appears his wit was not so quick after all. A heavy sadness had settled in his chest, as if he had lost something precious or discovered it held no value after all.

Tonight, they had eaten in silence. The meal was overcooked, as if her mind were on something else. Jack was not hungry but he ate it all the same and made no complaint, although he noticed that she had no appetite tonight either.

She finished washing the dishes. She looked pale and out of sorts, but he must not let that weaken what he had to do. It was too risky to have her beneath his roof. She listened, she followed, she had connections with smugglers and her brother might seek revenge through her. He had no choice but to tell her to leave.

'Jenna,' he said. She didn't hear him at first and he had to say her name again to break into her thoughts. She turned towards him, a brittle smile on her lips. 'Join me by the fire. I have something to say.'

Drying her hands she sat down before him. The fire cast a red glow upon her face, the bright candle reflected in her dark, almond shaped eyes. He swallowed, his throat felt dry but he would not look away. He realised that he did not want to dismiss her. Perhaps he would give her one more chance to tell him the truth. He came to the conclusion that he was willing to grab any lifeline she threw in his direction if it meant that his mistrust of her was wrong.

'How did you find Goverek?' Jack asked. She looked surprised at the question.

'Much the same as last time I visited, sir.'

'And your friend?' He noticed her gaze drop briefly before lifting again.

'My friend is well.'

'Did he like the sweetmeats?' Her eyes widened. 'There is no shame in visiting a debtors' prison, Jenna,' he continued. 'We all know someone who has been forced inside.'

She nodded. 'He did. I told him to save some for his wife and children.'

Jack felt his stomach turn. She was lying to his face. He knew that when he captured Silas on the request of his creditors, his wife and children were not with him. She had left him two weeks before, taking her children with her to seek sanctuary at her parents' home. Why would Jenna lie about something like that? Was nothing she said truthful?

'What is your friend's name?'

She got up to stoke the fire. Jack saw it for what it was – a tactic to buy her time to think.

'Silas.'

'His surname?' There was a pause as she prodded the fire vigorously. 'You must know his name,' he pressed.

He saw her hand begin to tremble, yet she said nothing.

'Smith?' he suggested.

She tucked a stray strand of hair behind her ear with the same trembling hand.

'Bolten?'

'No.'

'Or is it Cartwright?' Jenna stopped poking the fire and straightened. 'Why did you not tell me you were a Cartwright?' he asked.

'I am a Kestle,' she said, putting down the poker.

'Why did you not tell me you visited your brother?'

She placed her hand on the mantelshelf in an attempt to still her shaking. She had been caught out; there would be no escape from his questioning.

'I didn't want you to know.'

'That you are related to Silas Cartwright?'

She nodded.

'I told you I wanted loyalty. I need to trust you.'

'You can trust me.'

'Yet you hide the fact that you are related to Cartwright.'

'Are you going to dismiss me?'

His eyes narrowed. 'Why would you ask me that?'

'It is what you are thinking.'

'You know nothing of what I'm thinking,' he said angrily. He stood up and picked up the poker. Instinctively she

71

ducked her head. Jack frowned as he saw her whole body begin to tremble. He looked at the poker in his hand, then back at her. 'What sort of man do you take me for?' he asked in disbelief as he dropped it onto the floor. Shamefaced, she straightened. Seeing the guilty flush on her cheeks the furrows in his brow deepened. 'What have you done that you think I should beat you?' he asked.

Jenna looked away.

'Do I look the sort of man who would beat a woman?'

'A ... a woman cannot always tell ...'

He turned her towards him and took her face in his hands to search for the truth in her eyes.

'What have you done, Jenna?' he asked earnestly. 'Why do you fear me?' Even now he wanted her to be truthful.

She looked upset. How well you pretend to be the injured party, he thought. Her wide eyes, full of pain, were trying to persuade him to change his mind. If he forgave her, how she would laugh when she retold the tale to her brother.

'I have done nothing,' she replied solemnly.

'What do you plan to do?' he asked. A hesitation, a fearful glance away to look for an escape, he saw it all. She's thinking of a reply. His eyes dropped to her lips. He must put distance between them, he thought, letting his hands fall from her face and taking a step back. 'I want you to leave tomorrow. I told you I want loyalty. I cannot continue to employ someone I do not trust.

'Because I am a Cartwright?'

'Yes, because you are a Cartwright. Tell your brother that I have found you out.'

'Is there nothing more I can say to make you change your mind?' she asked him.

Jack shook his head as he picked up the poker and began to vigorously poke the brightly burning fire. He knew

Jenna was watching him. It was as if she had expected her dismissal and now that it had happened she was the calmer of the two.

'I will leave in the morning at first light, but I want you to know that although I am a Cartwright by birth, I have never stolen anything from you and never would.'

Jack placed the poker down and straightened. He saw the door slowly close behind her and listened to her footsteps as she quietly mounted the stairs. Tomorrow she would be gone and he could begin again with a clear head, free of her. Yet, this type of freedom did not give him a pleasant feeling. It felt like an aching sickness, which sapped his strength and made him want to retch.

Jenna blinked away the tears that were now free to fall in the privacy of her room. She thought she had become hardened to being dismissed as a Cartwright, but Jack's dismissal hurt more than any other. He was disappointed in her and she could not blame him. She had not been truthful and the fact that her evasiveness had come from years of prejudice against her would make no difference. He saw her as a liar and untrustworthy, which were not desirable characteristics in a housekeeper.

Jenna pulled out the clothing she had worn at Henry's hanging. She had hoped she would never have to wear them again, but she needed to earn money for Silas's creditors and doing what Silas had asked of her was her only option now.

She sat alone in her room, listening to Jack as he moved about downstairs. He sounded unsettled, and although she was tempted to go down to him and plead for his forgiveness, she knew she would not. She had begged at Henry's feet enough; nothing would ever make her beg again. Besides, even if he decided to allow her to stay, the money she earned was still not enough to free Silas and his family.

She heard him retire to his bedroom, but still she waited. For another hour she watched the remnants of her candle burn down until its flame extinguished in a pool of molten wax. Finally, the chime of the clock in the room below sliced into the silence of the night and told her it was time to leave. The men would be gathering, but at least she now knew that Jack would not be amongst them. She wiped away the last of her tears with a trembling hand, took a deep breath and began to unlace her stays.

# Chapter Six

Under the cover of darkness, twenty horses followed the track leading towards Porthenys Cove. Their acceptance of the sacking tied around their hooves told Jenna that these horses were experienced and had been used for a smuggling run before. They obediently followed the tail of the one in front, too tired from a hard day's work on the land to flee the men who led them.

Jenna lay in the coarse grass and listened to their muffled hooves, waiting for the right time so that she would be able to join unnoticed. The men who led them were as quiet as their charges. With their faces painted black they melted into the night like eerie shadows. Realising that her pale skin would single her out, she hastily dug her fingers into the mud and rubbed it on her own face, before lying flat again against the damp grass. The vibration of the ground against her cheek, caused from the horses' hooves, reminded her of another time when the thief-taker had pulled her out of hiding and put the fear of God into her.

'Your family have bad blood running through them,' said a voice in her head, 'and you will turn out the same if you don't mind your ways.' He was right, she thought, as she tasted the mud on her lips. The devil knows his children and he was calling her. She was as bad as Jack believed her to be. He was right to want nothing more to do with her.

A bat screeched above them, unsettling a horse at the front. It was the diversion Jenna needed. Breaking cover, she slipped into line near the back and grabbed a horse's head collar. Almost immediately the convoy began to move forward again. Head bowed, she effortlessly matched her footfalls with theirs, and unnoticed by the others, she became part of the moving line of shadows heading towards Porthenys Cove.

Silas was right; at least fifty men were gathered in the cove and already at work. Resembling a line of ants, they carried contraband from the shoreline and across the soft sand to the horses as soon as they arrived. Jenna had to admire their organisation. As soon as the first horses reached their destination, the first of the contraband arrived. There was no time wasted, or goods left unsupervised and it appeared that everyone knew what they were doing. In the distance, Jenna could just make out a number of rowing boats huddled together on the water. The jutting rocks provided shelter and calm water for them as they cut the ropes attached to the sinking stones and pulled up the hidden goods.

'Make sure you are a carrier,' Silas had told her. 'They will pay you on the beach where you will have less chance of them finding you out. If you stay with the horses you will not get paid until they drop off the goods at a holding house. There will be candles at the house and dawn will be breaking. They will see your face and know you are not one of them.'

A man arrived from the beach, his breathing rapid from running. Tied to his body were two tubs of spirits, one strapped to his back and the other to his front. A man helped him to remove them and passed a four-gallon barrel to Jenna so she could load it onto a horse. Aware she did not know how to, she rolled it towards the man at her side. Too busy to question her, he lifted the tub high onto a horse's back and tied it into place. Jenna grabbed the opportunity to leave and followed the other man onto the beach.

Although she was away from the horses, she did not feel any safer. As she ran along the beach, she passed men loaded with goods coming in the other direction. Either side of the runners were lines of large, stocky men standing guard and holding farm implements, their eyes focused on the cliff edges and ready for an attack from the preventative men. Pig sticking knives, wooden farm flails and scythes were deadly weapons in their hands, yet could easily be explained away by the rural workers if they were caught. These men have used violence before, thought Jenna, and they will turn on me if they discover I am not one of them.

The tide was out and left a damp sheen in its wake. The soft sand beneath her feet became solid and unforgiving as she neared the water's edge. A rowing boat, laden with tubs and wooden boxes, arrived at the shoreline. Immediately its cargo was unloaded by eager waiting men, while others steadied the bobbing boat. They worked in silence, fighting against the tidal water that hampered their speed as they waded back onto firm ground again with their booty.

Jenna grabbed a bale of tobacco, which was wrapped tight and made waterproof by oilskin, hastily turned and followed the others back to the waiting horses. As she ran she held the bale tightly against her chest and kept her eyes down to avoid looking at anyone as she passed them. She hated what she had become and silently cursed her brother under her laboured breath.

The hard sand turned soft again, sapping her strength with each step she took, but desperation and fear fed her determination so she continued on. As she arrived at the horses, she covered her small hands with her sleeves and handed the bale over to a waiting man before turning again and heading back to the shore. She was now one of many anonymous shadows on Porthenys Cove, all hardworking, focused, yet eerily silent.

Knee deep in icy water, Jenna began to shiver as she grabbed another bale of tobacco. She had lost track of time, but suspected that several hours had already passed. She was exhausted and wondered how long she could keep working. Her fingers, numb with cold, were blanched and clumsy, as she struggled to maintain her grip on the bundle.

She glanced up and saw a tall man approach, his face hidden behind a long beard, black markings and a low set hat. He looked down on the men scrabbling for goods around him, selected three with a firm touch on their shoulders and indicated that they follow him. Fearful she might be discovered, Jenna hugged the bale she was carrying closer to her chest and turned quickly to leave, but a wave pulled at her thighs and dragged her ankles from beneath her. She fell sideways into the water as the bale escaped her and began to float away. She scrambled to her feet and managed to grab the bale again, hoping she had not been seen.

'You! Boy! Follow me,' the man called.

Jenna froze in fear. It was the first time anyone had spoken and she was aware that inquisitive faces were already beginning to lift. She bowed her head and tried to ignore him, hoping he would try someone else, but the bearded man called to her again. Someone else nudged her to get her attention as heads began to turn in her direction.

'Job Blake wants you, boy,' muttered someone under his breath.

'He's one of the Blake brothers,' warned another. 'Best do as he says.' This time she felt she had no choice but to obey. Pulling her hat lower to cover her eyes, she dropped the bale back into the water and reluctantly followed, leaving the tobacco bobbing on the surface until it was grabbed by another.

She trailed behind the other men, as they left the main group and headed towards a cave entrance. Its gaping mouth was barely visible in the shadow of the cliff, as the cloud filled sky blocked out most of the moonlight above. Jenna's steps faltered, afraid she was heading for a trap. Job noticed her hesitation and called for her to hurry. Fearful of the unwanted attention she was causing, she had to do as he commanded.

'They hid some in here,' Job said as they entered the cave. 'We are nearly finished so we need to get this lot moved.'

'Lambskin adding to his collection again?' asked one of the others.

'Aye. Amos was sent word that they dropped the box so we need to check it. Better we say it never arrived than bring Lambskin damaged goods.' Job paused, causing those that followed him to stop too. 'If any of you blabber about what I just said,' he warned without bothering to look around and single anyone out, 'I'll make sure you will never walk again.' An uneasy silence descended as Jenna and the men followed Job deeper into the pitch-black cave.

Jenna heard the distinctive strike of a tinderbox. Flying sparks pierced the blackness and landed on a piece of charcloth in Job's hand. With gentle breaths, he coaxed life into the glow to encourage a flame, which another man used to light a candle inside a lantern. Jenna stepped backwards to hide in the shadows, but she need not have worried. The lantern they used was tailor-made for smuggling, with three sides blacked out whilst the fourth had a cone, which directed the beam.

'Hold this, someone,' Job demanded, holding it out

with a straight arm as he dropped to his knees. Without hesitating, Jenna grabbed it and held it steady, eager to ensure the beam was always pointing away from her. 'I want the light here, boy,' he ordered, indicating an area of sand in front of him. Jenna did as she was told and lit up his grimy hands searching the sand. He quickly found two shovels and handed them out. Without speaking, the other men grabbed them and began to dig.

It was not long before a shallowly buried wooden container jarred against their shovels. They immediately tossed their tools aside and fell to their knees, working furiously with their hands until the top of a box was exposed. Jenna watched in silence as they lifted it out and broke open the lid.

'Boy, bring it closer,' said one of the other men who had, up until now, not spoken. Jenna took a step closer and shone the beam of light onto the tightly wrapped cloth bundles. A knife was brought out and the twines holding them were quickly sliced in two.

'He's a strange one, to have such a fondness for fancy stuff such as this,' someone muttered.

A pair of turquoise, porcelain vases, on gilt bronze mounts, was exposed to the light of their lantern first. Each was decorated with an idyllic country scene of a gentleman wooing his love. What a contrast to my life, thought Jenna miserably, keen to look away.

The second pair of vases was of a different style. They were tall, bold, with a sculpted, bearded face decorating one side. Their deep red surface, which was interspersed with luminous flecks of white, shimmered oddly in the flickering light. Their strange style hinted at the foreign land of their origin and was not to Jenna's taste.

The last to be exposed were the paintings. These captured

Jenna's attention the most. Such skill. Such beauty. How could something so static depict such movement? For the briefest of moments, Jenna forgot where she was, until rough, dirty hands began to examine them. They were hurried and rudimental in their execution as they knew nothing of the real value of the objects they were handling. Although Jenna was no more educated, she knew that these items held a far higher value than the men understood. Satisfied that there was no obvious damage, they were hastily rewrapped and the light extinguished.

'Carry them to Amos. He's up by the ponies. He knows where to take them,' ordered Job. Without uttering a word, everyone in the cave took as much as they could carry and ran out onto the beach and back to the horses. Jenna did the same and this was repeated twice more before the cave was cleared. By then many of the other smugglers had received their payment and dispersed into the hills. Finally, Jenna was told to collect hers from Amos Blake. With her heart in her mouth, she lined up to be paid.

As she waited in line, her collar turned up and her head bowed, she watched the last two heavily laden horses be led away. In their wake a man brushed the ground with a large branch in order to wipe away their hoof prints. As she drew nearer to her turn she could see that the man handing out the money looked similar in size to his brother, with a solid frame, a great height and a long black beard to the level of his chest. A man at her side jostled her to move forward. She realised she was in the front of the line and it was her turn to get her money.

Jenna dared not look up as the coins were hurriedly thrust into her hands in the darkness and despite her dreading the moment, it was a rushed affair and quickly over. Within seconds she found herself walking briskly away to the safety of Jack's home, with the equivalent of a month's wage buried deep in her pocket.

She was halfway up the hill, and beginning to relax, when she heard a man's voice call out to her.

'Hey! Are you Ebenezer's boy?' Jenna knew no Ebenezer and vigorously shook her head without turning around. She held her coat tightly around her and quickened her speed.

'He won't like you being here,' he shouted. 'Stop when I'm speaking to you!'

Jenna broke into a run. The man gave chase, his grunting breaths indicating the speed of his steps behind her. Jenna followed an earthy track that snaked its way up the side of the hill, but already wet and exhausted, the steep gradient soon began to drain any strength she had left. As she grew weaker, her steps grew smaller. She dared not turn around and hoped he would soon tire, but like a dog with a bone, he would not give up.

The futility of her attempt at escape began to dawn on her when she heard more desperate, grunting breaths – and realised they were her own. Yet, despite the inevitable capture, she was still taken by surprise when her foot missed its step as he kicked it away from under her. She fell, sprawling forward, her chin hitting the ground with a sickening thud. She felt his knee press hard into the small of her back.

'I'm talking to you, boy. Show some respect!' he whispered through gritted teeth into her ear. She turned her face away as the smell of brandy and stale breath wafted over her face, but the action only angered him more. He grabbed her collar and some of her hair in his fist, and pulled her to standing. Jenna clamped her mouth shut to stop herself from screaming as strands of hair tore from her scalp.

'I can see I need to teach you a lesson in manners, lad,' he said, shaking her so roughly that for a moment her feet left the ground. She knew she had no strength to fight him, but she still had her wits. She reached behind her head for his hand and pulled hard on his little finger. He yelled in pain and his grip loosened, but just as she found her balance again, she lost it as he was pulled away into the darkness by someone unknown and thrown aside.

Jenna fell onto her knees, breathless and shaking, as her attacker sprawled on the ground beside her. Someone had intervened and, although she was grateful, she remained fearful that this new arrival would be just as dangerous.

She was about to run when she saw her attacker rise to his feet and challenge the man who had come to her aid. In reply, he received a single punch to his face. He stumbled drunkenly backwards, dazed and in pain. The newcomer advanced, spun him around by the shoulders, placed his muddied boot on his buttocks and shoved him roughly into the darkness.

'Scuttle back into the rat hole you crawled out of, unless you want my boot down your throat.'

Recognising the voice, Jenna scrambled to her feet in an attempt to escape. She stumbled and fell, but rose quickly again, desperate she would not be discovered, but it was too late. Her rescuer grabbed her sleeve to stop her, but as she tried to twist away she heard her shirt tear. The cold air on her exposed shoulder halted her in her tracks. The man tore off her hat and looked at her hair.

'Well, well. You are not a boy, but a maid. What a surprise,' he said, not sounding in the least surprised. He pulled her closer and roughly pushed the hat back onto her head as he looked about him. 'It is too dangerous to be out here tonight,' he said. 'You are coming home with me.'

He began to lead the way, but when he saw that Jenna was too tired to match his steps he grabbed her hand. Angry with herself at being caught, she shook him off, but he would not have it.

'You will do as I tell you. You have been lucky tonight, but luck has a bad habit of ending.'

'My luck ended some minutes ago!' she retorted angrily.

He paused and looked at her shivering body. 'You should be in bed,' he said tersely, before slipping his arm about her waist to hold her tightly. She held her breath, surprised by his close proximity. He did not notice. 'Come on,' he ordered, forcing her to match the speed of her steps with his own. 'We are too exposed on this track.' As they walked, the heat from his body began to warm her. She found her body, which had been tense with cold, begin to relax making the hill climb somewhat easier.

At the top of the hill she stepped away from him, to put some distance between them. He let her go, allowing her to claw back some dignity and independence. Side by side they looked down on the now empty cove below them to catch their breaths. With no form of shelter, the wind was stronger here and buffeted their bodies as they rested. He turned to look at her face covered in mud. The anger had left his, only to be replaced by disappointment. He reached for her hat again, and gently took it off her. Disarmed by his unexpected calmness, she did not resist. She watched him as he turned it in his hand to look at it, before drawing it back and throwing it over the cliff. The wind caught it, tossed it as if it were a toy, and carried it away.

'I knew you would be trouble,' he said as he glanced down at her clothes. 'I should have listened to my head and never have hired you.'

'I had my reasons,' she replied.

He did not want to hear it. 'There is no good reason for you to risk your life, Jenna,' Jack retorted.

They left the cliff edge and continued on towards his house. Her damp legs grew chilled and she began to tire again. Noticing she was lagging behind, he offered her his arm. The independence she had attempted to show earlier was gone and she reached for it. It gave her the support she needed, and for the first time that night she was glad that he was there.

'Wash that filth off your face,' Jack muttered, dropping a bucket of water down in front of her. Jenna watched some of the water slop over her boots and onto the floor. From the tension in his face, and the silence that followed, Jenna could tell that his anger had returned. The water was just another sign of how much she had disappointed him. It was ice cold, but she tentatively began to remove the dried mud from her face as he moved around the room, lighting candles. She shivered and Jack noticed. Saying nothing, he began to feed the fire with wood to bring it back to life. It did not take long and Jenna came to stand before it to soak in its warmth.

The silence was deafening; she had to break it.

'You are angry with me.'

He didn't answer and then, as if he could not bear to be near her, he left the room.

Jenna waited, unsure what to do. Finally he returned with a blanket and her nightgown.

'Take off those wet clothes and put this on before you catch a fever,' he said solemnly, dropping them unceremoniously at her feet. He turned his back on her to allow her some privacy. 'You have a lot of explaining to do,' he said.

'How did you know it was me?'

'I just did.'

'Did you know I had left? Did you follow me?'

'I did not. The fool that I am, I thought you were asleep in your bed.' He turned his head to the side so she would hear his next words clearly. 'Where you should have been.'

'Yet you knew it was me.'

He shrugged his shoulders. 'When I saw you running up the hill, you reminded me of when I first saw you running away from the gibbet. The way you moved looked the same, a sort of grace and fluidity in your movement that a man does not have.' He turned his head away again and lifted his chin. 'I knew it was you and did not question it.'

'Why were you out at night? Were you one of the smugglers?'

'It is I who should be asking you that question.'

The rustling of her clothes stopped, but she did not answer. He turned around abruptly for her reply, but he had turned too early. The white nightgown she had just put on over her head fell from her thighs to cover the rest of her legs. The unexpected sight of her shapely, bare legs surprised Jack, but it was the added bonus of being able to see every curve of her body silhouetted through her nightgown which rendered him speechless. He cleared his throat, which had gone noticeably dry, and reached for the blanket.

'You look cold,' he lied, determined not to let his hankering for a woman's body, this woman's body, muddle his thinking. He handed her the blanket. 'Wrap yourself in this and cover yourself up.'

She did as she was told, glad for the extra warmth, and sat on the floor to watch the orange and blue flames as they danced in the grate.

'I will leave in the morning,' she said quietly.

Jack pulled a chair up and sat down close to her. 'I think I deserve an explanation before you go.'

'I have none to give.'

'Let me be the judge.'

She glanced up at him with sad, brown eyes that reminded him of the dark hues of rosewood. 'I do not need you to judge me. I judge myself enough.' She returned her gaze to the fire.

Jack was glad. It would be easier to question her when she wasn't looking at him.

'They are fine words you speak.'

'It is the truth.'

'I think you would not recognise the truth if you saw it.'

His retort hurt, he could tell, but she tried not to show it and continued to stare into the flames.

'Let us start from the beginning,' Jack continued. 'Why did you follow me from Goverek and insist on working for me?'

'You paid for a day's work. I had nowhere to go and it was the right thing to do.'

'So I am to understand that a woman, who likes to masquerade as a boy, has the urge to do the right thing?'

'Yes.'

'Who happens to be out when a smuggling run is taking place?'

'Yes.'

'Why did you listen at my door when I had company?'

'That was wrong and I am sorry.'

'Perhaps it was not the right thing to do.'

Jenna fiddled with her blanket. 'You have missed your calling. You should be a barrister.' Jack said nothing. He did not find her retort amusing. 'You are right,' Jenna conceded, 'it was not, but I meant no harm.'

His heart softened a little at her admission. 'And yesterday you followed me again.'

She glanced up at him guiltily. 'You make it sound worse than it was.'

'Perhaps you were keeping watch for the smuggler's ship.'

'I did not know they were dropping off goods until I saw it arrive.'

'So it was me that you followed. You should watch what your shoes carry into the house. Your mistake does not make you a good spy.'

'I wondered where you were going in the middle of the night, no more.'

Jack leaned forward. 'Take care,' he said, allowing his gaze to wander over her hair as he mocked her reply. 'I may begin to think you have a concern for my welfare.'

'It was not a concern for your welfare that drove me,' she retorted.

Their faces had become so close he could smell the salt wind in her hair. How had he never noticed before? Perhaps tonight's events and her vulnerability were making a romantic fool of him. Her eyes, which had blazed with anger only moments before, turned from rosewood to the colour of black molasses as she looked at him. Beware, Jack. He moved back, a little shaken.

An uneasy silence descended while they mulled over their thoughts. Jack threw another log onto the fire; it was going to be a long night.

'So, you were surprised to see the ship arrive?' he asked her, breaking the tension.

Jenna nodded.

'Is that the reason you went out tonight? To see if the smuggled goods would be collected?'

'No, it was not. Was it yours?'

Ignoring her question, Jack let out a humourless laugh. 'Perhaps you were taking a midnight stroll? I hear it is good for the soul.'

Jenna got up. 'I'm going to bed if you are going to mock me.'

He grabbed her hand as she walked past and halted her. It felt soft and small in his tense grasp. He loosened his fingers and held her more gently.

'Then tell me the truth so I can believe you.'

'I went for the same reason as everyone else went there tonight. I went to take part and earn some money.'

'Not everyone, Jenna,' he said, drawing her back to face him. 'I did not. I hoped you would be truthful.'

Jenna knelt down beside his chair. The blanket fell from her shoulders, but she made no attempt to reach for it. 'It is the truth, Jack,' she insisted.

He should reprimand her for calling him by his name, he thought, but it had sounded too good on her lips to stop her saying it again. He looked into her almond shaped eyes, searching for the truth in her words. If he was not careful he could lose himself in their depths; it was best to remain wary. He looked down at his hand, which still held hers, and quickly released it, before he could draw it to his lips. The questioning began again.

'Do you have any connections with the local smuggling gang?'

Jenna looked at her own hand and he wondered if it felt cold and lost without his. She looked confused and frowned, as if she was trying to remember what he had just asked her.

'No ... no, I do not. I know people who have smuggled before in the past, but not I. In fact, I have never broken the law before tonight.'

Jack listened, but he did not believe her.

'It is true,' she urged. 'I slipped in line with the horses and no one noticed me. When I got to the beach I carried the goods as they were brought onto the shore. My brother told me that landed goods are not left long for fear they are discovered and that if I was a runner on the beach I would be paid at the end.'

Jack's eyes narrowed. 'The man who paid you, what did he look like?'

'He had a hat and a beard, much like the others. I did not look closely. I did not want him to see my face.'

Jack nodded. 'A wise thought,' he conceded, getting up and standing before the fire. 'Did you hear anyone speak about who had financed the trip?'

'It was rare for anyone to speak. Everyone knew what they were doing and there was no need for conversation. I followed everyone else and hoped no one would notice me.'

'You had luck on your side tonight, Jenna. Do you have any idea what they would have done to you if you were discovered?'

'I would rather not think about it.'

She looked frightened and Jack had to fight the urge to comfort her. He could not risk taking her in his arms, not how she was now, naked beneath a flimsy sheet of cotton. He had the feeling one embrace and he would be lost.

'I blame myself. I assume my dismissal of you and losing a good wage prompted you to take this risk. Well, it is over and you are safe. You can remain working for me so there is no need for you to be so foolhardy again.' He picked up her clothes. 'We must burn these before they are discovered.'

Jenna stood and grabbed her clothes.

'My money ...' she said, searching her coat pocket.

Jack looked down on her wearing nothing but her

nightgown, her blanket left discarded in a pool of cloth at her feet.

She opened her fist to show the coins, proving what she had just told him was true. 'You can't burn my clothes. I will need them for next time.'

'There will be no next time,' he said, pulling the clothes from her grasp, 'as next time you may be found out.' He threw them into the fire. Jenna immediately tried to rescue them, but Jack held her back. She was no match for him. They watched in silence, her body encased by his muscular arms, which held her tightly beneath her breasts. The cloth sizzled and steamed, before finally igniting into flames.

'I have to go again,' whispered Jenna so quietly he could hardly hear her. 'I have no choice.'

She felt so soft in his arms, he could feel her pain and worry in every tremble of her body. Jack released her, took her by the shoulders and made her look at him.

'Have to? Why do you have to?'

'I have to pay off my brother's creditors so he can leave the debtors' prison.'

'Your brother, Silas? Has he asked you to do this?'

Jenna nodded.

Jack gave her the blanket and raised his hands to the fire to pretend to warm them. 'Your brother is more reckless with his sister's welfare than he is with his money.' It was all making sense to him now. 'He told you what to do and what the ship's arrival meant when you saw him in Goverek, didn't he?'

Jenna nodded. 'I had to do it. I owe him my life.'

'You owe him nothing. He is a careless, selfish rogue and he has put you in great danger. Why do these men deserve such devotion from you?'

'Men?' she asked, confused at the sudden change in conversation.

Jack turned away from the fire and looked at her.

'Why does a woman sacrifice so much for an unworthy man? There are good men out there who are far more worthy and would never ask so much of them.'

'Silas is my brother and I love him. Who are the other men you talk of?'

'Your husband was no better and hanged for his crimes, yet you loved him so much that you risked your person to ensure he did not suffer.'

'I risked my person to grant his last wish and—'

'—put yourself at risk of being beaten by a jeering crowd. You are not a foolish woman, you knew the danger you put yourself in.'

'—*and* in doing so granted my own wish.'

Jack's eyes narrowed again. 'What do you mean?'

'I spent every day of my marriage in fear of him. He lifted his fist to me more times than I can remember. There was many a day I wished him dead. You think I was a foolish woman blinded by devotion and love. You are wrong. The hangman granted my wish too. By hanging from his legs I only hastened it.'

Jack sat watching the flames die in the grate. Jenna had gone to bed, but the floorboards creaking above his head told him that she remained awake as she restlessly moved about. It was understandable for sleep to elude them both; it was hard to settle after such a night as they had just experienced.

Jack mulled over the situation he found himself in. Jenna's presence, as his housekeeper, was initially a pleasant diversion for him and nothing more. Somehow, in a very short space of time, he had come to care for her more deeply than an employer should for his servant. His growing feelings for her had unnerved him, so it was easy to contain them behind a wall of suspicion, especially when his friend, Enoch, had laid the first brick.

Tonight, however, her honesty and bravery had torn it down and he was forced to face the fact that the concern he felt for her was more than an employer's obligation. Concern for her safety, anger at her brother, even admiration for her foolhardy bravery could be attributed to any friendship. And his desire for her body was just a natural urge any man would suffer when presented with a pretty woman. Yet all these emotions paled in comparison for the feelings of wretchedness he felt when she confessed her marriage was an unhappy one. Jack sat before the fire watching its flames lick the air, yet seeing none of it.

Until today, he had thought of her as a devoted wife who risked her own safety for the man she loved. He had believed it to be a marriage and bond that would still continue today, had it not been torn asunder by the long arm of the law. He thought her late husband was a memory, which would grow in perfection with each passing day. Instead Henry was a nightmare and Jack had not been there to protect her.

He had no reason to feel so wretched at her confession, but he could not call the emotion any other name. She deserved to be loved by a man who would give his life for her, not try to beat her life from her. A man who appreciated her qualities from the first day he saw her – a man such as him. Jack frowned as something stirred within him. He knew what it was, recognition that his feelings for her were even stronger than he had dared to admit. It felt like a door had opened that he did not even think existed and by doing so it changed the landscape about him. He must calm his thoughts. Just because a door had opened it did not mean it was right to walk through it. Soon he would have to move on again and leave her behind. It was not the time to be falling in love.

He turned his attention to the other man in her life. At least he could try to protect her from Silas's problems. Her brother's debts would hang around like a foul smell until they were brought to an end. She had already risked her life for the ruffian and she planned to do it again. He would be able to move on more easily if he knew she was free of the obligation.

Jack thought of her sitting before the fire. She looked so fragile in her nightgown with her blanket slipping from her shoulders. It was hard to believe that earlier in the night she was fearlessly working as hard as any man. Jack rubbed his temple to erase the image of her at his feet. Best to concentrate on what she had said, he told himself.

She told him she had been paid on the beach – an unusual method, but it made sense nonetheless. Only those who turned up and stayed the full night would be present to receive their money, and soon after everyone would disperse and disappear. Jack did not believe the top man would risk his life to be on the beach, but perhaps identifying and following the man who made the payment would lead Jack to him. Jack realised what he must do to keep Jenna safe and if there was an added benefit of finding the man that he sought, that was all to the good. It was time to talk to her.

The house was quiet and the floorboards above ceased to creak. The other rooms in the house remained chilled as the heat of the fire had not quite reached the farthest corners. He mounted the stairs quickly and went to her door. It was shut. Best that it stayed that way.

'Jenna, are you still awake?' he asked softly, addressing the grain of the wood.

'I am.' Her voice was quiet and far off. She was in her bed and preparing for sleep, he realised.

'If your brother's debts are paid and he is released, will his hold over you be gone?'

'He will always be my brother, but I will owe him no debt of gratitude. I have told him not to look for help from me again.'

'What has he done for you to owe him so much?' he asked.

Jenna did not reply.

'If you don't wish me to know then so be it, but blood should not tie you to someone who is prepared to let you risk your life for them. There are better bonds to make and live by. Bonds that nurture and strengthen you – not put you at risk.'

'I know that more than most,' she said. Her voice was nearer now, so close that only the door came between them. Her voice sounded gentle but sad. He could not help feeling it was a waste and should not be so.

'I will take your place and do the next smuggling run,' Jack said quietly. 'You can have my payment and some money I have saved so you can pay off your brother's creditors. He will be free to live his life, but more importantly, so will you.'

The door opened a little; her dark brown eyes looked at him through her tousled hair. She brushed it away with a hand.

'You would do that for me?' she asked.

He nodded and he found himself smiling at her surprised expression.

'But you can't ...'

'I can.'

'Why would you?'

'Why would I not?'

'I won't let you.'

'You have no choice in the matter.'

There was a short silence as she looked for signs of jesting. She found none, yet remained wary.

'What do you expect in return?'

'A simple "thank you" will suffice.' She frowned at him, confused. Perhaps a little explanation would help her to believe him. 'I don't want you to put yourself at risk. I could tie you up and lock you in the house, but that would cause more problems than it would solve. Although I could be persuaded if you think it would be better.' She lifted an eyebrow at him. 'No? Well, this appears the only way I can stop you then.'

'You are willing to put yourself in danger for me?'

'You sound like no one ever has.'

'No one ever has. How can I trust you?'

'I see why you are wary of my offer, but it is made in good faith and I am going to do it, whether you want me to or not.'

She covered her mouth with her hands as her dark eyes, filled with incredulous hope, watched him over the steeple of her fingers. Suddenly the door was opened wider and her arms were about his neck.

'Oh, Jack, thank you. You are such a good, kind man.' He felt her against his chest, her breath on his neck, her hair on his cheek. Initially shocked by her response, he now allowed himself to close his eyes and savour it, clenching his fists at his sides to help him fight the urge to hold her in return. He was a man, and like any man he wanted to touch her curves beneath the gown, but he knew if he did, he would not want to stop. It was not the right time to enter those uncharted waters; best free her of her brother so they could start afresh before it was time for him to leave.

'It is getting late,' he said, in a strangely husky voice he did not recognise. She let her arms drop and he stepped back, letting his gaze wander over her before he turned to leave.

'Forgive me. I should not have addressed you by your name.'

'Do not concern yourself. It no longer seems right to call me sir if I am to break the law for you.' He looked to the window. 'Dawn will soon be breaking so we had best get some sleep. Tomorrow is a new beginning, as I would rather forget about tonight.'

Jenna retreated behind her door to watch him stride away. He knew she was watching him, and thought he heard her speak, but when he turned the door was already closed and the passageway empty. A figment of his imagination, he told himself as he continued on his way. Yet if the words were uttered, there was hope for them after all, for he fancied that she said, *If Henry had been half the man you are, I would have felt truly blessed.*

# Chapter Seven

Silas's eyes narrowed as he studied the men around the
table. Jacob Timmons sat to his right, a willowy man, who
despite carrying himself with the grace and erect carriage
of a gentleman, now found himself in a damp hole full
of paupers. However, he was polite and quiet, and was
ridiculously pleased to have been invited to play. With the
enthusiasm of a kitten, he had joined them at the table, but
soon his fingers were trembling as he held his battered cards
and glanced nervously about him. Were these signs hinting
at his hand? Silas knew better.

Silas learnt early on that Timmons had a fondness for
gin. His love affair with the spirit had whittled away his
money and finally his creditors could stomach no more of
his promises. His family refused to visit him and reunite
him with his liquid friend and now he was suffering badly
for his abstinence. If his trembling fingers did not give him
away, his peculiar body odour did. Silas had smelt the foul
smell of poisons escaping the body before and he knew how
hard it was to concentrate when your body craved drink.
It would be easy to take advantage of such a situation and
Silas had spent his life looking for opportunities like this.

Opposite him was John, a nervous fellow who went out
of his way to avoid confrontation. Not an easy thing to do
when you live cheek by jowl with men who have nothing
left to lose, but meek and mild John somehow managed it
and Silas had noticed. He would be an easy man to cheat as
he did not have the will or courage to challenge.

On his left sat a stocky man who was aptly named
Smithy. He was a blacksmith by trade, whose means of

income had been destroyed overnight by a single episode of apoplexy. His sudden collapse allowed a spark from the furnace to grow unchecked and although he was saved from the fire, his business was not. If this had not been enough to destroy the man, on escaping the grips of death he found his vision greatly changed. Now he could only see directly in front of his eyes, and everything else was black. Although Silas showed concern on hearing of his condition, he stored the information away to be used on a day such as this. His peripheral blindness gave Silas room to swap his cards, which he did frequently with a smile on his lips and a slip of the hand. Yes, he had got to know these men well before suggesting a game. His parents would have been proud of him, and, after all, who could blame him for using the information to his advantage in order to win?

Smithy squinted at his cards. They were not what he had hoped. 'Is your wife visiting again today, Silas?' he asked.

'My wife has never visited. She has taken our children and now lives with her parents. It is my sister who comes to see me.'

'She is a dutiful woman. My family have disowned me,' said Timmons, rearranging his cards in the hope it would give him a better hand. It did not. 'To know you have someone on the outside who cares is a precious thing to have.'

'She is a good sister and I know of none better. We only have each other now.'

Smithy looked at him. 'You have no other family?'

'None. Our parents are long gone and our brothers have moved away.'

'I thought you said they were in gaol or transported?' Smithy challenged.

Silas looked up from studying his cards. 'They are not

around,' he replied sternly. 'Does it matter where they are?' He looked at the other faces around the table and smiled suddenly. 'The point I make is that we only have each other and as I have always looked after her, she naturally dotes on me.' He played his hand and claimed the cut up lengths of bootlace that substituted for money. Sullen faces watched him as he dealt the cards again.

'You have the luck of the devil tonight,' moaned Smithy.

'Are you saying that I am cheating?' Silas retorted, feigning indignation.

'I did not speak such words, but if that word comes to your mind, perhaps we should discuss it.'

Silas made to stand but John stopped him.

'Now, now gentlemen, let us remain civil. I'm sure he meant no such thing.' He patted Silas's arm, trying to calm things. 'Please, sir, continue with the game.'

Encouraged by Timmons too, Smithy relented and picked up his hand. An uneasy truce descended, as Silas dealt two more games. The first he lost on purpose, the second he won and recouped everything he had previously lost. With perfect timing, he noticed Jenna arrive. It was time to take his leave.

'Gentlemen, my sister has arrived. It has been most enjoyable.'

'For you, maybe, but not for me,' grumbled Smithy.

'Perhaps your luck will change tomorrow?'

Smithy grunted. 'If I had any luck, I would use it to get out of here.'

Silas was still smiling when he greeted Jenna and led her to their table.

'You look well, Sister,' he said, watching her as she took five pies from her basket. 'I see that the sea air agrees with you.'

Jenna blushed; a feeling of unease sent worms tingling up Silas's spine, as Jenna never blushed. He looked suspiciously at her. There was something different about her, he realised. Her skin was always smooth, but today her cheeks held a healthy glow and there was brightness in her eyes. What had caused this change? he wondered. What had she to hide?

'Have you been playing faro again?' she asked. Without waiting for an answer she slipped her fingers beneath his sleeve and brought out two cards. 'Have you no shame? You will go to hell, Silas.'

Silas hurriedly picked up the cards and hid them in his pocket. 'It passes the time, no more. Don't scold me, no one has been harmed.'

'Until you are out and claim your winnings from them.'

'If they are fool enough to be fooled it is no fault of mine.'

'You sound like Father,' Jenna said, handing him a pie. 'Eat your pie. These are for Nell and the children.' She looked around the room for them. 'Where are they?' she asked.

'The children are learning their letters and Nell has gone to watch.' The lie slipped easily from his tongue. He knew she would ask for them and this time he was prepared. To continue using illness to explain their absences was too risky, as Jenna would insist on seeing them this time. However, Jenna's delight made even Silas feel guilty.

'That is wonderful! Who is teaching them?'

'Someone.'

'Who?'

'Someone who can write.' What could he say? What did he know of such things?

Jenna folded her arms. 'Trying to get any news from you is like bleeding a stone,' she muttered, to which Silas only grunted in reply. Jenna ignored his sulk. Smiling mischievously she said, 'I am learning my letters too.'

He couldn't hide the surprise on his face. Is this what had changed his sister? Was she becoming learned?

'How? Who?'

'Jack is teaching me. He says that if I am to be a housekeeper I need to read and write, so I can make lists on what I need to buy.'

'Mother didn't need to.'

'I know. I think he just said that to give him a reason to teach me. It is easier than I thought and he says I make a good scholar.'

His sister looked pleased with the praise. Who was this man who offered to teach her and what was he getting in return?

Suddenly Silas felt an outsider. He had always been the most important person in Jenna's life. They had an unbreakable bond that even his wife and Henry were unable to weaken. Yet this Jack had wheedled his way into their lives and gained her trust right under his nose. Did he teach Jenna her letters by the fireside at night, with their bowed heads touching? Where did that leave her only kin? Outside in the cold, that's where.

He moodily looked through the other pies in her basket. 'I have taught you many things,' he said, trying to keep the sound of petulance from his voice.

'Not all good things.'

'Have I not always been by your side?'

'I never said you were not.'

'I have always looked out for you, Jenna.' Even to his own ears he sounded like a jealous child. He bit into one of the pies.

'As I have for you,' she soothed, taking his free hand. 'I did what you asked of me.'

Silas's eyes widened at her meaning. 'I thought you may not. I see you came to no harm.'

'I did not.'

'The money?'

'Be careful, Brother, or you will choke on your pie.' She was smiling at him again. She had smiled more in this short visit than she had in a long time, he thought. 'I have used it to pay one of your creditors.'

Silas did not return her smile. So this is what it has come to, he thought.

'You do not trust me with it?'

'Let bootlaces be your only currency until you leave here, or I will spend my life on the beaches of Cornwall trying to pay off your debts for you to only lose it on the turn of a card.'

'I have never lost at cards – unless I plan it to be so.'

'I have done it and it cannot be undone, nor would I want to. Anyway, Jack suggested it would be safer if I pay the creditors myself, and I agreed with him.'

'This man, Jack. Who is he?'

'My employer.'

'The one who pays you too much.'

'He pays me a fair wage that feeds your belly,' she retorted, withdrawing her hand.

'Even so, he must be after something. Why would he bother with someone like you?'

Hurt flashed across his sister's face, but the emotion only mirrored his own. He was not used to hearing Jenna speak of another man with such fondness. Now she was defending him as if he were blood kin.

'He's a good man, Silas, and I will not have you slander him or question his motives.'

'You defend him too readily, Jenna. You know nothing of the man.'

'I know that he has offered to take my place next time the lugger arrives so I do not have to.'

Silas sat forward and frowned. 'To pay off my debts?'

'Yes. He has even offered some of his savings too.'

Silas saw into Jack's plan. It was not because he was a good man, it was because he wanted to take his sister from him.

'And then ... you will be rid of me.'

Jenna looked guiltily away. Her action turned the pie in Silas's throat to sawdust. He dropped the remainder of the crust on the table with the others.

'He is a saintly man, to unburden you from your brother.'

She looked at him; her intense gaze held a steely determination. 'You will always be my brother, but I will not pay your debts in the future.' Silas sat back. 'I mean it, Silas,' she insisted. 'I want no more trouble knocking on my door.'

'You sound like Nell.'

'If it had not been for Jack, I may have been caught at Porthenys. I want to be free of this problem you have laid at my door. I want to live my own life ... a good, wholesome life where my children learn nothing of the evil in this world and are not dogged by the Cartwright name as we have been. Is that so wrong of me?'

'And where does that leave me, Jenna? Am I to be cast aside?'

'I do not cast you aside, Silas. I beg you to walk with me.' Her brother scoffed. 'But you won't, will you? Instead you consider me strange and you remain determined to continue on the path to the gibbet.'

Silas roughly wrapped the remaining pies in a cloth from her basket.

'This man, how will I know him? I would like to thank

him for teaching my sister her letters so she can look down on her family.'

'I do not look down on you, Silas. Have I not risked my life to help you?'

Silas sighed. 'I'm sorry. This is a rat infested hole that I have found myself in and although I want to be out, I do not like to feel beholden to a man I do not know.' He glanced up at his sister and resentment churned his stomach. This man, Jack, had infected her heart with kindness and although his sister was only the width of a table away from him, she felt unreachable. 'I am serious, Jenna, truly I am. I would like to thank this man for helping to release me.' He saw the distrust in Jenna's eyes. He took her hand in his and compared them, hers clean, small and pale, his grimy and scarred. He smiled and gave it a squeeze. She continued to look at him with a faint line in her brow as she considered his request. Finally she relented and told him what he wanted to know.

'His name is Jack Penhale,' she said. 'But you must address him as Mr Penhale and be polite when I introduce you.'

Years of gambling on the turn of a card had honed his skills in deception as he hid any signs of recognition he felt when he heard the man's name. Sweet, trusting Jenna.

Silas gave her hand a final squeeze and let it go. 'I will look forward to thanking Mr Penhale in person,' he said, gathering the parcel of pies. 'Now it is time for you to go home as we cannot risk displeasing your employer who has shown such kindness to us.'

They stood in unison.

'Stay by your fire on the night of the next run, Jenna. I want you to be safe. It was wrong of me to ask you to do what you did. Forgive me.'

Her smile broadened. 'You will soon be out of here, Silas, and we will start anew.'

After saying their goodbyes, he watched his sister leave, carrying her empty basket in the crook of her arm and with an optimistic spring in her step. What a foolish girl, he thought to himself, allowing a man such as Jack Penhale into her life. She had been a fool to marry Henry, and look how he had turned out. Now she was not seeing clearly again.

Had not their parents warned them, as small children, to beware of thief-takers? Yet, here was his young sister living beneath a thief-taker's roof. Silas now languished in this debtors' prison because of him, for he was the thief-taker his creditors had hired to capture him. While Jack Penhale was free to enjoy his sister's company, her brother lived, ate and slept in the dark. Well, he was not in the dark any more.

Silas returned to the table where Timmons, Smithy and John still sat.

'Smithy, will you lend me your boy to run an errand for me?'

Smithy looked up and smelt the food. 'For the price of a pie, I would.' Silas opened the cloth and tossed him one. Smithy caught it in his lap. 'This is a fine pie.' He looked up suspiciously. 'It is not like you to give away food. I will not have my boy harmed.'

'The errand is to ask a man to visit me and therefore deserves such a fee. When he has done this, he can have one himself.'

'This man, is he important?'

'He is. Not as important as what I plan to tell him. But it will come at a price.'

# Chapter Eight

Jack acknowledged the landlord's greeting and took his usual seat in the corner of the Tolbridge Inn. As he waited for the landlord to come over, his thoughts turned to Jenna, as they so often did.

This morning, under the pretence of shopping for supplies, she asked if she could accompany him to Goverek. Jack, not minding her company, agreed, but he knew better than to think it was only supplies that tempted her to town. The real reason, he believed, was her desire to visit her brother, but knowing that Jack did not like the man, she had the good sense not to say.

Jack was torn on how he felt about her visits to him. Loyalty was an admirable character trait, but her loyalty to Silas was not. He imagined Silas's smug face when he learnt someone else was willing to pay off his creditors. The irony that it was the same man who had put him away would add to his joy. A muscle twitched in Jack's jaw. The farce would be more bearable were Silas grateful for his help, but he would not be, and would show no remorse for the trouble he brought to people's doors. No, Jack was glad he did not question Jenna about her reasons for accompanying him, or he may have let his frustration show.

'You are the only customer I have who has only one drink,' said the landlord as he began to fill his tankard with beer.

'Good day, Klemmo. Are you the only one working today?'

'My wife and maid are out at the back. We may have a wedding in the family very soon. A young man has taken an interest in Melwyn. He walks four miles to see her each Saturday and she has a fondness for him.'

'She is a pretty girl.'

'She was. Her choice of suitors is more limited now.'

'You will miss Melwyn when she is wed.'

'I will be glad when she is away from here and safe.'

Jack glanced up at Klemmo's guilty face. He had said too much and was already regretting his slip. Jack grabbed his wrist, unwilling to let the opportunity pass.

'Klemmo, talk to me. I have watched your family and know what you sell.'

The landlord bent forward so no one else could hear. 'I will tell you no more. It is best it stays that way. I cannot tell what you want to know.'

Jack would not let go. 'Cannot or will not?' Klemmo tried to look away, so Jack tightened his grasp. 'My family was like yours once. I know what it is like to be caught in a web that you cannot break free from. I need information, Klem. I can put an end to this.'

Klemmo pulled his hand free. 'Leave well alone, Jack. You will put yourself in danger and there is nothing you can do. They are too powerful for the likes of us.'

Jack watched Klemmo hurriedly walk away. He was nervous and watchful, afraid that someone may have seen.

Jack took a drink of his warm ale. Over the last few weeks he had cultivated his friendship with the landlord, but today he may have pushed it too far. He had come to believe that Klemmo was an unwilling receiver of smuggled goods. If he was right, the landlord might be willing to help him. Jack thought the landlord was beginning to trust him, but he may have miscalculated. It appeared that Klemmo trusted no one, and certainly not a man who he had only recently come to know.

Jack sat back in his seat to moodily nurse his beer until the outer door opened and another man entered. The stranger's furtive glances as he surveyed the room piqued Jack's interest. He did not know him, but he realised that Klemmo did, and was not pleased to see him. Jack straightened in his seat to obtain a better view just in time to see him grab Klemmo's shirt and push him through to a back room. Jack pushed away his tankard. Seeing the man manhandling Klemmo meant that he had no choice but to get up and follow.

Unnoticed by the other drinkers, he followed the angry voices to an outhouse at the back of the inn and listened from a recess in the yard.

'You will have ten kegs,' shouted the stranger angrily.

'The price is too high,' argued the landlord. 'Bring it down and I will reconsider.'

The sounds of a scuffle made Jack step closer.

'The price remains as I have told you. Ten kegs on Friday and another the following week.'

'I cannot hide that amount and I do not have the means to pay for so much.'

'You will do as you're told or I will slice your daughter's face, as *he* did.'

Jack heard the sound of fighting and a body hit the brick wall. He heard Klemmo cry out in pain. The landlord was no match for the younger man and it was evident that he was not winning. Unwilling to hear any more, Jack entered the outhouse to find the younger man kicking a crumpled body on the floor. Jack grabbed him by the coat and dragged him backwards away from his victim, before roughly turning him around to face him. Their eyes locked momentarily, before Jack punched him in the face. The man staggered back, momentarily dazed, before lurching forward at his unknown attacker with an amateur swing. Jack was ready for him, dodged his punch and came up with another to the bottom of the younger man's chin. The man toppled backwards and landed heavily on a pile of logs behind him, before sliding to the floor at Jack's feet. Jack did not have the patience to wait for him to get up. Lifting him up by his arm, he marched him out to the alleyway and shoved him into the street.

'Get out and don't come back or next time you will not have legs fit to walk away on,' he warned.

Klemmo, half stooping, followed him into the alleyway. 'He will be back.'

'Not for a while,' Jack said, picking up his hat from the floor and brushing off the dirt. 'He will not have the courage to tell the Blake brothers that he has failed in his task. He will keep his mouth shut and hope you will buy the ten kegs.'

The men's eyes met as Klemmo dabbed his bleeding nose.

'How much do you already know?' Klemmo asked warily.

'Some, but not all. I need to know who finances the smuggling gang. When he is gaoled you will be free of them. Do you know who it is?'

Klemmo shook his head. 'No and if I knew I would not tell you.'

'You do not trust me?'

'I trust no one, Jack. People are not who they seem to be. I know of one who talks to both sides.'

Jack's eyes narrowed. 'Who?'

'I have said too much and have an inn to run. Go on your way, Jack. It is too dangerous here.'

The landlord retreated inside, leaving Jack standing alone in the alleyway. He had thought Klemmo was about to unburden himself, but it turns out he was wrong.

'He needs time,' said a woman's voice behind him.

Jack turned to see Melwyn, leaning against the doorframe. She stepped into the alleyway, shutting the door carefully behind her. Despite a jagged scar upon her cheek and wearing a large sackcloth apron, her youthful looks still shone out from beneath its coarse weave.

'I do not have time, Mel, and what I have seen here today shows me that they do not care who they hurt.'

'Father is afraid for us. They have increased the prices every month and Father now makes little profit in it. They threaten us if we do not do as they say.'

'And I can see from your face they do more than just threaten. Speak to your father and persuade him to tell me what he knows.'

Melwyn's eyes brimmed with tears. 'He won't, he is too afraid.'

Jack put his arm around her to comfort her. 'I understand. Fear is a powerful thing and it can cripple a man.' He gave her a friendly hug and patted her shoulder. 'Take courage, Melwyn. It will not be forever. I am here to stop it and I have every intention of doing just that.'

Her lip began to tremble like a child's so he reached for her again and held her close to comfort her. As her head rested beneath his chin he looked over her head to the street beyond the alley. He wondered what he should do next, until he realised he was looking right into the eyes of Jenna.

So this is what he does with his time, thought Jenna. Feeling flustered, she turned around a little too quickly and started heading in the wrong direction. She heard him call to her. Realising her mistake, she abruptly changed course, narrowly missing a horse and cart as it passed her by. He called again, but she pretended not to hear him and surged on towards what she hoped was the stables.

The woman looked too young for Jack, she thought as she marched along. The woman pawed at his chest like a needy dog and, despite the distance, Jenna was sure she had a simpering smile. How could Jack find her attractive? She would bore him quickly and he would soon look elsewhere. Jenna did not like feeling jealous, but there was no other name for the uncharitable thoughts that were rushing through her head.

She heard him call again. This time she slowed her step. There was no point trying to outrun him, she realised, as they were to share his horse for the journey home. She had also forgotten the direction to the stables, although she would never let him know that. It was embarrassing to catch him embracing another woman, but to show him how much it disturbed her was far worse. She turned and smiled at him, ready to play the happy housekeeper pleased to see her employer.

Jack walked calmly towards her, his dark eyes watching her steadily from beneath the brim of his hat. She could not decipher his mood. Was he angry she had disturbed him in his courtship? If she had not would they be kissing now?

He has such a beautiful face, she thought, as he approached her. How could she bear another woman to kiss it? She felt sick at the thought and her brittle smile weakened. She must not let Jack know what she was thinking. She had no right to feel such loss at seeing another woman in his arms. He was not hers to lose.

'Your silence is like the wrath of a scorned woman,' said Jack from behind her.

She could not argue with him. She tried to pretend she

did not care, but a mile into their ride home she had fallen into a sulky mood. The image of him with his arms wrapped around another woman would not go away.

'If you continue to avoid telling me what is the matter, I will have no choice but to guess.' Hearing no answer, he added, 'She is the landlord's daughter and she was upset. I was comforting her.'

Heat rose in Jenna's cheeks. Was she so transparent to him? Despite her embarrassment, she could not stop herself wanting to know more about her rival, for that was how she saw her.

'What was she upset about?'

'I cannot say.'

'You are at liberty to find comfort where you wish.'

'I was not finding comfort, I was giving comfort.'

It was more than mere comfort she was experiencing, thought Jenna.

'You can call it what you like, it is no concern of mine.'

Silence returned, but for the rhythmic beat of his horse's hooves on the track.

Eventually, Jack said, 'She is sixteen. No more than a child.'

'She is no child.'

'To me she is. I do not wish to talk about her again.'

'I am only two years older,' muttered Jenna.

'Are you?'

She turned in the saddle to look at him. 'You sound surprised.'

'I thought you were older.'

Jenna frowned; for a moment the landlord's daughter was forgotten. It was hard to think of her when Jack's face was so close to hers and a tilting smile curved his lips.

'How old did you think I was?' she asked, looking at his mouth.

'I feel like I'm being interrogated,' teased Jack.

Jenna reluctantly turned around again to stare moodily at the track.

'I thought you were forty.'

'Forty!' Jenna said, swinging around angrily to face him. He stifled a laugh. She turned away again, frowning furiously. He became quiet, although she could still feel his laughter through the movement of his body. She tried not to smile.

'You are teasing me. That is unfair.'

'But well deserved. I will not put up with moody sulks. It does not suit you, Jenna.'

'I was surprised, no more. You did not tell me you were meeting a woman.'

'I did not tell you because it was not a woman I visited. It was a man – her father.'

And yet you were providing comfort to *her*, Jenna wanted to challenge. Instead she bit her lip and remained silent.

'How was Silas?' Jack asked.

'How did you know?'

'You are the only woman I know who goes out for supplies with a basket full of food.'

'I did not want you to know. I thought the less you heard about him the better.'

'I see.'

There was a short silence. 'Why did you visit her father?' she asked.

'It is better you do not know why.'

A sense of unease swept through her. His reply was a reminder of how little she knew about Jack Penhale. She wondered how well the other woman knew him.

'Then I will not enquire further.'

'Good. I am glad to hear it.'

'Jack ...'

'Yes?' he said, sounding content that his name came naturally to her now.

'Do you really think that I look forty?' She felt him move behind her, as he attempted to stifle more laughter. She waited patiently for his answer. Finally it came.

'No, not forty,' he replied seriously. 'You look far too old to be forty.'

# Chapter Nine

A late November gale howled outside the windows, rattling the salt-stained glass within their metal frames and sending the occasional puff of black smoke back down the chimney. Outside, twigs and debris were tossed and rolled by the wind, littering the picturesque coastline and haphazardly flattening the lush grass in the fields beyond.

To Jenna, the harshness of the weather outside only enhanced the sense of warmth, safety and peace within the house. Sitting at the table, practising her letters, a particularly strong gust broke into her concentration and made her glance up at Jack. Jack did not notice and continued to read his book before the open fire. His immersion into the words on the page was so complete that she noticed even his expression changed slightly as he absorbed their meaning. It was endearing and Jenna found herself smiling as she watched him.

She dragged her gaze away from him and dipped her quill in the ink. Carefully, just as Jack had shown her, she touched the edge to let the excess fall back into the pot before taking it to the paper. J-e-n-n-a, she wrote carefully, her bottom teeth pinching her lip in concentration as the ink flowed onto the page. She sat back and looked at it. She had written her name several times, but this time the letters were smooth and shapely, just like Jack's writing above them.

'You look pleased with yourself,' Jack said, abandoning his book so it lay half open in his hand.

'I am. I have written all the letters in my name and it no longer looks a mess.' He put out his hand and she immediately went to him.

'You see,' he said, taking the sheet to look at it. 'You can write. You just needed to be taught.' He handed it back to her with a flourish of the hand and a sincere smile on his lips.

Feeling ludicrously happy, Jenna forgot about her lesson and sat down opposite him.

'I have never been encouraged to learn, and I knew no one who could teach me.'

'No one in your family could read?'

Jenna arched an eyebrow. 'No, if you knew my family you would understand.'

'I know Silas. He thinks stealing is an honourable profession and would see no use for writing.'

'My parents and four brothers are cut from the same cloth. They have quite a reputation and it is not for their intellect.'

'Tell me about them.'

Jenna sat back in her chair and looked at him. 'And you will not judge me?'

Jack held her gaze. 'I will not.'

Jenna cleared her throat nervously. She had always hidden her background from her employers before, but Jack's gentle tones were encouraging.

'I loved my parents, but they were thieves. I cannot pretend otherwise. They thought, by teaching their children to do the same, they were passing on a profession. They believed they were doing the right thing.'

'Do you look like your mother?'

Jenna settled herself into her seat. 'People say there is a likeness. My mother did not look like a thief. She was pretty and claimed to have French blood. She did have a French name. Marguerite, but I suspect it was a name she chose to call herself, rather than one she was given. She spent her life deceiving people and my father was no different.'

Jenna began to comb her hair with her fingers, unaware that Jack watched her. Her memories had taken her to another time, as she remembered the life she would normally want to forget.

'I was the youngest of five,' she continued. 'There were twelve years between me and my two oldest brothers, David and Paul. When I was about four, they were caught stealing and taken to gaol. I never saw them again. Silas thinks they left the county after their release, but I do not know for sure.'

'And your other brother?'

Jenna smiled. 'Mark was more like me and wanted a different life. When he was thirteen he ran away to sea. I often wonder what happened to him. I was young when he left and can no longer remember his face, but I often think of him.'

'Many men do run away to the sea to escape the law. Fighting ships are littered with men from dubious backgrounds.'

'And Mark will be one of them. I hope he has found his sea legs.'

'What happened to your parents?' asked Jack, leisurely stretching out his legs and crossing them at the ankles.

'One night, when I was fourteen, they went out and never returned. Silas was the only one left. He did not desert me. We were always close, but after that day he took me under his wing and gave me a home. I lived with him and his new wife, Nell, for a few months until I could find live-in work. It was difficult to keep a job, when you have a family like mine, so I was often dismissed. Silas took me in every time. He was like a father and brother all rolled into one, but I felt a burden to him and his wife, so I married Henry, hoping it would solve all our problems. It did not.'

'You have had a difficult life.'

Jenna tilted her head to consider his words. 'I don't think I know how to live any other way. Life is difficult, isn't it?'

Jack's eyes softened. 'Not always,' he replied, a slight smile curving his lips. 'Life can be good too.'

'Tell me about yours then. Who taught you to read?'

Jack closed his book, although his finger remained on the page he was reading.

'My mother was a governess until she married my father and became a farmer's wife. She loved the farm, but I think she had fond memories of her time in employment so she used her skills as a governess to teach the only pupil she had, which was me.' Jenna stopped hugging her knees and looked at him with a renewed curiosity. 'You look surprised that my mother was a governess.'

'I am surprised you are a farmer's son. You have not bought a plough yet. The fields need to be ploughed if you want to seed them.'

Jack laughed. 'I am in no hurry to plant crops.'

'How do you earn your money?' The question was a bold one, even by her standards. A housekeeper had no right to ask her employer such a question, but then if things were as they should be, she would not be sitting opposite him now and he would not be offering to break the law for her.

'I am employed here and there to undertake certain tasks and when they are done I am paid. I move around a lot.'

This news did not surprise Jenna. The first thing she noticed when she arrived at the house was the lack of personal items that bring their own peculiar comfort to a home.

'Do you like to travel?' she asked.

'No,' he said sadly, but then he suddenly brightened. Lifting his book again he said, 'But I like to read about it.'

Never having read a book, his meaning was lost to her. 'I don't understand.'

'When you read a book, you can be transported to another part of the world, even another time. I think you will enjoy the experience.'

'Is that what you were doing before? You were sitting in front of the fire, but you appeared to be somewhere else in your head.'

Jack nodded, pleased she understood.

She leaned forward, her elbows balancing on her knees, her hands held together as if preparing to plead. 'Take me with you,' she asked him suddenly.

His smile faltered as he looked at her expectant face. 'Where?'

'Anywhere.'

'You must have a preference.'

She shook her head. 'I do not care where. I just want you to take me.'

He did not answer at first. The fire continued to crackle in the grate and the wind still howled outside, yet the atmosphere had subtly changed, cloaked with his silence. Jack swallowed; his smile was gone and there was gravity in his gaze.

When he finally answered his voice was softer than before and there was a stark absence of any irony or teasing in his words. He leant forward too, their knees almost touching as the fire warmed the sides of their bodies.

'It is a request that would be hard to deny.'

Were they still talking about reading? She was unsure of Jack and even less sure of herself.

She spoke before she thought; she did not care how it might sound, it was what she wanted to say so she said it.

'Then don't deny me.' Her own voice had changed too.

The words slipped from her lips like silk in a way she had never heard before. Their dance of words excited her and turned her voice to the throaty sweetness of a seductress. The book still lay in his lap, but neither thought of it.

His lips look soft, she thought, as she imagined what they would feel like against hers. She found herself swallowing, just as Jack had done a few moments before. Was he sharing the same shameful thoughts as her? His gaze dipped and lingered upon her own lips. Yes he was, she thought, hardly daring to breathe, and she was being drawn to him like no other.

The fire belched a small puff of black smoke into the room, coming between them and breaking the spell. Jenna tried to hide her smile as Jack cursed the fire and waved the smoke away. He poked at it needlessly and fed it more wood before finally settling in his chair again.

'The chimney needs sweeping,' he grumbled. 'The view from here may be fine but the sea winds can be too strong.' He was allowing his attention to remain diverted, she thought, as he made a show of finding his page. He did not want the intimacy they felt to return, or perhaps it was only in her mind and he was now embarrassed for her. She made to leave.

'I will read you this chapter,' Jack said suddenly. 'The book is a diary of a man's expedition.' He looked up to see her standing. 'I thought you wanted me to read to you.'

She sat back down, feeling foolish. 'Yes, I do.'

Jack appeared not to notice her discomfort, as he noisily cleared his throat.

'He has travelled to many islands to collect specimens for his scientific research, but by accident he has discovered a tribal village.'

Jenna eased herself back in her chair to listen. She felt

silly, yet Jack had dismissed their moment of madness and was back to normality. He began to read and she watched his lips move and his fingers caress the page, but she did not listen to his words. Instead she watched the man as his hair shone in the firelight and his eyelashes fanned his cheeks.

His hair and complexion were dark, hinting at a line of foreign blood in his ancestry that she had not noticed before. She had heard tales of sailors from the failed Spanish Armada being washed up on the shores of Cornwall. Was he descended from someone like this? She could well believe it for he had the darkest brown eyes she had ever seen and the air of mystery of someone from a strange land.

His voice was lovely to listen to – intelligent and learned, but comforting all at the same time. She closed her eyes so she would no longer be distracted and began to listen to the story he read.

Within minutes she was transported into the world that lay within the pages of his book and an island far away. Away from a country brutally divided by class, where aristocrats looked down upon the poor majority and where a criminal underbelly grew unchecked. Away from a county where winter made its presence felt daily, and her brother and his family languished in the squalor of a debtors' prison. For the hour that followed, Jenna was transported to a mystical vibrant island called Fiji, and by her side walked a man named Jack.

# Chapter Ten

Captain Henley took off his hat and dipped his head below
the doorframe. The air inside the passageway was foul,
causing his nose to wrinkle in distaste as the smell clawed
at his throat.

'Do you have a room where we can be alone with him?'

The keeper nodded, but did not move. His open hand
waited for a coin, which Captain Henley reluctantly
presented. The coin changed hands with a flick of two
fingers and the keeper, satisfied, finally showed them the
way, leading the two officers down the narrow cobbled path
to a door at the end.

The small room beyond the wooden door was no better.
Green moss grew on the walls and black mould darkened
the corners. Captain Henley and his deputy, Tilbury, waited
in silence as they let their eyes wander over their grisly
surroundings. They could hear the cries of the prison inmates
in the distance and the rustle of rats scurrying behind the
walls. They stood awkwardly in their smart uniforms of
blue and white, unaccustomed to being summoned to such
a place and a little fearful of dirtying their white breeches.
It was a necessary evil, Henley thought to himself. When a
message was sent offering them valuable information, the
temptation was too much to resist.

After some moments the door opened and in walked
a man with filthy, ragged clothes and skin ingrained with
grime. Yet, despite his appearance, his eyes were bright
and he had a smile upon his face. He sat down at the table
as if he were a lord, straightening his sleeves and brushing
some dirt off his breeches. The men watched the inmate

and wondered if they had been made a fool of by coming here.

'You asked to see us,' Henley said finally.

'Aye, I did,' said the man, enjoying the attention he was receiving. 'I hear that you want information. I hear you have been asking around. I have what you want and I am willing to give it to you.'

Captain Henley forgot his clean white breeches and sat down opposite him. Tilbury moved to the door to guard it.

'What information do you have?' Henley asked.

'The sort you want.'

'I will be the judge of that.'

Silas laughed. 'There is only one judge we should be fearful of.' He looked up to the ceiling and winked. 'Only one.'

The man is enjoying this, thought Henley. He resented his toying but this might be the breakthrough he was waiting for.

'What is this information? Tell us, man.'

'I will ... for a price.'

Henley reached in his pocket and once again flipped over a coin. Silas looked at it and snorted in distaste.

'A coin will not get me out of here. I have one creditor left that needs payment. I want my debts paid and some money for my pocket.'

'You place great value on the information you have.'

'I do.'

'And if I should agree to this, what will I get in return?'

Silas's smile left his lips. Glancing up at Tilbury he said, 'I want him out of here. I will only tell you.'

Henley considered his condition before giving Tilbury a curt nod, indicating for him to leave. Reluctantly he did so.

Silas waited until he was satisfied they were alone. Finally, he leant forward towards Henley, sending a waft of his breath into his face as he spoke. Henley hid his repulsion.

'When I walk out of these prison walls and leave these rats behind,' Silas whispered. 'I will tell you.'

'Tell me what?'

Silas laughed, enjoying his position of power. 'How to find out where the next run will be.'

Henley attempted to mask his reaction, but the lack of it told Silas all he needed to know. Underneath, the man was as eager to learn more as a dog seeking a bitch.

'How do you know this information?' Henley asked in a measured tone.

Silas raised an eyebrow.

Henley answered his own question. 'You have helped carry contraband.' He watched Silas give a single, leisurely nod of his head. 'I am listening.'

'I will not tell you until I am free or you will leave me to rot in this hole after you have heard what I say.'

Henley was barely able to conceal his frustration. The inmate held all the cards and he had no choice but to bow to his demands. His eyes searched Silas's face as he considered the deal. This man was his first informant. If he rewarded him well, it would not only give him the information he sought, but pave the way for other informants to come forward. However, Henley did not intend to be made a fool of.

'How will I know you are not feeding me lies?' he asked.

'I will speak the truth.'

'A gambler's tongue does not know how to speak the truth.'

'But he knows which stake to place his bets on.'

Henley fell silent. It might just work, but he would ensure that the money went direct to his creditor and not pass through this man's filthy hands first. He would only fritter it away.

Henley nodded his agreement. 'I will arrange for your creditor to be paid.'

'And some money for my pocket.'

'Money you will gamble away.'

'I need to live.'

'Then find employment.'

'I see that I'm wasting my time.' Silas stood and prepared to leave. 'Perhaps my information is best kept to myself.'

A muscle worked in Henley's jaw. 'A month's wage for your disposal, but no more.'

Silas sat down again and smiled smugly.

'But the money will be split,' added Henley. 'I will give you half for the information and the other half when it has been proved right.'

Silas grinned at him. 'It will be good to breathe clean air again.'

His smile was not returned. 'Meet me at the Dog and Duck tavern when you are out and we will talk further. I will pay you the first instalment when you have told me what you know.'

'Come alone. There are ears and eyes everywhere who will sell what they know. Do not tell anyone, not even your soldiers until the night of the raid.'

'The King's men are not corrupt,' snapped Henley.

'Everyone can be corrupted if the price is right.'

Captain Henley narrowed his eyes. 'You have little faith in mankind,' he replied. The wretched man opposite him did not answer. 'But perhaps you have good cause. I will come alone.'

Silas put out his hand and Captain Henley reluctantly took it in his. The deal was done.

'You will be betraying a large number of people for your freedom. I hope you make good use of it and avoid returning to this pit,' Henley said, scraping back his chair to stand.

'There is only one person I am interested in and he will be on the beach at the next run. When you make your move on the landing gang you will remove him from my life. If others die in the process, so be it. I owe them no loyalty. I only care about my sister and myself. The rest can rot in hell.'

Jenna picked up the abandoned breakfast plate from the table and looked at it. The uneaten eggs, cooked how she knew he liked them, were now cold, sunken and stuck to the plate. She wasn't used to wasting food and for a moment she wondered what to do with them. Jack did not usually leave anything, preferring to eat whatever dishes she chose to give him, even the ones that had not turned out as well as she had hoped.

As she hesitated over the mundane decision, she could hear him pulling on his boots in the next room. The sound of sharp tugging was filled with frustration and energy, not the usual gentle sound of leather sliding over cloth. She often saw him put on his boots. It was a confident, unhindered routine that was mesmerising to watch, but this time she did not stay, sensing that he wanted to be left alone. He did not have to ask this of her, she just knew and gave him the solitude he desired. Jenna bit her bottom lip, his plate temporarily forgotten in her hand.

She had discovered that her sensitivity to his needs came naturally to her. It was not something that she was forced to develop in order to survive, as with her late husband. It was an innate understanding of his soul, encouraged by desire, curiosity and a willingness to learn about him. It was like a lesson that was continuous and constantly evolving but without the need for study. His behaviour this morning suggested that something was troubling him, and Jenna had a growing realisation of what it might be. She dropped the plate and eggs in some water and went to him.

He was looking for something, tossing papers and books aside as he did so. 'You are not hungry?' she asked.

'No,' he replied, finding his tinderbox and slipping it in his pocket. 'The weather has hampered my work these past three days but now I have things to do.'

'Is there anything troubling you?'

He ignored her question and continued his searching. 'I pity the fishermen who have to work in such winds. There will be many uprooted trees on the track to the north and roof slates in need of repair, I wager.'

'Where are you going?'

'I have a meeting this afternoon and won't be home until late. Although the worst of it has passed, I suggest you keep the drapes drawn to keep in the warmth as there will still be a chill in the air when the sun goes down.'

'Has it turned?'

'Yes, the weather has turned. I feel we are in for a calmer spell now.'

'You know that is not what I mean,' said Jenna. Jack looked away, but Jenna would not be put off. 'Has the weathervane turned?'

Jack straightened. A single nod of his head confirmed what she suspected. A rush of prickly fear swept over her. 'Which way does it point?'

'Tudor Cove,' he replied solemnly.

His searching came to an end, for in truth he was not looking for anything of importance. His offer of help was now becoming a reality and true to his word he was going to take her place on the beach tonight. Tomorrow her brother would be free. Yet Jenna felt no relief that it would soon be over, only a sickening anxiety welling up in her chest. She twisted her fists into her skirts to keep the tension she felt in check.

Jack glanced up and noticed. 'I will be back before you know it.'

'Tudor Cove is so near.'

'Not a ten minute walk from here.'

'Are you sure?'

'I saw the lugger drop the goods last night.'

'I did not hear you leave.'

A slight smile curved his lips, but there was no happiness in his tone. 'I am glad I did not disturb you.'

'Were you planning to leave without telling me?'

He did not answer.

'You believe there will be trouble?'

'There will be no trouble.' He sounded so sure. Was he trying to reassure her or perhaps telling her the truth? It is easy to believe such words when desperation fills one's heart. Eagerly she took up the mantle of reassurance.

Jenna smiled nervously. 'If I, a woman, can masquerade as a smuggler, I am sure you can.'

'I do not plan to fail.'

'Everyone is involved in one way or another. I'm sure the tea at Sally's shop is delivered in the dead of night.'

'Keep the light low when it grows dark and use only one candle. Don't let them know you are up.'

'And then there are those who supply the horses and turn the weathervane.'

'Go to bed early tonight,' Jack said, putting on his hat and making for the door.

'And then there are all those fishermen who allow their boats to be used. There cannot be many in Cornwall who have not had smuggled goods pass through their hands.' Jenna followed him. 'Silas says that no one has been convicted here for twenty years.'

'They have the luck of the devil,' Jack said, reaching for the latch of the door. Jenna stepped in front of him, barring his way.

'I'm afraid for you, Jack. Don't do it.'

Jack looked at her clenched fists entangled in the cloth of her skirts and gently placed a hand on each.

'You often do this when you are worried. Did you know that?'

The warmth of his hands relaxed her, causing her to slowly unfurl her fingers beneath and release the crumpled cloth of her skirts. He is so close, she thought, if she dared she could step into his arms and lay her head upon his chest. She could hear him breathe, as he could her, their chests rising and falling with each mirrored breath they took.

'And if I don't do this, what then?' he asked her softly as he looked down upon her hair.

Jenna could not answer as she had no words that he would wish to hear. If the debts were not paid, Silas would remain in prison and his burden would remain with her.

Jack smiled. 'As I thought.' He lifted her hands in his and looked at them, turning them in his palms and stroking them gently with a brush of his thumbs. 'Your hands are too soft to carry such heavy cargo again and your face should not be hidden by mud.' He looked up. As he held her gaze his eyes grew black. The moment stretched and her throat grew dry. He was going to kiss her, she thought hopefully, but instead he gave her hands a reassuring but brisk squeeze. His smile broadened. 'Don't fret all day. It is the truth when I say that for the most part I am in a meeting and in no danger. For the latter part I intend to avoid any trouble.' His sudden cheerfulness sounded forced and was fleeting, but it succeeded in doing what had to be done as it broke the spell between them.

'Silas will want to thank you himself.'

'I care nothing for him.'

'Then it is I who should thank you. Were it not for me—'

'Do not feel any guilt. I have my own reasons for doing this.' He gently moved her aside and opened the door. 'Keep yourself warm. As I said, there is still a chill in the air.'

'I will not be able to sleep until I know you have come home safe.'

Jack did not appear to hear her. Instead he looked across at the rugged coastline that stretched for miles into the distance.

'No, I do not envy the fishermen. The coast has fine views but the winter winds are harsh.'

'Please take care. If they discover you are not one of them—'

'They will not.'

'What if something goes wrong?'

'I will send word. There is money in a pot in the cupboard should you need it.' He began to stride away, leaving her to stand in the doorframe alone.

'I will not need it,' she called after him, 'for I know you will come back.'

He did not answer, his mind being elsewhere. She watched him walk away until she could see him no more. He was gone and although she believed he would be back, his remark about the money ran a prickle of fear across her skin that his departure had a threat of permanence about it. She carefully closed the door on the empty track he had followed, in the hope to stop such thoughts and shut them out.

Jack collected his horse from the field and headed towards Goverek town. Although his horse was fresh and willing, the journey took longer than he expected. Three days of rain had saturated the turf making a cross country route hazardous. Therefore, to avoid his horse suffering an injury, he chose to travel by road, which, although quiet, added unwanted time to his journey.

For the most part, the ride was not unpleasant as it followed a swollen, brown river littered with fallen branches, which added interest to his journey. Sunshine peeped out from fast passing clouds to cast welcome, warm sunbeams on his skin, while flocks of starlings from Northern Europe seeking a milder winter climate gathered noisily in the distant fields.

He thought of Jenna, wishing the circumstances were different and that she could be with him now, enjoying the sights the storm had left in its wake. He thought of her face as he was leaving. Although etched with fear, it remained beautiful to his eyes and he wondered if she ever noticed his growing desire for her, despite trying to hide it. It was best if their relationship was kept in check for now, he thought, as their lives were entangled more than she knew.

If he were to confess his involvement with her brother he risked damaging something that had yet to blossom. What woman would fall in love with the man who had committed her brother to prison? To make matters worse, she thought he was helping her brother for *her*, but he did not deserve such praise because there was another reason he was taking her place tonight. To confess to her that he was spying on the smugglers might put her at risk as she would know too much. Yet not confessing meant he took all her praise, which he did not deserve. He could only hope that when her brother was free again, she would look more kindly on him when he finally told her the truth. He knew that she had a kind heart. This morning it had taken all his strength not to tell her how he felt and kiss her goodbye. Had he lost the battle to keep his distance, at least he would have had the taste of her on his lips right now.

His thoughts were getting him nowhere so it was with a sense of relief that he finally arrived at Goverek. Sir Enoch Pickering had sent word that he wished to meet him at the only remaining coffeehouse in the town. Jack disliked coffeehouses. Once an all-inclusive social meeting place, they had been numerous and frequented by many. Now their popularity was waning and many had closed. Those that remained open excluded all but the educated gentlemen, who valued their own opinions more highly than those of others around them. These men chose the form of debate to show off their knowledge as they supped their bitter coffee in wood panelled rooms. Jack found no pleasure hearing their wisdom, if at the end of it nothing ever changed. However, Enoch had insisted on meeting him at Salwes Coffeehouse, so reluctantly Jack agreed.

He climbed the narrow stairs to the room on the first floor and paid his admission fee. Grinding his teeth in frustration at the sounds of a political debate greeting him, he took off his hat and entered the poorly ventilated room.

The young man commanding the attention of the crowd was no more than twenty years of age. Jack could not help but be impressed by his fine words if not their political content.

Enoch's tall, lean frame broke away from the crowd and walked over to greet him. 'He is a fine orator, is he not?'

'He holds their attention,' Jack conceded.

'I was once an advisor to his father. He is staying with me for a few days and expressed a wish to come here. He sneaks into Parliament to listen to the members in order to hone his speaking skills.'

Jack raised an eyebrow. 'Parliament?'

'This man was practically born in the building. His father was the First Earl of Chatham. He died last year. Ah, he has finished and is coming over to us. Do not be put off by his aloofness, he is a kindly fellow but he does not mix easily.'

The serious young man was almost upon them, weaving his way through the gentlemen coffee drinkers as yet another loud debate broke out about him. Jack understood what Enoch meant, for despite his confidence only moments before, he now spoke or acknowledged none of his listeners as he approached them. He had a large nose, an ill-defined chin and neat fine lips, yet despite the absence of strength in his features, he had a presence that many men failed to achieve.

'This is William Pitt. William, this is the man I have told you about – Jack Penhale.'

The men shook hands.

'William Pitt,' Jack repeated. 'The same name as a past prime minister.'

'He was my father,' the man replied in a curt tone.

Enoch interrupted to explain further. 'Unfortunately, last year he collapsed suddenly in the House of Lords and died shortly afterwards.'

Perhaps the man's impolite tone was due to his grief, thought Jack. He tried again to make conversation. 'It must have been a shock when you heard.'

'I did not have to wait to hear, I was there at the time.'

Enoch laughed nervously and patted the young man

on the shoulder. 'William, here, will follow in his father's footsteps one day. I have no doubt about it. I'm sure your father hoped it to be so. It is for this reason I wanted the two of you to meet.'

'And do you?' asked Jack. He would remain polite even if the man's tone was not.

'Do I what?'

'Wish to follow your father into politics?'

'At the moment I study law, but politics is in my blood and I take every opportunity to take part.'

The two men had little in common. Once again Enoch interrupted to smooth the waters.

'William believes that until the country's purse is sorted we cannot grow as a country.'

Surprisingly, Jack found himself agreeing. 'It makes sense.'

'Which is why I wanted to introduce the two of you. You both also have an interest in reducing the smuggling trade. Jack, you often tell me, "What is the use of debate if nothing changes?" I say that if you talk to someone who will one day be in power, there is a possibility that something may change.'

Jack looked sceptically at the young man in front of him. If this youth ever came into a position of power, it would not be for a long time yet. Nevertheless, Jack had time to kill before the run tonight. Talking to this man would at least maintain a distance between himself and the woman who waited for him at home. Seeing Jack nod in agreement, Enoch placed his hands behind both their shoulders and guided them away from the debate.

'Let us discuss the matter somewhere quieter. There is a table behind this wall that will suffice.' They sat down and almost immediately three drinks were served.

Enoch took a sip. 'What a foul liquid,' he complained, examining his dark coffee. 'I much prefer tea.'

'You would say that,' Jack said, looking at his own drink. 'You are in the pocket of the Indian Tea Company.'

'True, they have asked me to reduce the smuggling, which is why I employ you. And a very good job you do of it.'

Jack lifted his cup and drank a mouthful. 'You expect too much of me and I am not worthy of such praise.'

'You are too modest.' Enoch turned to William, who remained silent. 'This man has spent the last eight years travelling the south coast and putting smuggling gangs behind bars. Unfortunately, the people in this area are more stubborn and unwilling to expose the perpetrators. We are also having difficulties keeping them under lock and key when they are found.'

'Why?' asked William.

Jack put his cup down and pushed it away. 'Last year, before I came to the area, four members of the Blake brothers' gang were captured. It was deemed that there was not enough evidence to convict, so the judge brought a halt to the case. I will not be outdone, but I fear the task is ultimately a hopeless one.'

'Why?' asked William again, allowing his guard to drop and his interest to show. Perhaps, thought Jack, he just required time to relax.

'We are approaching the problem the wrong way. As soon as one gang is caught, another comes to fill its place. There is deprivation everywhere and great need breeds desperate men who will take desperate measures.'

'Do you have an alternative?' William asked, pushing his cup aside too. Only Enoch continued to drink. 'The country needs the tax on imports. We have a national debt which continues to grow, thanks to the revolution in America.'

'I have several suggestions that will help. On the matter of America,' Jack replied, 'I think we should stop fighting and allow them to have their independence.'

There was a short silence. 'You think it is an unjust war?' asked William.

'Indeed I do. I also think that it is a war we cannot win.'

Enoch laughed. 'You see William, I told you Jack has some novel ideas.'

'They are not so novel,' replied Jack.

'I would be interested to hear how you might tackle the smuggling, Mr Penhale.'

'Smuggling is rife. It has become a normal part of people's lives, but it has a dark underbelly, which involves torture and murder. It can only be tackled effectively from the top down.'

William frowned. 'Go on.'

Enoch answered for Jack. 'Jack thinks that taxes should be cut so the profit made by smuggling is slashed. I am not so sure. What do you say, William?'

'It is an interesting idea. I hoped by visiting the county where the trade is so prevalent I would learn more about it. I did not expect to hear advice from a thief-taker on how to run the country.'

'Not all thief-takers are corrupt. I know that my chosen profession has a bad reputation, but there are many thief-takers who are honourable, honest men. Like me, they dislike the villains who roam our towns and want to sweep the streets clean.'

William nodded in agreement. 'I seem to have met a kindred spirit. I also have a desire to sweep our world clean of corruption and dishonesty, only I hope to do it in the halls of Parliament.' Jack raised an eyebrow. For the first time the young man smiled. 'A corrupt man can just as easily be found wearing a cravat of finest silk and silver braid upon his waistcoat.'

Jack was beginning to like the man after all. 'How do you plan to rid Parliament of such unsavoury characters?'

'By example. One day I hope to become prime minister by being honest and truthful with the electorate. The people are tired of dishonest politicians. When the time comes they will vote for someone they feel they can trust.'

Enoch laughed. 'You see, Jack, coffeehouses are not so bad. The coffee may not be palatable, but its medicinal elements are many and the conversation is stimulating.'

'Stimulating, but not useful – unless something comes from it.'

Smiling at Jack's honesty, William said, 'I agree to a certain extent. However, I do find that places like these allow me to practice my public speaking.'

'What use is speaking at people if no change is made?' Jack challenged.

'It has a valuable use. When a man can raise the passion of many with a fine speech, or show commitment to their concerns with some well-chosen words, he will obtain their support and ultimately the power to lead his country. When that happens, it is possible to change things.' William finished his coffee and stood. 'I must leave, gentlemen. I have had a tiring day and my physician suggests a daily glass of port to ward off my troubles. With your permission, sir, I will return to your home for a rest and a drink, as I'm sure you gentlemen have matters to discuss. It was a pleasure to meet you, Mr Penhale,' he said, bowing his head. 'Your ideas warrant further investigation and I will not forget them.'

Enoch and Jack watched the younger man walk away. There was a slight limp to his gait that Jack had not noticed before.

'He is a nice enough fellow,' Enoch said, scratching his head underneath his powdered wig. 'Although rather serious and driven. He takes no interest in finding a wife, preferring the company of men to stimulate his mind. I believe he will be called to the bar next year, but I think politics will remain his only mistress and pull him more strongly. Mark my words; he will not remain in law for long.' Enoch turned to Jack. 'How are things with you? Do you have any more news?'

Jack did a cursory look about them. Content no one could hear him, he said, 'I know how the smugglers communicate.'

Enoch frowned. 'That is good news. You have done well. We must inform Captain Henley immediately so they can capture the rogues in action.'

Jack shook his head. 'No. There are informants everywhere and I trust no one but you. If it is discovered that their code has been broken, they will only change the method and we will lose our advantage. I told you before, the only way to stop the trade is to get the people at the top who supply the money.'

'So what do you propose to do?'

'I am going to become a smuggler.'

At first Enoch laughed, but when Jack did not join him he realised he was serious. Enoch sat back in his chair. For a moment he was rendered speechless.

'A smuggler. You have gone quite mad,' he said finally, bewildered at what he had just heard.

'If I can follow the trail of money it will lead me to the man at the top. The first step is finding out who pays the men on the beach.'

It was Enoch's turn to look around for unwelcome ears before leaning forward with hunched shoulders.

Lowering his voice, he said, 'Jack, you run too big a risk.

If you are found out, they will not take kindly to having a stranger in their midst. Should it be discovered you are a thief-taker and a spy, they will show you no leniency. I do not want to learn that your body is lying broken at the bottom of a cliff, or has been dragged behind a horse.'

'You need not warn me of this. I know from experience what such men are capable of doing.'

'Forgive me. I spoke out of turn. Even so, dear friend, this is risky. What has possessed you to do this?'

'When I learnt how they paid the men, it seemed too good an opportunity to miss.'

'Is there nothing I can say to persuade you differently?'

Jack shook his head.

Enoch sighed in exacerbation. 'When is the next run?' he asked miserably.

'I will not say.'

Enoch raised his eyebrows. 'Dear Lord! I thought you said you trusted me, but it seems that there are limits to your trust.'

'I have to be careful. I hope you understand.'

'I am paying you to end the free trading here. I have given you no cause not to trust me fully.'

'I want as few people knowing as possible.'

'You think I will tell Henley when the next run is taking place?'

'Do not persist, Enoch, or I will think I have a just cause to be careful.'

Enoch appeared visibly shaken. 'We are in a dark place if friends become distrustful of one another.'

'We are indeed.'

'Yet you are prepared to have a Cartwright under your roof.'

Jack frowned. 'I did not tell you Jenna was a Cartwright.'

'No, but I felt it was my duty to investigate the woman.'

'And what did you discover?'

'That her kith and kin are thieves and rascals.'

'And what of Jenna? Has she ever been brought before the magistrates?'

'No, she has not.'

Jack let out the breath he was holding.

'Then let us not tar her with the same brush as her family.' Jack noticed the light from the window was fading fast. It was time that he left. 'Let us not part on bad terms, Enoch. When I have more information, I will let you know.'

Their chairs noisily scraped along the wooden floor as both men stood. Jack could see Enoch remained unhappy.

'I do not like what you are doing,' his friend said, 'and I am affronted that you do not trust me. I understand the reasons behind your decisions, however, I cannot help feeling concerned for you and that you will not allow me to supply you with some support.'

'By only involving myself, the blame lies with me if anything goes wrong. Only I will be subjected to their punishment.'

'That is what concerns me, Jack. I see great potential in you and I don't wish it to be destroyed by their barbaric revenge.'

'Potential?'

'Politics needs someone like you who can look at things differently for the good of the country.'

Jack smiled. 'Then you do not know me well at all, Enoch. I have no desire to enter politics.'

'Then what is your desire when this is all over?'

'When I am ready to settle, I would like to live the same life as my father did, before the smugglers came and destroyed it.'

An argument broke out between two gentlemen nearby,

diverting their attention. It inflamed the emotions of others around them and quickly spread to involve all at the table. One irate gentleman stood and began to gesticulate rudely at another, which developed into ineffective pushing and calls for a duel.

'I have seen people behave better in the Tolbridge Inn,' muttered Jack.

'It will soon die down. I am used to such behaviour. I have seen far worse in the corridors of Parliament.'

Enoch and Jack weaved their way through the remaining rowdy customers and just as Enoch predicted, by the time they were descending the stairs the angry argument began to subside.

A man entered the passageway and began to head towards them. Enoch stopped abruptly.

'What is wrong?' asked Jack.

'You see the man approaching us?'

Jack looked up. 'He is hard to miss.'

'His name is Charles Buller or perhaps I should say The Honourable Mr Justice Buller. Since discovering I was a parliamentary advisor to the former prime minister he has courted me as if I were a duchess with money. I believe he has political ambitions. I have no interest to enquire, but he is beginning to feel like a leech that I cannot shake off.'

'Why have you wasted your time trying to persuade me into politics when you have this man wishing to engage with you?'

'There are some men one likes and others one does not. He is one I have an intense dislike for. Perhaps it is because he reminds me of a black rook waiting for a rotten corpse to pick over or maybe it's the fact he has overly long fingernails. Both these features repel me and it is hard to trust someone who stirs such a vivid emotion inside me.'

'Strong words, Enoch.'

'Strong indeed.'

Charles Buller was fast approaching them. Dressed in black, he appeared to Jack like a man of two halves, as his broad shoulders and large, hard belly were in stark contrast to his spindle-thin calves and unusually narrow feet. His small, wide-set eyes and long straight nose also did him no favours and, put together, Jack had to agree with his friend's comparison to the devious, black-feathered bird.

'Sir Enoch! What a pleasant surprise!' he bellowed.

'A surprise for me, but perhaps not for you,' replied Enoch solemnly.

Buller smiled. 'You are an astute fellow. It is one of many qualities I admire in you. It is true, I heard that the former prime minister's son was speaking here and had a mind to come. I am told he is staying with you.'

'Your messengers are efficient today.'

'It does a man well to keep abreast of things.'

'On that we are agreed.'

Buller turned to Jack. 'How are you finding these parts?'

Jack frowned at the strange question. 'I find them the same as others. People do not change so much, all have similar struggles to contend with.'

'Indeed they do, sir. Indeed they do.'

'I'm sorry we cannot stay to talk,' interrupted Enoch. 'My friend has other commitments, as do I.'

Buller's smile left his lips. 'You are always a busy man, Enoch, which is why I would like to invite you to dinner one evening.' To Jack's surprise he turned to him again adding, 'I would like to invite you also.'

Enoch answered for the both of them. 'That is very kind of you. We will await the invitation.' He made a show at looking at his pocket watch. 'We must be going. Time does not wait for us. Good day to you, sir.'

Buller smiled broadly, satisfied that he had achieved what he set out to do. 'I will look forward to your acceptance. It will be an enjoyable evening, eh?'

The men bowed their heads and went their separate ways. One with a self-satisfied swagger, the others walking briskly for the front door.

'You are going?' asked Jack, amused at Enoch's discomfort.

'He has only invited me to further his own ambitions. I find his deceit rather repugnant as we will never be friends. However, I think I would find it rather amusing if we did accept his invitation.'

'Why do you say that?' asked Jack. 'Do you think I would embarrass myself in such austere company?'

'I have every faith you would carry yourself well in such company,' Enoch replied as they entered into the street and put on their hats. 'However, I believe he thinks you are William Pitt, son of William Pitt, the former Prime Minister of England and it would be amusing to be present when he finds out he is mistaken. In fact, I would consider paying to see his face fall when he discovers he has a lowly farmer's son and thief-taker in his expensive home, eating at his laden table and conversing with his idle friends. Eh?'

Jack laughed. 'Masquerading as a relative to a politician would be the nearest I would ever get to entering politics. I find the prospect tempting, but I would not wish to spoil his dinner party.'

'Sometimes young people do not know how to enjoy themselves,' Enoch teased.

'Eating to excess at a table laden with silverware is not high on my list at the moment, Enoch.'

Jack's words sobered them and Enoch became serious.

'Have a care, Jack. Do not place yourself in unnecessary danger. Unpaid taxes on tubs of French brandy are not worth a man's life, especially someone like you.'

Jack swallowed down the emotion that rose quickly in his throat. Unable to voice his appreciation at the kind words, he nodded and curtly bowed his head goodbye, before walking briskly away.

Jack had heard those words before. They caught him off-guard and stirred memories that he preferred to forget. Suddenly he was a boy of seventeen again, hearing them whispered through his father's bloodied lips. The feeling of holding him in his arms, and the smell of his blood at the back of his nose, came rushing back to him as he walked.

As a boy he had tried to be strong and attempted to comfort his father as he lay dying. He had felt useless, knowing that his words of reassurance were lies. When his father died, Jack's composure abruptly abandoned him. Alone, he broke down and wept over his body, until his throat felt raw and his body ached. On that day the youth became a man and he vowed that he would cry no more. Sorrow was replaced by a desire for revenge, and it was this familiar companion that drove him now.

# Chapter Eleven

Jenna felt as if her insides had been taken over by snakes. Anxiety always had this effect, making her restless, queasy and prone to hand wringing. To calm her nerves she busied herself cleaning the cottage from top to bottom. It worked for a while. Cupboards were emptied, dusted and refilled, floors were brushed and mopped, and windows washed until they glistened in the November sun. However, the cleaning chores were insufficient to fill the hours spent waiting for Jack's safe return. Her pent up energy made short work of them and soon everything was clean and in order.

At midday she began looking around for another challenge to occupy her and stop the snakes in her belly tying themselves into knots. Rolling up her sleeves, Jenna started to bake and within hours she had made a golden-crusted onion pie in the bake kettle, cooked turnip soup over the fire and prepared a dish of apples and bacon. Jenna surveyed all the food laid out on the table. She had been excessive, and although it looked and smelled delicious, she had no appetite for any of it.

Her gaze wandered to the window and the darkening sky outside. The day had turned to night and soon Jack would be on the beach. Remembering his instructions, she carefully pulled the drapes over the windows, ensuring there were no gaps to allow the light from her candle to shine through. There was no more she could do. The wringing of her hands began again as she sat by the dying fire and waited for his safe return.

The first time Jenna heard the faint knocking on her door she dismissed it as a branch tapping against the window nearby. The second time was louder and there was no mistaking the sound. She scrambled to her feet, almost tripping on her skirts, and ran to the door.

A boy with a runny nose stood shivering on her doorstep.

'I have a message for Mrs Kestle,' he announced.

'I am she.'

'A gentleman wants you to go to Lanros Inn as quickly as you can.'

His message delivered, the boy immediately turned and ran away, disappearing into the night like a ghost.

Was Jack in trouble? Was he injured and needing her help? Without hesitating further, Jenna grabbed her shawl, a lantern and followed the route the boy had taken.

Jenna did not see the boy again. She felt quite alone as she ran along the cliff path towards the village of Lanros. The distant roar of the ocean was her only company, as the sea wind wrapped her skirts around her legs and dragged at her shawl. It was only when she saw the lights of the village lamps in the distance did she know for certain she was running in the right direction. With red, windswept cheeks and tangled hair, she entered Lanros Inn in a flurry and was greeted by the sudden warmth of a large, roaring fire.

Situated on the main coastal route of Cornwall, the inn at Lanros was a popular resting place for travellers. Faces briefly looked up at her entrance, but quickly dismissed her. The inn was busy with people drinking and eating, whilst others stood waiting to take delivery of their trunks before retiring to their rooms for the night.

Jenna looked round the crowded room searching for Jack. No one looked familiar and she began to feel a sense of unease.

A man, dressed in fine clothes and partially in shadow, called to her from the adjoining room. He sat alone at a table laden with dishes, his hand beckoning to her to come forward.

Jenna stepped into the room, her eyes squinting in the low light. The room, set aside for patrons able to pay for solitude, was quieter, causing Jenna to shut the door on the noisier travellers behind her. She cautiously approached the gentleman, but it was only when she was close to him that she could finally trust what her eyes were telling her. The man in fine clothing did not have a fine pedigree running through his veins. He had the tainted blood of the Cartwright line.

Silas smiled. 'Do I not look fine, Sister?' he said, smoothing his waistcoat.

Jenna carefully sat opposite her brother and looked at him. His serviceable, but ragged clothes had been replaced with a three piece, beige suit made of fine wool and beneath he wore a white linen shirt that looked freshly laundered. She glanced down and saw that he wore woollen stockings on his legs and new leather shoes decorated with large, impractical buckles. Even his hair, which he often neglected, was now clean and tied back at the nape of his neck with a black, silk ribbon. The sense of unease grew inside her.

Jenna looked around for Jack, hoping that he would saunter across the room with a smile on his face and explain how he had managed to pay Silas's debts so quickly. His absence unnerved her. She looked back at Silas who had begun to eat.

'How did you know where I lived?' she asked him.

'You told me when you brought the sweetmeats. Do you remember when we were children and we would pretend to have a feast like this?' He lifted a chicken leg. 'Now the feast is here and tastes better than any dream we had.'

'Has Jack already paid your creditors?'

'In a roundabout way. Come, Jenna, join me. I have bought enough for the both of us.'

'And more besides. Where are Nell and the children?'

'At her parents'. Eat, eat,' he urged, his mouth dripping with chicken fat.

'I would rather not until you tell me how you have suddenly come into so much money,' she replied stubbornly.

'Well, this is a fine greeting. I thought you would be pleased I was now free, rather than locked away in the prison all alone.'

'You were not alone – you were with your wife and children.'

Silas guiltily glanced up and for the first time stopped eating. Jenna grew suspicious.

'They *were* with you, weren't they?'

Silas winced.

'You lied to me!'

'It was only a little lie.'

'A lie is a lie!'

'Would you have helped me if I told you the truth? Would you?' he persisted. Jenna looked away. 'I thought not, and I do not blame you.' Silas began eating again. 'It was no one's fault but my own that I was in debt. When Nell found out that the landlord wanted us gone, she took the children and left me. I needed your help, Jenna.'

'You should have told me the truth!'

'Can you not look kindly upon me?'

'I risked my life for you and I would have done it again.'

'And I am ashamed for asking you to help in that way, but I was desperate.'

'And I was a fool.'

'You were never a fool. Kind, thoughtful—'

'—and easily taken advantage of.'

Silas tilted his head and his eyes softened. 'We have always been close, Jenna. For years there were just the two of us. Even Nell knew better than to come between us. I would never have asked you to smuggle if I did not think you could do it. You have a gift for melting into the background so no one notices you.'

'It was no gift, just a skill I developed out of a need to survive.'

'Whatever you think, we are both survivors.'

Jenna snorted in reply.

'I can see that I have hurt you. I promise, before God, I will never lie to you again.'

'You should not jest about making promises before God, Silas.'

'I do not jest. Now let us enjoy my good fortune with a glass of port.' He poured her a glass and she reluctantly took it, cradling it in her hands, but unwilling to taste it.

'Who paid your creditors, Silas?'

He sighed and carefully put his own glass down on the table. The toast would have to wait.

'My debts have been paid. It does not matter who paid them.'

'We can play cat and mouse all evening, Silas, or you could just tell me.'

He sat back and folded his arms. 'I arranged my own payment.'

'Which included fine clothes and all this food?'

He lifted his chin in defiance. 'Aye, and bed and board with a view of the sea.'

'A pretty sum. How much did you steal and from whom?'

'I did not have to steal,' he said, leaning forward and tearing off some bread. 'It was honest payment for honest work, so there is no need for you to worry.'

Jenna's eyes narrowed. Her brother did not know what honest work was.

'It is the nature of the work that worries me, Brother.'

'You are always suspicious when good fortune calls,' he muttered, popping some doughy bread into his mouth. Jenna lifted an eyebrow but did not reply. Silas discarded the rest of the bread; it was difficult to enjoy his meal under his sister's reproachful glare. 'I had some information that someone was willing to pay for.'

The sound of her own heart began to beat loudly in Jenna's ears. 'What information did you have that was worth so much?' she asked. 'What knowledge would a thief, smuggler and gambler have? Have you told the smugglers that Jack is an imposter?'

'If I told the smugglers I had information to sell them they would use force to get it from me. No, best tell someone who could arrange my liberty.'

Suddenly she knew what he had done. He had told how the smugglers communicated and where the next run would be.

'Oh, Silas, no! Who have you told?'

'The Head of the Land Guard.'

'But the run is tonight! They will attack them!' Now she understood why he had invited her here. It was not to share a feast with her but to keep her out of harm's way and away from the beach. She felt no gratitude for his keeping her safe, only anger that he had placed Jack in such danger. 'Jack will be on the beach tonight.' Grabbing his wrist she whispered through gritted teeth. 'He is risking his life for you!'

Silas slipped his wrist free and continued eating. 'Pity it is too late to tell him not to go.'

'Don't you care? He is doing this run to get money for you!'

Silas scoffed. 'He cares nothing for me. Either he is a fool or has reasons of his own. Is he a fool, Jenna?'

'He is no fool,' she replied, not trying to hide the tenderness she felt for him.

Silas heard it too.

'I see he has charmed you. The trouble with you, Jenna, is that you are charmed too easily. Henry saw that flaw in you and used it to his advantage. Penhale is doing it too.' He picked up his chicken leg again and waved it at her. 'Don't trust him,' he warned her. 'It is people like him that took our brothers away.'

Jenna got up and picked up her lantern. 'I'm not staying here to listen to you any more.'

Silas looked up surprised. 'Where are you going?'

'Where do you think?'

'To him?' Silas grabbed her skirt. 'I have always looked after you, Jenna, and made sure you had enough to eat when our parents disappeared.' Jenna tried to pull her skirt free from his grasp, but he held it fast. 'It was me that comforted you at night when you dreamt of the thief-taker coming to get you.'

'Let go, Silas.'

'It was me you ran to when you needed help.'

Jenna pulled her skirt free. 'That was when we were children.'

Silas stood and tried to take the lantern from her. Jenna refused with a jerk of her hand making the lantern swing precariously.

'It's too late, Silas. I am a grown woman now.'

He grabbed her arm, halting her. 'I looked after you and now you want to risk your life for a man you barely know.'

'Let go,' said Jenna, pulling her arm away.

Silas's grip tightened. 'All I hear about is this Jack Penhale.'

'Let go, Silas.'

'Stay here and eat with me. Let us be friends like we used to be. It is not safe to leave now.'

'I have to warn Jack,' Jenna replied crossly as she wrenched her arm away. 'You have betrayed us.'

A muscle worked in Silas's jaw.

'There is too much food here. Sit and eat,' he commanded.

'I would rather starve than eat with you.'

'I am your brother!'

'You are no better than Judas!'

'Now you are being foolish.'

'I *was* a fool, but no more.' Jenna turned to leave.

'If you go there, you might be killed,' he called after her.

'Then my blood will be on your hands!' she shouted over her shoulder as she walked away.

Jenna left him with his dishes and opened the door. Remaining oblivious to the heat and noise that greeted her from the other room, she weaved her way through the crowd, stopping and starting as people crossed her path and trunks were placed in her way. Finally her frustration got the better of her and she pushed a portly man out of her way. He glared furiously at her, but she did not care. She had other things on her mind. She had to warn Jack.

She left the muted sounds of Lanros Inn behind its closed doors and headed towards home. Her concern for Jack's safety gave her a new spurt of energy and she ran quickly along the track leading out of the valley. However, the steep gradient soon took its toll, and to her frustration her pace began to slow. By the time she reached the top, she was exhausted and could go no further without a rest. She reluctantly stopped and allowed her chest to heave in the precious air her lungs craved. Only the stamping of her feet and her hands on her hips showed her frustration at having to wait. Gradually her breathing and heart began to settle, and as soon as she was able she picked up her skirts and began to run again.

As she ran, she could hear the waves crashing on the rocks of Porthenys Cove below her. Tonight she knew it was empty. Free of men's boots churning up its grains, its sand would remain tranquil, smooth and glistening in the moonlight tonight. Jenna saw Jack's house in the distance, its black silhouette standing out against the inky, star-studded sky. She decided she would check to see if he had returned, before going further towards Tudor Cove.

The house was empty, but for the buzz of a single stray wasp. Duped into remaining active by the unusually warm autumn, it busied itself feasting on her apples and bacon. She looked at the dish she had made for Jack, enjoyed by an insect that should have died weeks ago. Jack should be here, she thought, not risking his life for her. Tears threatened. She called Jack's name, desperate, yet still hopeful, that he would appear safe and well. For a moment silence greeted her, until the loud buzzing of the yellow and black pest began again.

Jenna found another candle to replace the one in her lantern and within seconds she was running along the narrow cliff path towards Tudor Cove. Ignoring Jack and Silas, she was heading for the place they had warned her not to go, and holding a lantern to light her way.

By the time Jenna arrived at Tudor Cove the coastal wind had dropped significantly. An uneasy stillness had replaced it, while a palpable tension emanated from the sandy cove below. Yet, all was quiet, far too quiet, for smuggling activities to be in progress. In fact, if a casual passer-by were to walk the nearby road, he would be forgiven for thinking the cove was deserted.

Concerned she had been duped, Jenna drew closer and looked down over the sand dune. The beach was far from deserted. The dune's sandy walls had succeeded in muffling the sound of the smugglers below. There was a whole new world down there and Jack was amongst it.

Jenna surveyed the scene. The packhorses had already arrived and waited patiently on the firmer sand. Some appeared exhausted from their day working the land and hung their heads low as they tried to rest. Two or three horses were less experienced. They stamped their muffled hooves and repeatedly tossed their heads to dislodge the rags their handlers had tied around their mouths to silence them. Small groups of men stood nearby, waiting for the arrival of the first load, their heads bowing and turning now and again as they whispered the odd word. But for the most part they stood in silence, watching, waiting and waiting some more.

Jenna turned her head and peeped through the reedy grass, which had made the inhospitable dry sand its home. She searched for Jack. She kept her lantern hidden beneath her shawl as the cloudless sky above carried no barrier against the soft light of the moon. At least fifty men, with blackened faces, were waiting for one of the small rowing boats to arrive on the shore. Jenna could not tell which one was Jack as their merging, shadowy figures all looked the same in the darkness. For the first time, Jenna realised the enormity of her task. If she ran onto the beach to look for Jack and warn him of the imminent attack, she would soon be caught and questioned by the other men on the beach. They would want to know how she came by such information and why she chose to only warn Jack. She would not only risk her own well being by such a foolish act, but her brother's and that of the man she wanted to help.

Jenna heard a man's cough. She looked to her left and saw a figure standing alone by a pile of bracken, slowly swinging an unlit torch in his hand to pass the time. She realised he was a lookout waiting to light a warning beacon should a preventative man be seen. In that instant Jenna realised what she must do. If she warned everyone on the beach she would not be looked upon with suspicion as she would be helping them all. Mayhem was sure to follow as everyone tried to escape. The chaos would allow her to slip from sight and no one would ever know who she was. She took her lantern from beneath her shawl and started to run towards the man. He looked at her, the light from her lantern shone on his shocked face, temporarily blinding him and forcing him to squint.

'The preventative men are coming!' she yelled. 'Light the beacon. Warn them all!' The lookout did not move. Jenna was almost upon him, before she realised that he was not a man, but a boy of sixteen frozen by fear. From his sickly complexion, he looked too weak to carry goods so had been placed out of the way with a lighter task. To his horror, the task he was set was now upon him. Trembling, he began to fumble with his tinderbox in order to start a fire.

Her sudden cry had disturbed the horses and they began to stamp and pace in agitation, but the men on the beach heard nothing and continued with the run.

'Light it!' she urged, fearful that the preventative men may have heard her. Sparks finally began to fly from his shaking fingers, but the bracken refused to burn. In frustration, Jenna flung her lantern onto it. Her lighted candle fell out of its casing and landed on its side. The flame on the candle grew taller, but the bracken still did not light. Jenna cried out in frustration and headed for the beach.

As she ran down the sand dune, the grains cascaded

around her and slipped beneath her feet causing her strides to lengthen and her speed to increase faster and faster.

'They are coming! The preventative men are coming!' Jenna yelled as she tried to remain on her feet. New faces looked up and one man started to run away, but the majority of men were at the shoreline in the distance and could not hear her cries against the roar of the sea.

A man grabbed her arm as she stepped onto the beach and pulled her roughly towards him. She fell at his feet but was immediately pulled up again so her captor could look into her face.

'What say you? Who are you? How do you know?' His fingers dug painfully into her arm as another man approached them wielding a flail.

'The preventative men are coming. Run for your lives!' she urged.

'I don't believe you,' the man snarled, twisting the cloth of her dress into his fist.

'Look!' said the other. 'The beacon's been lit!'

Three faces turned to watch the flames of the beacon reaching for the sky. Jenna felt his grasp loosen and she fell back down onto her heels. The men needed no more warnings. Jenna was instantly forgotten as they ran to escape, along with the sickly youth on the cliff top. As the men around her scurried like rats from a sinking ship, Jenna picked up her skirts and ran in the opposite direction towards the shoreline to warn Jack and the others.

The word began to spread from man to man. Horses began to panic and pull at their handlers, some breaking loose, others flailing their hooves as they reared.

An officer's command to his soldiers was heard clearly on the wind. A line of dragoons emerged from their hiding places and began to descend down the sandy slopes into the cove. Their battle yells merged with the warning shouts of the smugglers and the two came together in the middle of the beach.

By the time Jenna reached the shoreline the men were already beginning to scatter and the rowing boats were turning to head back out to sea. The cove began to resonate with musket fire causing Jenna to look back to the beach in horror. In the moonlight she could see puffs of gunpowder smoke as men collapsed to the ground. Jenna watched, desperate to find Jack alive and well, but in the poor light and confusion every man was faceless and every shape familiar. The men's yells and cries seemed quite distant until she heard a man close by call to her. She turned smiling, believing it to be Jack.

The shadowy figure stood tall in the darkness, his head tilted strangely and his arms held high. The moonlight grew brighter casting new light on the man. Jenna's stomach lurched – it was not Jack but a dragoon in uniform, high on excitement and ready for battle. In that moment time appeared to slow, hindering her ability to think, understand and move. He looked at her through one narrowed eye as he carefully aimed his musket at her face. Her smile left her lips. I am about to die, she thought, as she looked down the barrel. Fear drained from her body, leaving her calm and ready to accept her fate. Lifting her chin she looked him in the eye and waited for him to fire.

A sudden blackness engulfed her, propelling her backwards to the ground. The back of her head hit the firm sand with a thud, as the sound of his musket fire echoed in her throbbing brain. Jenna opened her eyes to see the musket smoke rise harmlessly into the star-studded sky above her. She tried to speak, but nothing came out – her breath had been taken from her.

# Chapter Twelve

The musket smoke continued to rise higher in the sky, leaving Jenna earthbound. This realisation surprised her, as did the heavy weight pressing down on her body and pinning her to the ground. She tried to move.

'Play dead,' a voice whispered in her ear. 'He would rather chase the living than waste time on the dead.'

Feeling Jack's words brush against her skin was almost too much to bear. She turned her head and found herself looking into his eyes in the breaking dawn light. It was not a dream – it was him, and he had just saved her life.

She wanted to speak but heard footsteps approaching, so did as Jack instructed. She remained still, locked in a gaze with Jack and seeing in their inky depths that he was willing her to remain strong. Knowing he was next to her gave her the courage she needed.

The soldier stopped and looked down on their bodies. Together they lay as if dead, neither flinching when the soldier prodded them with his boot. Time dragged as they heard the soldier above them tear and spit his cartridge before priming his musket. To Jenna, the noise seemed strangely loud compared to the distant shouts of the others. He was taking his time and Jenna's eyes began to sting and fill with tears. She wanted to blink but she remained strong and kept her eyes steady and fixed on Jack's. She took comfort in feeling Jack's heart beating against her own and the warmth of his body providing shelter against the chilly night air. What had initially felt like a heavy weight was now comforting and protective and she longed to reach up and hold him as he held her. At last the soldier's muffled footsteps were felt vibrating through the sand, signalling that he had left. Jenna closed her eyes in relief and felt Jack's forehead touch hers.

'It is going to be all right, Jenna,' he whispered reassuringly. 'He has gone.'

She felt him brush a stray hair from her cheek, a gentle gesture amongst so much carnage. Her body began to tremble, as she wrapped her arms around him and buried her face into his body.

'Oh, Jack. I was so afraid.'

'Do not be afraid,' he whispered into her hair.

She opened her eyes, wanting him to see the honesty in her face. 'I was afraid for *you*, Jack ... not for myself,' she said, placing her hand against the stubble of his jawline. 'I was afraid they would catch you ... that they would kill you.'

He tried to smile. 'They did not,' he reassured her, 'although we cannot stay here much longer.' In the dim light, she could see his expression remained troubled.

'You want us to run?' The thought of standing and becoming a target filled her with dread. Her hand fell from his face.

'Yes, we must.'

'But I can't.'

'Why? Are you hurt?'

She shook her head, not thinking to ask him the same.

'Then we must leave now,' he persisted, grabbing her hand. 'Before he comes back for our bodies.'

Suddenly the warmth of his body left her and he was pulling her up. Taking her firmly by the hand, he led her towards the cliff.

'Where are we going?' Jenna asked.

'Back to the cottage, but not by the route that you came.

The track will be littered with dragoons and smugglers, and at this moment we are friend to neither. Hold on tight,' he told her as they entered a cave. 'I don't want to lose you.'

The cave's gaping mouth provided instant shelter as they stepped inside its eerie void. The sound of their rapid breathing broke the silence inside and echoed around them. Jack tightened his grip slightly and led her towards the darkness.

He came to a halt and searched for something in his coat. After finding it, he tried to use it, but failed. She heard him curse, before pressing whatever it was into her hand. 'Make a spark, Jenna. I have a candle for you to light.'

She recognised it as a tinderbox and did as he asked. The sudden bright spark in the darkness temporarily blinded her, before it grew into a small dancing flame whose only flaw was to cast eerie shadows on their faces. Jack lit two candles and used some melted wax to stick one of them onto his hat to light their way. He gave the other to Jenna to carry.

'Keep it tilted so the hot wax does not burn you,' he said, taking her hand again.

She followed as he led her down into a narrow passage framed with dripping rock.

'What is this place?'

'It is a tunnel leading straight to our house. The wooden panel at the back of the pantry is a false wall. This tunnel leads straight to it.'

'Why?'

'The tale I told you about a sea captain's wife waiting for her husband to return is true. What I did not tell you is that the captain not only carried legitimate cargo, but also a small quantity of smuggled goods. His wife had a fondness for silk and he had a fondness for French brandy. He employed four miners to dig this tunnel so he could drop off his supplies before he reached the harbour. She waited for her husband, but she waited for her fine bolts of silk too.'

Jack's footsteps slowed which allowed her to look around and marvel at the miners' workmanship. The incline of the floor began to steepen until it finally gave way to steps chiselled out of the rock. After a while the tunnel changed again. The walls crowded in around them, squeezing the path narrower, pressing the ceiling lower and sapping the freshness from the air. Mineral trails lined the rock surfaces above and beside them, whilst the distant sound of dripping accompanied their journey. Eventually, the steps changed abruptly back to the same steep gradient as before. The abrupt change caught Jenna unaware and she almost stumbled. Jack looked back, concerned. After reassurance, they moved on, finally arriving at the foot of a ladder, which marked the end of their escape.

Jack took off his hat and gave it to Jenna, before climbing somewhat clumsily up the few rungs. Carefully lifting her candle so that he could see, she watched him gently ease a wooden hatch free and climb out. Placing his hat on her head and blowing out the second candle, she lifted her skirts and followed him.

It was just as he said; she was looking into the pantry through an open false wall. Jack stood in the room beyond looking at her.

'We must clean your face,' she said, taking his hat from her head, walking into the room and reaching for a bowl. 'The dragoons may want to search here and they hang people for having a blackened face at night.'

Jack leant against the table. He was unusually quiet as he allowed her to clean away his camouflage.

'I'm so sorry for asking you to do this,' Jenna said, tenderly wiping his face. 'Please forgive me.' She sensed he was watching her as she cleaned, but she dared not look directly into his eyes, fearful that if she did, she would not feel able to finish. She could see his eyes were crinkled with worry and his handsome mouth was held in a firm, straight line. The stubble on his jaw quietly rasped against her cloth as she worked and blamed herself for the trouble she had caused. She swallowed and tried hard to concentrate on the task at hand. When she had finally finished, it was he who spoke first.

'There is nothing to forgive,' he said quietly. 'I told you, I had my own reasons to go. Do not concern yourself.' His balance faltered and he steadied himself.

'Jack, what ails you? You look so pale. Let me take off your coat, it feels wet and you will catch a chill.'

She reached for his coat and eased it off his shoulders, causing Jack to flinch. Jenna looked at the coat, which felt wet and sticky in her hands. She looked up at his shirt, which she could now see was stained with his blood.

'You have been shot! Oh Jack, why did you not say?' She began to undo his shirt. 'No wonder the dragoon thought we were dead. He saw your wound.'

'I will be all right.'

Jenna would not be put off.

'We must stop the bleeding and then I must clean it before it festers.' She pulled the shirt carefully away from his body, exposing the gaping wound for the first time. She hesitated as she saw the enormity of her task, before rolling the shirt to form a pad and tying it in place with her shawl.

Jack began to sway. 'Take me to my bed. I will pass out if I don't lie down.'

Supporting him under his good shoulder, they carefully

163

made their way up the stairs where he collapsed onto the bed. Jenna ran back downstairs, hid his coat, cleared away the bowl of water and quickly returned to his room. She looked at him lying on the bed, thankful that the colour was beginning to return to his face.

'I must hide your boots, they are covered in sand,' she said, pulling each one off him and hiding them in the wardrobe with her own. She covered him with the blankets.

'I wish you had told me.'

'It would have made no difference. We are home and that is all that matters.'

'Let me look at your wound.'

He shook his head. 'I can hear someone approaching.'

Jenna heard something too and ran to the window. Tentatively she lifted a drape away from the wall so she could look down at their door.

'There are four dragoons outside,' she whispered, just before they banged so loudly on the door that the windows vibrated in their metal frames.

Jenna began to undress.

'What are you doing? They will be here soon.'

Jenna stepped out of her dress and threw it under the bed.

'My father taught his children the art of distraction. He told us that if we learnt the skill, in all its forms, we could pick a pocket with ease.' She started to untie the lace of her stays. 'Mother said a woman could distract a man with greater ease than a man could.'

Jack watched her warily from across the room.

'A playful smile, a flirtatious look ...' Frustrated she could not undo her laces quickly enough, she picked up Jack's razor blade and cut them in two. Jenna smiled triumphantly as her stays fell limply to the ground at her feet. She dropped the razor on top of them with a flourish. 'A razor will add a sense of passion,' she said matter-of-factly as she stepped over them. Her petticoats were the next garments to fall to the floor.

Jack moved his head more comfortably on the pillow. 'Your distraction technique is working.'

'I hope to distract *them* – not you.'

They heard the front door bang open and sandy boots shuffle on the wooden floorboards of the parlour below.

Jenna climbed into his bed.

'I want them to think we are making love and have not been on the beach tonight.'

'I have a hole in my arm that says otherwise.'

She covered his bandaged arm with the blanket. 'Close your eyes, while I pull down my shift.'

Obediently he did as he was told just as the shift slipped from her shoulders and pooled at her waist. Satisfied with the effect, she climbed on top of him and lifted its hem to expose a thigh. Jack groaned beneath her as she ruffled her hair.

'You don't have to do this, Jenna,' he said. 'I don't want lecherous dragoons seeing you like this.'

Jenna looked down on Jack's face as she heard footsteps gathering at the bottom of the stairs. His brows were knotted in pain, but his eyes remained tightly closed.

'It will embarrass and confuse them, no more. It is worth a try.'

'Did you smile to distract me on the first day we met?' he asked suddenly serious.

She heard the soldiers' voices downstairs.

'Hush. It is time,' Jenna warned him. She touched his jawline with her fingers.

'If you did, your smile worked. I let you go and you ran away from me.'

'The pain is going to your head. Hush, Jack, and rest. I will do the acting.'

Jenna heard a boot on the bottom stair. She looked at Jack's handsome face shadowed in evening stubble. His lips were well shaped and inviting. Dear Lord, she was about to kiss him! She placed her lips on his. Her kiss was chaste and awkward. She was playing the role of a passionate lover, but she had little experience to draw from. It was a painful charade to be part of, especially with Jack. What must he think of her?

She expected Jack to play a passive role, but she soon discovered that he had no such thoughts as he responded with a kiss of his own. Henry was the only man who had kissed her. Rough and self-satisfying, his kisses were never a pleasure to receive. It was how she thought it must be and expected no more, but Jack's kiss was different, causing Jenna to freeze in surprise.

It was a gentle kiss and the knowledge that such a kiss could exist at all confused her. She began to withdraw, wanting to touch her own lips with her fingers to stop the strange tingling sensation that she felt there. Jack, she soon realised, had no plans to let her go.

She felt his hand briefly touch the naked curve of her waist, before sweeping up her back to cradle her neck. It left a trail of exquisite, burning embers of pleasure in its wake. His kiss followed her withdrawal and deepened, casting a spell and inviting her back to him. She stilled and allowed herself to drift into the sensuality of his kiss as he asked. Any resistance she felt dissolved in that moment and she found herself drawn back to him until his head lay back down on the pillow. They were now together, with no resistance on either side and she allowed herself to take part in this new, lovers' game he was playing. It was a game that was foreign to her, yet natural to play.

She heard irregular gasps and moans, and realised they came from her. Their kisses deepened still further and took on a life of their own. Jack was good and she wanted more of him. Her kisses grew more demanding and she heard his breathlessness match her own. She felt triumphant as she forgot the soldiers' advance.

Through the fog of pleasure, she heard a man shout. They sprang apart, surprised to see four soldiers in the room and the door swinging on its hinges.

The first soldier stopped abruptly, causing the other three to bump into him in a disorganised line. Musket barrels clashed with hats, dislodging them at precarious angles to resemble ships sinking out at sea. The men looked at the tangled bed sheets and the partially clothed couple. The intimate scene was enough to cause two men's faces to redden, one man to snigger and a fourth to abruptly leave. From their reactions it appeared Jenna's plan was working, yet she felt no joy.

She covered her breasts with her arm and quickly pulled her slip over her shoulders with trembling fingers. She dared not look at Jack, suddenly feeling shy now that reality had returned and cast a harsh light on what was taking place. Their kisses were for the soldiers to see, yet their presence now cheapened them. Jenna's resentment muted her. Jack, though, played the role to perfection and she had to admire the anger he feigned.

'What is the meaning of this?' he shouted at the remaining men. 'Get out or I will report you.'

The lead soldier hesitated and began to apologise.

'We did not mean to disturb you and your wife but smugglers have been seen in Tudor Cove. We have orders to search the properties in the vicinity.'

'Do I look like I have been smuggling?' Jack asked.

Jenna slipped from the bed and wrapped herself in a blanket. She forced herself to look at Jack. He looked dishevelled and played the frustrated lover well. She looked away.

'You are right, sir. We are sorry to disturb you.' They turned to leave when more booted footsteps mounted the stairs. The soldiers moved aside as another man in uniform approached. He was taller and older, with a commanding presence that filled the room when he entered. His gaze efficiently took in the scene with a few well-aimed glances – the bedding, the cut stays at his feet and the quiet woman wrapped in a blanket in the corner.

Jenna felt the heat rise to her cheeks as she saw in his face the judgement he passed on her. This man was different to the young soldiers who spent their careers doing what they were directed to do. This man would not be so easily distracted and would want to know what lay hidden beneath the blanket placed over Jack's arm. Jenna held her breath as she watched the man turn to Jack and their eyes lock. An unspoken challenge passed between them, until finally the man's gaze dropped to the blanket over Jack's arm.

He knows, thought Jenna, expecting him to rip away the cloth, but to her surprise he abruptly turned to his men, gave a curt nod to the door and ordered them out.

Suddenly Jenna and Jack found themselves alone. They looked warily at each other from across the room as they listened to the soldiers leaving. Neither spoke. Memories of their passionate kiss lingered between them like a great mythical creature that had broken its chains and been briefly set free. Jenna trembled from the shock and embarrassment of her body's reaction to Jack's role playing. What must he think of her? What was going on behind those dark eyes of his? Jenna was the one to look away first. She made the excuse that his wound would need cleaning. Jack agreed far too quickly and was keen to let her go.

Jenna watched the men ride away and let the drape drop. The small amount of time that had passed was enough for her to regain her composure and see their kiss for what it was. An act to fool. It almost fooled her. She had hoped her plan would work, yet its success still surprised her. She finished buttoning her dress, then lifted the pot of boiling water from the fire and placed it on the table. Carefully she took three kitchen utensils from the boiling water and placed them onto a clean cloth. She placed it onto a tray next to clean bandages made from a sheet, a bread and milk poultice, and some boiled water for cleaning.

She carefully carried the laden tray up to Jack's room and placed it by his bed. She noticed beads of perspiration had formed on his forehead during her absence. Any earlier embarrassment was now well and truly extinguished by her concern for him.

'They have gone. Is it very painful?'

'It is getting worse by the minute.' His face was etched with pain, but seeing her worried expression he attempted to make light of it. 'Perhaps you should try distracting me again.'

Jenna did not feel like laughing. 'The time for playing games has come to an end. Your wound must be tended to.'

'I will see no surgeon. He will raise too many questions and the ones I know are too quick to pick up a saw.' He managed a slight smile. 'I am rather attached to my arm and have no wish to lose it now.'

'Which is why I brought this,' Jenna answered, waving a hand across her tray.

Jack looked at the knife, fork and sugar prongs and sniffed the bread and milk poultice.

'What do you plan to do with that? Eat it off?'

Jenna broke into a smile, the first in many days. His joke lightened her spirits and dispelled any awkwardness between them.

'My brothers and father were often wounded during their ...'

'... law breaking?'

'We could not afford a surgeon and even if we could it would ...'

'... raise too many questions?'

Jenna nodded. It was always difficult to talk about her family's unsavoury ways of earning a living.

'So my mother learned how to tend to them and reduce the risk of infection. She found that by boiling everything it seemed to work. I don't know why but it does.' She carefully arranged the utensils. 'I am going to use these to examine the wound.'

'Then I hope your mother taught you well.'

'It was the only thing I was willing to learn from her.' Jenna began to undo the makeshift bandage and laid it carefully into a clean chamber pot.

'It has stopped bleeding, but it must be thoroughly cleaned. If a musket ball is still in there, I need to get it out.'

'Do what you need to do.'

'It will be painful.' She poured a large glass of brandy from a decanter and offered it to him. 'It is best if you drink yourself into a stupor.'

Jack shook his head. 'I stay away from too much drink. It loosens the tongue and I must stay on my guard.'

'And I need you to stay still or your arm will become useless and lie flaccid at your side.'

'Give me my razor's leather strap. I will bite down on that.'

Reluctantly she handed it to him. 'I need you to be still, Jack. Grimacing as you bite down on this will not stop your body writhing away from me. It is a natural instinct that a man cannot stop.'

He scowled at her. 'I will not move,' he retorted, biting down on the strap.

Jenna raised an eyebrow. 'You are being foolish, but fooling no one.' She dipped a cloth into the water in readiness to clean the wound. 'This will hurt. Are you ready?'

Jack prepared himself and nodded for her to continue. Jenna sighed and began to clean his wound with the cloth. Deep inside the wound she could feel the metal of the ball at the tips of her fingers. The movement caused Jack to arch and cry out in pain.

He spat out the strap. 'Cat's teeth, woman. That hurt!'

'I told you it would! Have the brandy.'

'I will not!'

She attempted to clean the wound again but Jack arched again at her touch. 'What in the devil are you doing?'

'I am trying to remove the musket ball with the prongs. Keep still or more damage may be done.'

'And if it is not removed?'

'It will fester and eventually the fever will travel to your head.'

'And then what?'

'You will die.'

Jack covered his brow with his forearm and thought for a moment.

'You are afraid of what you might say when you are drunk?' His silence told her what he did not voice. 'I ran on the beach to warn you tonight. If you cannot trust me, who can you trust?'

'True, you did risk your life.'

'As you did for me.'

He smiled at her. 'We are a fine pair. Both willing to do good but ending up on the wrong side of the law.'

'And you are gravely injured and I am to blame for that. It is a heavy burden to bear. Let me help you.'

'The blame lies with your brother and his debts – and this musket ball in my arm.'

'If you move you run the risk of having a useless arm. It will make life difficult for you.'

'I can ride a horse one-handed.'

'Earning a living would be difficult.'

'I am not afraid of working hard.'

'You will not be able to wrap your wife in a passionate embrace ...'

Jack's jaw tightened. 'I have no wife.'

'... or lift your children high in the air to make them scream in delight.'

'Give me the glass,' he said irritably, taking it from her and gulping down its contents. He looked at her uneasily. 'I do this against my better judgement,' he added, reluctantly holding the glass out towards her again. Silently he watched her refill it. He took another gulp. 'Do you miss your mother?'

'I have not seen her for a long time. I am afraid I will forget what she looks like.'

'It must have been hard.'

She smiled. 'Silas looked after me. You look surprised. I know he is a foolish scoundrel, but he has been the only constant in my life. As a child he was my playmate and protector. When I was frightened it was he who comforted me.' Jenna thought of the day the thief-taker took her older brothers away. It was Silas who crawled from his hiding place and held her hand to comfort her. 'People do not know Silas as I do. He has a soft heart, which he rarely shows, and he is prepared to do anything to protect me.'

Jack emptied his glass and reached out for a refill. Jenna obliged.

'I would not ask my sister to smuggle.'

'Dodging the law is his way of life. It is nothing abnormal for him. It is no different than you asking a sister of yours to do a job to earn some money.' The drinking continued; each time his glass was emptied it was immediately refilled. They lost count of how many he drank, as the aim was to have him unconscious.

'You call Silas foolish, but he is no fool,' Jack continued. 'He knew what he was asking you to do. But you love him and love can make people do things they would otherwise not consider doing.'

'You sound like you speak from experience.'

'I loved my father. When he died I wanted revenge. I came close to being no better than the men who killed him.'

'Did you get your revenge?'

'Yes – but not in the way that you think. I killed or injured no one.'

'What did you do?' Jack looked at the contents of his glass and said nothing. 'You are not going to tell me. You see, you are not as loose with your tongue as you say.'

He smiled at her, saluting her with his glass. 'You are quite a woman, Jenna. Your brother will surely miss you when you set up a house of your own and have your own family to care for.'

'I have tried that and it did not work. I do not see it happening again.'

'Are you adamant you will not remarry?'

'No decent man would want to marry me. I have no wealth, I do not come from a respectable family and I have a brother called Silas.'

They both smiled. 'That is what I like about you, Jenna. You have a sharp wit.'

'Some would call it a sharp tongue.'

'And you are trusting and courageous.'

'Naive and foolhardy,' she countered, pouring him another glass.

'Courageous – and beautiful.' She stopped pouring. 'It's true,' he insisted. 'When I saw you running away from the crowd I thought what a courageous boy you were.'

'And when did you think I was beautiful?' she asked, carefully putting down the decanter as her heart began to thud in her chest.

Jack dropped his head heavily back onto the pillow and looked up at the beams above. A whimsical smile lifted the corners of his lips. 'When I discovered you were not a boy.'

'I think the brandy is talking.'

Jack laughed. 'It is true. When I saw your big soulful eyes looking down at me with that gentle smile, I realised you were no boy. However, you have hurt my pride now that I know that your smile was no more than a trick to distract me.'

'It was a thank you for helping me.'

'It was a trick so I would not forget you.' Jack closed his eyes to shut out the spinning room. 'It worked.' He tapped his temple. 'You were trapped in here. Thought I was imagining you at the Mop Fayre. It took all my strength not to hire you that day,' he mused.

Jenna took the brandy away from his partially open hand and took a small sip herself, feeling the need for some too.

She watched him over the rim of the glass, waiting for his next confession.

'I had to go back again ... had to find out what happened to you ... couldn't let that lecher take you ...'

'Thank you for stepping in.'

He waved his hand precariously in the air. 'Men like that have no respect for women.'

Jenna put down the glass. She had something to say and it was important he heard it.

'Jack, I want you to know that I have never undressed to trick a man before. I would not want you to think badly of me.'

He sighed. 'I do not think badly of you, Jenna. Henley took his men away so your plan worked.' He tried to touch his lips but missed, the effort was too much and he let his hand fall once more. 'I have a confession to make and you may think badly of me when I tell you.' He was slurring his words and Jenna was afraid she would miss something. Frowning, she leaned forward.

'What do you have to confess, Jack?' she asked. Her heart began to thud again so loudly she felt he must surely hear.

He sighed again. 'You told me to close my eyes,' he said slowly, each word an effort for him to form, 'but I didn't.' A smile returned to his lips. 'The temptation was too much – I peeked.'

# Chapter Thirteen

With a lot of gentle manoeuvring and concentration, Jenna finally managed to remove the musket ball from Jack's arm. However, infection remained the greatest threat, so she remained by his side for the rest of the night, vigilant for any signs of a fever. She sat wrapped in a blanket, hugging her knees to ward off the chill as she watched him peacefully sleep off his liquor. She thought of the risks he took to help her, and how he had saved her life with no thought of his own. She remembered his caress and their kissing, and the nice things he said in his ramblings. She hugged her knees tighter. She had almost lost him tonight and the realisation sickened her.

At some point she fell into a fitful sleep and finally woke to a sunbeam breaking through a gap in the drapes. She got up to close them so they would not disturb Jack, but stayed a moment to look at the sea. Jack thought she was beautiful. The compliment, just one of many, pleased her to such an extent that the countryside outside the window appeared more colourful than when she usually looked upon it. It was a ridiculous reaction to a few drunken words, but it confirmed what she suspected last night – that she was in love with the man.

Jenna noticed a young woman striding across the grass towards the cottage. After checking Jack was still asleep, she slipped from the room and made her way quietly down the stairs to the door. She opened it before the woman could knock and their eyes locked. It was the girl from the Tolbridge Inn.

'Does Jack live here?'

Jenna, unsure of the purpose of her visit, felt protective towards Jack and ignored her question.

'Who are you?'

'My name is Melwyn. Jack said that I could come here. I need to talk to him.'

Jenna lifted her chin. Melwyn looked prettier than Jenna had first thought. There was no simpering smile and even the scar on her cheek did not distract from her healthy glow. No wonder Jack found himself comforting her. A pretty face that is not etched with a brother's troubles is easy to look upon.

'Mr Penhale is not receiving visitors at the moment.'

'So he is here,' Melwyn said, brushing past her into the house.

Jenna shut the door to keep in the warmth.

'Tell me and I will tell him later. He is asleep and I will not disturb him.'

Melwyn's smile slipped from her face. 'My words are for his ears only, not for his housekeeper's,' she replied curtly.

Melwyn had put her in her place with a few well-chosen words and Jenna felt herself bristle at the truth of them. While she spent the night realising how much she loved Jack, her position in his household had, in reality, remained unchanged.

'If you will not tell me, then you will have to return another time. I speak the truth when I say he is not receiving visitors.'

Melwyn raised an eyebrow. 'He will see me. We have an understanding.'

Jenna imagined herself grabbing Melwyn's hair and pushing her out of the door. She realised her feelings were not as noble as simply wanting to protect Jack. It was jealousy she felt and she saw Melwyn as a rival.

The floorboards creaked above them. Jack was awake.

Jenna forced a brittle smile. She could not turn her away now.

'I will speak to him and ask if he is willing to see you.'

'He will,' replied Melwyn confidently, holding Jenna's gaze. 'And he will want to see me alone.'

Jenna watched a self-assured smile curve the young woman's lips before turning to leave and closing the door nosily behind her.

Jack was already out of bed and struggling to pull on his boots.

'You should be resting.'

'I heard voices,' he said. He swore under his breath. 'Help me with these.'

Immediately, Jenna went to help him. 'How are you feeling?'

'Like I have been kicked in the head by a horse. It has reminded me of the other reason why I do not drink to excess.'

'I meant your arm.'

He smiled, 'My arm is considerably less painful.'

She did not believe him. 'It is only the landlord's daughter. I can send her away.'

'Melwyn?'

The woman's name lit up his eyes. He sounds pleased to see her, thought Jenna.

'Yes. She wants to talk to you.'

'I'll come down stairs and see her alone.' Jack stood up, 'My shirt ... help me with my shirt.'

Jenna found it and eased the sleeve over his bandaged arm. Melwyn was right, she was just his housekeeper and she would remain so if she did not let him know how she felt.

'Do not let her visit tire you out. Tell her to go if you do not feel up to it.'

'I am glad she has come.'

Why? Why are you glad she has come? You said you had no interest in her, yet you are eager to see her.

He attempted to button his shirt, but found bending his arm too painful. Jenna saw him wince.

'Let me,' she said, taking over the task. She instantly regretted her offer of help as each button she worked upon lay on his bare chest. It took all of her willpower not to tremble and make a mess of it. Thankfully, he did not watch her, preferring to look over her head and stare at the wall.

The task finally came to an end and they found themselves standing too close with no purpose. They both turned awkwardly away.

'Jenna ...'

'Yes?'

'I want to apologise for yesterday. I should not have reacted to your kiss as I did. I did not consider the consequences. I was not thinking clearly.'

Jenna picked up a pillow and held it to her chest. 'I was not offended,' she muttered miserably.

'You should be. I took advantage and grew loose with my tongue. I would not wish to make you feel uncomfortable working for me.'

Any happiness she felt had gone. Melwyn's visit had seen to that.

'I do not,' she said quietly.

'My response was quicker than my wit,' he said. It was a poor attempt at a joke.

Jenna looked away. 'I will stay in here and change the sheets,' she said, looking at his empty bed. 'I will not eavesdrop.' Jack did not reply; she could see that his mind was elsewhere and he wanted to see the woman downstairs.

After he had gone, she stood alone listening to their muffled greeting below. Just as she suspected, she could not make out what they said. She looked around her and saw evidence of yesterday – the musket ball she'd left in a dish and fresh bandages ready for redressing his wound. Yet, despite it all, he behaved as if he was ashamed there had been any closeness between them.

She was not ashamed and would not forget. She was in love with him, but he did not know it and, if his ramblings were only half-truths, he had a liking for her too. If she wanted things to change she needed to let him know how she felt. But how? What did she have to draw on in life? Every relationship she had ever had with a man was based on blood ties or fear. How does a woman convey to a man that she wants him? How does she encourage his interest in her when he is reluctant to even acknowledge he has one when sober? Whatever experience she drew upon, she had to do it quickly, before Melwyn stepped into his arms and took her chance away.

Jack paused on the last step to ensure his bandage could not be seen. His wound hurt like hell, but he did not want Melwyn to know about it. The less people that knew, thought Jack, the better. He pasted on a smile before entering the room where he knew she would be waiting for him.

'Hello, Melwyn. I did not expect to see you here.'

He offered her a chair and was glad when she accepted and sat down. He had begun to feel lightheaded already and needed to sit down himself.

'Does your father know you have come?' he asked as he settled himself carefully in the wooden chair opposite her.

'No, he does not,' replied Melwyn, sitting stiffly, her eyes darting about the room whilst her hand twisted the weave of her skirt. She was nervous, he could tell, so waited patiently for her to speak.

She noticed him looking at her and jerked her head upwards to the room above. 'I didn't think I would get to see you,' she said. 'Your housekeeper was not best pleased to disturb you. If she was a dog she would have snarled.'

Jack's laugh morphed into a wince before he had a chance to guard his reaction.

'Are you hurt?' asked Melwyn, her nerves overtaken with concern.

'I fell from my horse yesterday and now have a bruise to remind me of my stupidity.' Jack smiled. 'It is not something I wish to dwell upon, Melwyn. Tell me why you are here.'

Melwyn began to worry the thread of her dress again. 'Your housekeeper won't tell anyone I have been here, will she?'

'Jenna is very loyal and will not gossip.'

Melwyn considered his reply. 'She seemed very protective. She wanted to send me away so I gave her the impression we had an understanding. I hope you don't mind.'

'An understanding?' queried Jack.

'A liking for one another.'

Jack raised an eyebrow. He wished he had been present during *that* conversation.

'You find that funny?' asked Melwyn, with a curious look upon her face.

Jack straightened in his chair. He had forgotten Melwyn felt self-conscious about her scarred face. Why did women ask questions that had no right answer?

'Not in the least.' It was time to get down to business. 'Melwyn, why are you here?'

Melwyn shifted uneasily in her seat. 'There is talk that the preventative men attacked the smugglers last night at Tudor Cove.'

'News travels fast,' said Jack, noncommittally.

'Father hoped that would be the end of them, but it seems most got away. Why, even this morning Job and Amos Blake sent someone around to us. They want Father to take more kegs. He doesn't want them or have the money to pay, but the Blakes are forcing his hand as they don't want to risk carrying it across country to one of their holding houses.'

'Will he be a witness against them?'

Melwyn shook her head. 'He is too scared. And nor will I. You don't know what it is like to live in fear, Jack.'

He did, but now was not the time to share his own life story. 'I can't bring them to justice without evidence or witnesses. I need help, Mel.'

'Which is why I am here.'

Jack straightened. Suddenly the pain in his shoulder no longer mattered. 'Tell me.'

'There is someone who speaks to both sides.'

Jack let out the breath he had been holding. 'There are many who speak to both sides,' conceded Jack. Had her father not already told him this?

'A man in authority. A man no one would suspect.'

This was different to a sly creature like Silas. 'What man?'

Melwyn hesitated. 'I don't know his name, but I know he has connections to the highest in the land. He has inside knowledge, Jack, so he can warn the smugglers.'

'But he did not warn them last night.'

'You do not believe me?' asked Melwyn, a little hurt.

'I believe you,' said Jack. 'I just don't know if what you have been told is correct. Where did you hear this?'

'I don't know their names.'

'You must do.'

'I don't. I was working and overheard some men talking as they supped their ale. They spoke of being warned about the preventative men on a previous drop. So they changed the landing place to avoid capture.'

Anonymous drinkers, earning a coin or two with the odd bit of smuggling. However, their loose words brought out by drink may be of some use.

'I had better go,' said Melwyn, getting up. Jack stood too. 'You have been good to us Jack, I hope what I have told you helps in some way.' A little frown darkened her brow. 'I am leaving home soon as I am to be wed. I don't want my parents spending their final years worrying for their own safety.'

Jack gave her arm a reassuring stroke. 'I will do everything in my power to help,' he told her. 'Now take that frown from your pretty face and go home to them. Try not to let the last few weeks you have of their company be marred by others. Time with your family is precious and you can never get it back. Take it from me,' he added sadly. 'I know about these things.'

Melwyn went to the door, but paused with her hand on the latch. She turned to look at him and he saw her struggling with the thoughts in her head. Finally she spoke, her voice determined and clear. 'The man who speaks to both sides is a preventative man, Jack. I know this because my father is warned each time there is to be a search for smuggled goods. Only a preventative man would know that information. Please don't tell anyone that you have heard it from me.' Before Jack could reply, Melwyn had lifted the latch and stepped outside. He went to the door to speak further to her, but she was already walking briskly away with no intention of looking back.

Jack looked down at the neatly secured bandage around his arm. It had been a week since the night he was shot and the wound beneath was almost healed. Jenna was right when she said he would recover quickly. Her tender care, good food and rest had all played their part, as did the musket misfiring as a result of damp gunpowder from the sea air. Without any of these things, he may have lost his arm, if not his life.

He tentatively moved his fingers. Apart from a slight pulling sensation, he felt no pain. This was a great improvement from when he first stirred from his drunken stupor. He had opened his eyes to the sound of women's voices and was surprised to find himself in an empty room. His head ached and he initially remembered little of the evening before, but when he saw a musket ball on the table by his bed, some of the memories came flooding back.

He turned the musket ball in his fingers. It appeared innocuous now it was extracted, but he would keep it as a reminder of how fragile the gift of life could be. The near death experience had changed him inside, and he suspected it had changed Jenna as well.

Since that night her eyes seemed brighter and she smiled more often. He couldn't stop himself commenting on her good mood.

'I have much to be grateful for,' she had said, passing him a slice of buttered bread. 'You are healing well and will soon be back to normal.'

'And what is normal for you?' he had asked.

Initially she had dropped her gaze, but at the last

moment looked up at him through her lashes. 'To be your housekeeper,' she had replied. He wondered if that was what she really meant, for she had a strange opinion on the duties of a housekeeper.

What housekeeper would lie half-naked in his bed to distract the dragoons? It was wrong of her to place herself in such a vulnerable position, yet having her so close felt anything but wrong. Somewhere along their journey together, she had stepped outside her role – and he had helped her to do it. He had taken advantage of her when she was only trying to help him. He had been too free with his compliments when she had never encouraged him. On waking he had made up his mind to redraw the line between employer and employee. It had taken all his strength to do it and even more to abide by the decision. Each day it grew harder and for a very good reason.

He paused briefly to listen to her singing in her bedroom, before snuffing out a candle in preparation for bed. It was not only her lightened mood that was different. He noticed another change had come over her, causing unspoken messages to fill the air between them. He saw them sent by other women and he knew what they meant. She was not an innocent maid who did not know the language of nature. She was married once and no doubt used it before. Jack did not respond but it was getting harder to ignore – a lingering touch on his hand, another bashful look through her lashes and a playful tone to her words. She was flirting with him and the line he had drawn was fading fast.

Her singing stopped and the house became still. It cleared his head and gave him a moment to think. Perhaps he was misreading her signals and he was only seeing what he wanted to see. It was a sobering thought. He tried to console himself that any man can have moments of delusion. Any man can see attraction in a woman's eyes when in reality it is no more than kindly interest sparkling in their depths. He would go to his own bed, he decided, and ignore his fanciful thoughts brought on by the fact that he had not lain with a woman for several months.

Jack frowned as he realised he had not even looked for a woman since Jenna came into his life. She had much to answer for, he thought, as he snuffed out the candle and watched the plume of fragile smoke rise in the air. He had suspected that hiring her would cause him trouble, but he did not consider what it would be like to live with a woman he found so tempting.

Jack straightened his shoulders as Jenna's soft lyrical tones began to waft through the floorboards again. Damn those floorboards, he thought. He looked up and wondered if fate was stepping in with a beckoning hand. Only moments before he had decided to be sensible. Unfortunately, where Jenna was concerned he realised a sensible choice was no choice at all.

Jenna stopped singing as she realised she was failing miserably. Jack had not mentioned his drunken confession all week. At first, she tried to encourage him by providing the right atmosphere that might stimulate such feelings again, but her attempts got her nowhere. Like a blind man, he saw none of her gentle approaches and left her wondering if he was attracted to her at all. Any sane woman would have asked him if he meant his compliments, but she had been afraid that he would disown them. Instead she had become devious in her cowardice and tried using tricks that she copied from women who loitered around the entrance of Goverek Inn.

She should not have used them on Jack, but her desire to touch and be touched by him had grown over the last few days and made her reckless. She should have known he would not respond. He would be too mindful of his position as her employer. Her attempts were now bordering on embarrassing and tomorrow she must stop. His brandy fuelled words were just a memory that would fade over time. It was no wonder the song she had just sung was a sad ballad about thwarted love. It was how she felt: desolate, empty and undesired.

Jenna heard the door of her room creak open and was surprised to see Jack filling the doorway, a hand resting on the latch, the other against the frame. Jenna put down her hairbrush and slowly stood up. He avoided looking at her, preferring to stare intently at the floor.

'Tell me to go if I am wrong to come here,' he said quietly.

Jenna's heart began to thud in her chest and her mouth grew dry, leaving her silence to hang heavy between them.

'I have made a mistake,' he muttered briskly. He was leaving, and so were the kisses he could lay upon her skin.

'You are not wrong,' Jenna blurted out a little too loudly. She felt her face redden. Her abrupt reply sounded more like a fishwife than a seductress.

Jack hesitated, turning his head as if he thought he had misheard her.

She tried again, but more quietly and heartfelt. This time, her reply came easier to her as it was how she truly felt. 'You are not wrong, Jack,' she said softly. 'I am glad you are here.'

He paused, allowing her words to linger in the air, before closing the door with a push of his hand and a click of the latch.

Jenna's heart began to race. 'What about Melwyn?' she asked. She had to know.

His black eyes held hers. 'There is nothing between us.'

'But you like her?'

'She is barely out of childhood,' he said as he allowed his gaze to slowly sweep over her body. 'I want a woman,' he mused, lifting them again to snare hers. 'I want you.'

Three strides and he was framing her jaw with his fingers and kissing her face. His soft kisses deepened before hungrily trailing down the line of her neck. She found herself smiling, as his hands slid down her back to span her waist, before rising again to her breasts. He wanted to feel her, but she remained encased within her stays. They would have to go.

Without uttering a word, they both watched as he pulled at her laces with impatient fingers, their foreheads touching as their shallow breaths mingled in the cold night air. Jenna's body softened beneath and began to tremble as Jack finally eased her stays from her and impatiently cast them aside. He began to caress her breasts beneath her shift, as he kissed the curve of her neck.

'Tell me to go ... if you want me to stop,' he whispered hoarsely as he slid one shoulder of her shift down to expose her skin. His lips felt soft and warm, while a sensual graze of his teeth sent shivers up her spine.

'I don't want you to go,' Jenna whispered as her skin's sensitivity heightened, tightening her nipples to a painful ache.

Jack eased the other shoulder of her shift away and guided it down to rest on her hips. He lifted his gaze to look into her eyes.

'Then I will not stop,' was his sultry reply.

Jenna gasped as his lips followed every curve of her body. She closed her eyes and threaded her trembling fingers through her own hair, for she knew he was about to take her on a journey she had never experienced before.

Jenna opened her eyes and saw the unfamiliar wooden beams above. She smiled as she realised she was in Jack's bedroom and he was lying asleep next to her. She rolled to face him so she could watch him unnoticed. His lovemaking was perfect and he was perfect, she thought happily. She did not know a relationship between a man and a woman could be this good. Her smile threatened to turn into a giggle as she remembered how they came to be in his room. She clutched the sheet to her mouth to stifle it and he felt the movement. He opened his eyes and smiled at her. Delighted he'd woken, she snuggled against him to enjoy the lazy caress of his hand on her arm.

'You look happy,' he said, looking at her from the corner of his eye.

'I am,' Jenna replied. She reached across to let her hand rest on his chest. She could feel his heartbeat through her fingers. It was steady and solid, like him.

'I am glad,' he replied, placing his hand on hers and caressing her fingers. 'I could be dead now, but I am here with you. I am fortunate indeed.'

He lifted her fingers to his lips and kissed the tips, before encasing her hand in his and sliding it back to his heart.

'Such tiny hands,' he mused.

Jenna smiled. 'Would you like them larger?' she teased.

'No, your hand fits in mine as if it were meant to do so.'

Jenna lifted herself up on her elbow and stared down on him. She looked at his hand over hers, strong, masculine and surrounded by a scattering of dark hairs on his chest. She wanted to thread her fingers through them, yet did not want to withdraw from his hold.

'Do you believe people are made for each other, Jack?'

He opened his eyes to look at her. 'Do you?'

'I asked you first.'

He thought for a moment. 'I think some people are more suited than others,' he replied, closing his eyes. Easing her fingers apart, he slipped his between them and began to caress her skin, sliding them up and down to the rhythm of her breaths.

*I am made for you*, she wanted to say. *Only for you.*

He squeezed her hand. 'Jenna?'

'What?'

'I asked if you think people are made for each other.'

'I didn't used to,' she replied as she looked at him lying next to her, his eyes closed, his lashes fanning his cheeks, his stubble darkening his olive skin. She felt the familiar ache of desire rise up inside her again. 'Perhaps you could persuade me.'

He smiled. 'I hear mischief in your tone,' he said, opening his eyes, 'and see mischief in those dark eyes of yours.'

They fell silent, each content to just look at each other's face. The glint of mischief died in Jenna's eyes.

'You almost died trying to protect me,' she said quietly. 'I should never have let you go in my place.'

'Your brother should never have asked you to go.' He closed his eyes and his fingers stilled. 'He brings you unhappiness. You deserve more from life.'

'I am happy now.'

'But for how long? You are too kind-hearted and will be paying his debts again before long. Let your brother get himself out of prison. He does not deserve your help.'

'He is already free.'

'Free? How?'

'His creditors have been paid.'

Jack fell silent and his fingers fell away from hers. Jenna felt a subtle change in the air and she shivered. She snuggled up to his warm body. It felt unyielding to her touch.

'How did you know the dragoons were coming, Jenna?' Jack asked.

She had no reason not to tell Jack the truth. He was her future and she wanted no lies between them.

'Silas told me. He sent a message asking me to meet him at Lanros Inn. There, he told me how he bought his freedom by telling the dragoons how the smugglers communicated. I am sorry, Jack. I tried to warn you as soon as I knew.'

'And he told you this to keep you away from the beach?'

'Yes.'

Jack was silent for a moment. When he finally spoke his tone was measured.

'Did he know I took your place? Did he not think you would try to warn me?'

'Yes, he knew you would be on the beach, but I don't think it crossed his mind that I would warn you. I'm sorry for what he did.'

Jack fell silent again. The steady rise and fall of his chest remained, but his body felt tense beneath her fingers.

'Your brother will reap the rewards for his betrayal.'

'What do you mean?' Jenna asked.

'Smugglers are ruthless. They do not like to be made fools of.'

Jenna did not like the sombre mood that was wheedling its way into the room.

'For the most part they are ordinary folk who see an opportunity to make some money to feed their families.' Jenna wondered who she was trying to reassure, Jack or herself, but she continued on. 'They accept that dodging the preventative men is part of the game.'

Jack's frown deepened. 'You think that smugglers are local villagers who will be happy to wait for the next tide,' he said. 'Smuggling requires large numbers of people and mules to bring goods across the sea and have it distributed. Brandy and tobacco have to be sold on.'

'As do spices, silks and paintings.'

'Paintings?' Jack asked, surprised.

Jenna turned onto her tummy and rested on her elbows so she could look at Jack more clearly. 'Yes. There were paintings and vases for a man called Lambskin.'

Jack was thoughtful. 'They are branching out and are no longer content with dodging the import taxes. This work takes organisation by ruthless gangs. With so many people involved, they have to keep their silence through fear and violence. Silas has much to fear and will be made an example of.'

It was Jenna's turn to frown. 'You seem to know a lot about smuggling. By the way you talk one would think you would like to be the one to silence him.'

'He is no friend of mine. His talk almost cost me my life.'

'And now you are well. Silas has smuggled before. He knows the risks better than we.' She moved closer and stroked his chest, enjoying the contour of his muscle as it spread to his shoulder. 'Let us forget Silas,' she soothed. 'Let us enjoy the here and now. Let us enjoy each other.' She moved to lie on top of him and looked down at his face. His eyes darkened as he looked at her.

'You are right,' he replied, reaching for her. 'This is no time for such talk.' He rolled her onto her back and rose above her, his silhouette shielding the early dawn light spilling through the window and hiding his expression.

He began to kiss the curve of her neck and the smoothness of her shoulder causing her breath to quicken. Instinctively, she turned her head to expose more flesh for him to kiss. She heard him groan at her invitation. 'Damn the free traders,' she heard him mutter as he looked down upon her. He started kissing her skin again, running his lips across the curves of her ear. 'Damn them all,' he whispered hoarsely as he reached beneath the sheets to feel more of her.

For Jenna, their lovemaking was as perfect as before. In the morning, she woke and turned to him. The perfection ended when she found he was gone.

# Chapter Fourteen

Lanros Inn dominated the main road of the village. The building had grown in splendour over recent years as a direct result of the lucrative coach route that ran by it. Although it provided work for the villagers, its popularity and noise built resentment in those who remembered quieter times. This meant that as stagecoaches waited to depart, they were routinely subjected to sidelong glances of frustration and scorn by the villagers themselves. The inn's height, while casting a shadow over the pedestrians below, offered fine views to guests inhabiting the rooms on the upper floors. It was through one of these windows that Silas now watched the lives of others unfold beneath him.

The rain finally stopped, leaving muddy puddles to form on the uneven road surface below. Those who had sought shelter were finally venturing out into the daylight and Silas watched in silence as one final trunk was heaved aboard an overloaded stagecoach and tied into position. Passengers climbed in and a thud sounded within to signal they were ready. Silas watched silently, his thoughts more occupied with his sister than the scene below. He had waited a week, hoping she would contact him first, but this morning he could wait no longer and had sent her a message asking her to visit. Why had she not sent him a reply? Had she been hurt on the beach or was she still angry and just refusing to come?

Silas's money was beginning to run out and soon he must move on. If she did not call upon him soon, he would have to go to her. The horses whinnied and the driver shouted a command, dragging Silas's attention to them once more.

With a stamp of their hooves, they began to pull on their harnesses, dragging the carriage behind with the turn of their wooden wheels. Its long awaited departure revealed a man on the far side of the road dressed in black. His tricorn hat obscured his face, but the determination in his step as he crossed the road appeared familiar to Silas. On reaching the other side of the road the man stopped and slowly looked up. His confidence told Silas he must have been watching him for some time, as he knew in which window to find him. Their eyes locked and Silas stepped back. He had expected this visit, yet he was not prepared when it came. Looking up at him, with a predatory stare, was Jack Penhale and Silas realised there was no place to hide.

Silas nervously raked a hand through his hair as he waited. He considered running, but Penhale may have news of Jenna and his desire to know his sister was well for once outweighed his cowardice. He heard his arrival and the landlord's muffled tones outside his door. Penhale's words were clearer, dismissing the man in a manner that evoked no argument. It was evident Penhale wanted to see him alone. Silas fingered his neck cloth and prepared for the confrontation, but whereas yesterday his fashionable clothes made him feel confident, today they choked and mocked him.

The door opened and Jack stepped inside, taking off his hat as he did so. His face was impassive, but his relaxed manner told Silas that he had no bad news of Jenna to tell. Silas knew he should be grateful for this small mercy, but he wasn't. While he had spent the past week concerned for her welfare, this man had her in his life. Penhale knew more about Jenna's life than her own blood kin, and that thought sickened him. Feelings of jealousy, which had festered in his gut ever since the day his sister had first mentioned Jack Penhale's name, rose up inside him.

'We meet again,' Jack said coldly as he glanced about the room. 'But this time you have money in your pocket instead of creditors at your door.' He let his gaze wander over Silas's foppish clothes and a slight smile curved his lips. 'You appear to have joined the aristocracy?' he teased.

'What do you want, Penhale?'

Jack smoothed a few raindrops off the brim of his hat. 'Information. Your tastes are expensive and your purse is not deep. I have a little money, which I was planning to use to pay some of your creditors ...'

'Jenna told me you were willing to help me.'

'I was willing to help her, not you,' Jack corrected him.

Silas tilted his chin at the retort. 'I hear that you played at being a smuggler. How is the free trading these days?'

'I know you told. Was it for money or was it to get your revenge on me?'

Silas shrugged. 'Both and more.'

There was a short silence as Jack considered his next words. It gave Silas time to study the man who had turned his sister's head. Gifted with good looks, good physique and intelligence, his sister had been easy prey for his charms. Did she not realise she was betraying her family by falling for a thief-taker? He had a hold on Jenna, Silas thought. He gritted his teeth as he resolved to do all in his power so this man would not win.

Jack looked up. 'The money I have I am willing to give you, if you can supply me with the information that I need.'

'You have flexible morals. First you earn money to capture people like me, now you are willing to pay for my services. You tore me from my family and landed me in prison!'

'You broke the law and your wife had already abandoned you.'

'We all know what thief-takers are like – they report false crimes, bring innocent people to court and make up evidence.'

'Your crime and evidence was not made up and you have not been innocent since you were in swaddling clothes.'

'People like you took two of my brothers away – Jenna's brothers – and were probably involved in the disappearance of our parents.'

'If your brothers were taken because they broke the law then they deserved it. I am not corrupt. I am an honest thief-taker.'

Silas almost laughed. 'If you were as honest as you say, you would not be able to carry out your work. A spy cannot be honest to everyone they meet. Does Jenna know?'

Jack looked away.

Silas snorted. 'I thought not.'

'I am here to help you. I will pay you well for the information I need.'

'What information?'

'I want to know whose money finances the smuggling.'

Silas laughed. 'I would rather spit on your money. If I told you that, do you think I would survive for very long? They would come and find me.'

'They will, which is the other reason why I am here.'

Silas went to the window and looked down on the road below. Another carriage had arrived and travellers were unloading.

'What do you mean?' he asked warily.

'Word will get back to Amos and Job Blake and their financier that you were the one who sold out to Henley and the dragoons. They will make you pay dearly.'

Silas turned away from the scene below.

'You must think I am a fool. I only told Henley. I ensured no one else was present.'

'He came alone?'

'With one other but I sent him out.'

'You need to leave Cornwall. They will come for you and you will be lucky if you survive.'

'I told you, only Henley was present.'

'There are ears and eyes everywhere. They will know someone has told and your new-found wealth will have caused gossip. It is only a matter of time until they find you.'

'Your concern touches me.'

'I care nothing for you, but Jenna will be distraught if anything happens to you. It is a shame you do not have the same concern for her safety as she does for yours.'

'I have been my sister's protector since we could walk. You have known her for only a few months. How fortunate that your housekeeper could provide you information about the free traders. Did you hire her before or after you discovered that her late husband and her brother helped with some runs? Were the sweetmeats to soften her tongue? Next you will be bedding her so she would be fooled into thinking you love her.' Silas saw a flash of anger in Jack's eyes.

'If you were any other man,' he replied menacingly, 'I would force your words back down your throat with my fist, but you are Jenna's brother so I will hold my temper. I see that you will not help me, and I understand that, but I stand by my warning. It is not safe for you to stay here and you should leave. With the money you have left, travel north and do not come back again.'

So this was his plan, thought Silas. He wants to scare me into leaving. He wants me out of my sister's life. Silas's lips narrowed. Well, he could play the same game of deception and drive a wedge between this man and his sister.

'I no longer need your help,' Silas said, opening the door. 'I want you to leave.'

'So be it, but you cannot say that I did not warn you.'

As Jack turned to leave, Silas clumsily slipped his fingers into Jack's pocket and lifted his purse. Jack grabbed his wrist and looked at the purse dangling in the air.

'Even now, when your life is threatened and you are offered a way out, you return to your sewer rat ways.' Jack ripped his purse from his fingers and shook the contents out. Coins fell over Silas and onto the floor around his feet. 'Keep the money, Cartwright. Perhaps, when I am gone, you will think better of your decision and leave Cornwall.'

'It would suit you if I were to go.'

'You are right. I would like you gone. Jenna has a strong sense of family loyalty, which ties her to you. But those ties are no more than shackles that will drag her down and blight her future. It is not the life she wants. It is not the life she deserves. She is a good woman, Cartwright. If you love her you will leave.'

Jack stepped out into the passage and Silas angrily slammed the door behind him. He took a deep breath to calm himself as he listened to Jack's footsteps receding. He looked down, but it was not the coins at his feet that brought a smile to his face. In his open palm lay two buttons ripped from Jack's sleeve.

He straightened his waistcoat and combed his hair with his fingers, admiring his reflection in a mottled mirror above a wooden chest of drawers. Then he positioned himself with care and began to count to three. On the fourth silent beat he bent forward quickly to smash his face on the unforgiving wooden corner with a sickening thud. He stood up, slightly dazed, and looked into the mirror again. His cheek, bright red from the impact, quickly began to swell and deepen in colour. Red fragile threads spread across his eye as his smile broadened. What a tale he would have to tell Jenna. What a yarn he would spin. Her fledgling fondness for this man would turn to hate when she saw what he had done to her brother.

The sound of a commotion outside his room caught his attention. He stopped examining his face and nervously looked out the window. From his vantage point on the upper floor, he could see Penhale riding away. He looked nervously to the top of the street and noticed Jenna making her way through the muddy puddles. She had received his message and was coming to see him.

Men's voices stopped outside his room. A prickle of fear rose up and flowed along the back of his neck. What if Penhale was right to warn him? What if the Blake brothers had come to get him? With trembling hands he tried to open the window in order to shout for help, but his fumbling made him too slow. The door swung open and banged against the wall. Two bearded men, with fists like boulders and bodies as solid as granite stone, stood in the doorway. It was Amos and Job Blake and they had violence on their minds. The moment of silence and calm was fleeting, before they rushed into the room and dragged him to the floor. No time was given for him to beg for leniency or make his escape. Their fists and muddy boots rained down upon him, and throughout his ordeal not a word was spoken or an explanation sought. Both sides knew why they had come, and both sides accepted the outcome.

It was her scream reaching his subconscious that told Silas he was still alive. He opened his eyes. Through narrow slits he saw Jenna in the open doorway with her hands covering her mouth. The look of horror on her face told him how bad he must look. The pain that racked his body told him he was lucky to be alive. Jenna ran towards him and fell to her knees by his side. She had come as he had asked and not let him down.

'Oh, Silas ... Silas ... Who did this to you?' Her concern made the pain more bearable. His plan had gone momentarily awry, but now it was back on track. He relaxed in her arms and found the strength to talk.

'Penhale,' he mumbled through swollen lips.

'Jack? No, you are mistaken. He would not do this.'

Her denial fed his hatred for the man and gave him strength to carry on. 'He was here,' he retorted hoarsely. 'He did it with his own hands.'

He saw Jenna look to the doorway where the landlord's large body stood filling the space.

'Fetch a surgeon. Quickly!' she shouted irritably, before turning her attention back to him. 'I know Jack. He would not hurt you like this. It is not his way.'

Even now, he thought, when I, her brother, am badly injured, she protects *him*. Silas grew angry and his anger gave him strength.

'Look in my hand, Sister – buttons from his coat.' He winced in pain as he opened his fingers. 'I tried to protect myself, but he was a man possessed.'

Jenna took the buttons from his bloodied hand and stared at them. Silas saw her frown change to sadness. Doubt had begun to grow in her mind, he thought triumphantly. For a brief moment he forgot his pain.

'He wanted information.'

Jenna glanced up. 'What information?'

'Who supplies money for the smuggling runs.'

Jenna shook her head. 'You are confused. He does not want anything further to do with smuggling. He only did it to help you.'

He was right to think she does not know how Penhale earns his money. The revelation spurred Silas on.

'It is his business to know. Penhale is a thief-taker.'

She shook her head again. 'No.'

With a trembling hand he clutched at her dress, forcing her to brace herself to stop falling on top of him.

'The likes of him took our brothers away,' spat Silas through the pain. 'You can't trust a thief-taker. They will sell out their friends to earn a coin.'

'No ... he can't be.'

''T'is true. It was he that sent me to prison.'

Her expression changed again. He saw the range of emotions cross her face like clouds on a windy day. Each new hurt was his triumph and Penhale's loss.

He released his grip to look at the blood on his hands. 'Thief-takers ruined our family.'

'Our family ruined themselves,' she retorted.

Silas glanced up at her; even now she was defending him. How deep this man has wormed his way into his sister's heart, he thought angrily.

'He is using you, Jenna. He wants to know about Lambskin.'

'I know nothing of Lambskin or smuggling. Jack knows more than me.'

'You are a widow and sister of men who have smuggled. You are easy prey to wheedle the information he seeks. All he has to say is a few kind words, buy a box of sweetmeats, teach you to read ... perhaps even speak words of love.' A sudden sharp pain caused him to stiffen, tearing and gnawing at something deep inside.

'Don't say any more. Save your strength,' Jenna soothed as beads of perspiration began to form on Silas's forehead. 'It will not be long now. The surgeon will be here soon.'

As suddenly as it began, the pain moved on. Silas rested a moment to catch his breath before lifting his head to spit bloody saliva onto the ground at his side.

'He is ... no good ... for you,' he whispered hoarsely. 'He has kept the truth ... from you. Didn't I promise I would always protect you?'

Jenna nodded, tears blurring her vision.

'I am only keeping my ... promise,' he added weakly, letting his head fall back against her. Why was it getting harder to talk? He felt tired and more breathless, and his sister looked defeated. She was attempting to clean some blood away with the hem of her dress, but it was futile. Silas waved her help away and placed his hand on hers.

'He ... has ... used you ... Jenna.'

Jenna's eyes glistened in the morning sun as tears began to fall. Silas sighed with relief. He could see in her eyes that the doubt he had placed in her mind was now growing with each memory she had of him.

He felt her hand withdraw from under his so she could cradle him in her arms. It felt comforting and he relaxed, until another sharp pain caught him and took his breath from him. He attempted to exhale the pain away, but this time the pain lingered and grew. He looked at Jenna's worried face. She believed his injuries were too great for her skills. Suddenly, Silas understood what this meant and it frightened him – he did not want to die.

'Keep away from *him*,' he wanted to say but no words came out. He frowned in confusion and felt Jenna stroke his brow. Why was the light fading at this time of day? His mouth became dry and his mind turned foggy. Although he felt Jenna's arms about him, her soothing tones seemed so far away. He was leaving her already, he realised, and he did not want to go.

Silas mustered what little strength he had left in one last effort to drive a wedge between her and the man that still had a life to share with her.

'Tell Lambskin ... about Penhale,' he whispered hoarsely through blood-cracked lips. '*He* will make him pay.'

# Chapter Fifteen

Jack put the tray of glasses on the table and began to fill each with port.

'No housekeeper to attend us?' asked Enoch, looking at the ashes in the fire.

'I found her gone when I returned this morning. I suspect she is buying supplies for the larder.'

'Administering to your needs as any good housekeeper should,' Enoch said with a smile, taking the glass Jack offered him.

'Or administering to someone else's needs,' muttered Henley as he reached for his.

Jack kept hold of it and left Henley's hand to linger in the air. 'I trust her more than some,' he said pointedly, before handing him his glass.

'What do you mean by that?'

'I mean that a uniform does not mean that the man behind it can be trusted.'

Henley bristled and turned to Enoch. 'I have guarded this coastline for many years without this man's help. He comes here and has the gall to accuse me of double-dealing.'

Enoch opened his mouth to play peacemaker but Jack interrupted him.

'The day after I was shot I was given a message by an informant that there is a spy in your ranks.'

Henley snorted. 'Most of your informants accept smuggled goods. Hardly trustworthy sources.'

'I can trust this one,' said Jack, picking up his glass.

Henley snorted again. He had heard that before.

Jack tipped his head back and drained his glass. 'There

are many who were willing to buy smuggled brandy at first, but after your searches they want no more involvement.' He toyed with his empty glass as he contemplated having another, smudging his fingerprint with a rub of his thumb. 'Unfortunately, smugglers only get their profit when the goods are sold and they do not take kindly to losing a customer. They force landlords to buy by threatening their wives', sons' and daughters' lives.' He placed his glass on the table. 'The fear of what they might do costs the landlords dearly as the smugglers can increase their prices at will.'

'How does your informant know there is a spy in my ranks?' asked Henley.

Jack looked at him. 'Through idle gossip,' he replied evasively. 'Besides, even I have suspected that the landlords are warned when there is going to be a search.'

'And this informant was willing to confide in you?' asked Enoch, refilling his own glass. 'How does he know he can trust you?'

'Because I understand the risk this person runs should they refuse, and I think they saw that in me.' Jack refused Enoch's offer of another drink with a curt shake of his head and took a seat opposite them to stare into the ashes.

Jenna would have a fire warming the room by now if she was home, he thought, but instead three men sat around its grey ashes feeling the cold. Stubbornly, he had not lit it himself, as to do so would accept she was not coming back. He should have woken her before he left, but she had looked so peaceful in her slumber he had not wanted to disturb her – or tell her where he was going. Now she was angry that she had awakened alone and he was paying the price for his insensitivity.

Jack dragged his gaze from the ashes and back to the meeting in hand. 'If they catch up with Silas we will know my informant speaks the truth and there is someone playing both sides.'

Henley held up his glass in a mock toast. 'Says the man who is bedding the widow of a smuggler. How much have you learnt from her?'

'She is not like them,' ground out Jack. 'She is a good woman who tries her best to lead a law-abiding life. Her brother drags her down but I believe she now has the strength to resist him. I trust her. She risked her life to warn me about the dragoons that night.'

'You would like to believe that,' retorted Henley, 'but the reality is that she warned fifty smugglers at the same time. Perhaps it was them she wanted to warn, not you.'

Jack clenched his fists. 'You know nothing of Jenna.'

'I know she has a strange view of what housekeeping duties are,' said Henley. He turned to Enoch. 'The last time I saw her she was lying half naked on her employer.'

Jack's jaw tightened. 'She is a fine housekeeper,' he replied in a menacing tone.

'She is a slut,' retorted Henley.

Jack leapt to his feet and dragged Henley to his. The small table toppled and Jack's glass smashed on the slate floor at their feet.

'Mind your tongue, Henley,' warned Jack, 'or you will have to fish it out of your throat.'

Enoch stood and with feeble arms attempted to break them apart.

'Gentlemen! Gentlemen! This will not do! Jack, put the man down!' Jack's fists loosened, allowing Henley to pull away. 'We are all on the same side. Fighting each other will help no man,' Enoch scolded.

Henley straightened his clothes as he moved to put some distance between them. He had goaded Jack before but the man had always remained calm under his sarcasm. Jack's sudden anger today surprised and frightened him. He must choose his words more carefully in the future, particularly where his housekeeper was concerned. He filled another glass of port and emptied it to steady his nerves. He turned to Jack.

'I went to the prison with Tilbury, but sent him out of the room to keep guard. I was the only one who heard what Silas said and I told no one. The dragoons did not know their mission until the night of the attack.' He pointed to his chest with his thumb. 'I am the only one who knew, and I told no one where I got my information from. This will be proved by Silas remaining unharmed.'

'Money is a source of corruption. Men from all classes can be bought for the right price,' Jack said, turning away and righting the table.

'Not this man,' argued Henley, putting on his hat. 'It is time you began to trust me, Penhale. Had I been told that you would be on the beach that night, I would have warned my men.'

'I knew the danger I risked,' said Jack. 'Besides, they would not have been able to recognise me if they were warned of my presence. The darkness of the night turns all men into shadows.'

'Even so ...'

'Gentlemen, what is done is done,' interrupted Enoch. Turning to Henley, he said, 'Jack has been informed there is someone in your ranks tipping off the smugglers as to which part of the coast will be guarded by the preventative men. It is useful information to know and should not be dismissed. Let us have another glass of port and plan what to do. We have an enemy, and it is not one another.'

Jenna looked down on a deserted Porthenys Cove. Below

her the sea rose and fell rhythmically within the narrow channel, breaking occasionally on jutting rocky outcrops to form trails of white foam. In turn each strand of foam was whisked up and diluted by the murky waves that came behind. Although she watched the tide coming in intently, she took no pleasure in it. As the sea wind chilled her skin and knotted her hair, all she could see was her brother's battered body in her arms and hear his words of warning in her head.

By the time the surgeon arrived, Silas was already growing cold. The landlord of Lanros Inn took pity on her and agreed to keep Silas's body in his cellar until he was buried. She remembered watching him hastily gather the scattered coins on the floor for payment. His kindness and sympathy did not last long. Within minutes Silas's body was wrapped up in a sheet and removed so the room could be cleaned and made vacant for other guests.

As they carried his sagging body past her, kindly hands guided her away from her brother's room to a quieter one. Lukewarm broth was offered to bring colour back to her pale cheeks, but she had no stomach for it and refused with a shake of her head. A man, a stranger to her, came to sit next to her to ask questions about Silas's beating. She had little she wanted to tell him and finally he admitted that she was not the only one struck dumb. He could find no one who was willing to bear witness to the murder and the culprits would probably not be caught.

Jenna did not share who her brother accused. She did not know the man asking so many questions and she needed time to absorb what her brother had said – and asked of her. She lost track of time as Silas's traumatic death turned to mere gossip and was passed from person to person around her.

Eventually, her presence in the inn was forgotten and she was left quite alone. Unseen, and still feeling bewildered, she got up and wandered out into the street, leaving the bustle of the inn behind her. She remembered looking about her and feeling confused that nothing appeared to have changed. How could the street seem so normal when, for her, everything was different?

A gull screeched angrily at another bird as it tried to steal its catch. The sudden noise shocked Jenna out of her memories and she looked about her in bewilderment once again. She found herself standing dangerously close to the cliff edge. A minor landslide would easily carry her away, like flotsam on a tide of earth and down to the rocks below. The danger set fear coursing through her veins and stopped the numbness that had encased her body and frozen her tongue. She stepped back to safety.

Turning away from the cliff she headed back to Jack's house, her thoughts focused on what her brother had told her. Had Jack been gaining her trust all this time for his own purposes? Had he used her and beaten her brother so badly that now he was dead? The revelations were too great to be easily believed. She needed to know if her brother spoke the truth and the only way to do that was to speak to Jack.

Jack's cottage rose up on the horizon as she approached. A man riding a grey horse was just leaving and heading towards her. As he passed, deep in thought, his horse's hooves flicked mud into the air and muddied her dress. She glanced up and instantly recognised him as the Head of the Land Guard who had ordered his men to leave Jack's home, but today he wore no uniform, suggesting his visit was a social call.

She remembered Jack called him Henley when he was drunk. The realisation that they were acquainted before the night of the smuggling brought colour to her cheeks that the broth had failed to do. She had stripped to save Jack from the dragoons, when in fact he did not need saving at all. The dragoon on the beach had tried to kill her not him. Jack probably knew them all by name. How stupid she must have looked in his eyes. Yet even with such evidence that Jack had misled her, she wanted more proof. Wrapping her shawl tightly about her she trudged onwards to the cottage.

Jenna quietly lifted the latch and entered into the hall. She heard the quiet tones of Jack's voice and realised he had another visitor. Dropping her shawl, she followed the sound to the drawing room where she tilted her head to listen at the door.

'Do you think it is Henley?' said his visitor. Jenna recognised the cultured voice of his friend who had visited before.

'No. He would not have arranged for the dragoons to attack if it was. I believe this man Tilbury has questions to answer.'

This was no social call, thought Jenna, as she heard Jack's voice. She pressed her ear closer and quietened her breathing.

'But he was not present when Silas told.'

'He knew of the visit. It would not require too much thought to realise a connection between the intelligence of the landing place and Silas's freedom.'

Jenna turned to rest the back of her head against the door as she continued to listen. She had told Jack it was Silas who had informed the dragoons. If she had not Jack would not have gone to the inn to find him. Silas might still be alive if it had not been for her loose tongue.

'You should not have goaded Henley,' said Jack's visitor.

'He goads me enough. Anyway, until he lost his temper, I did not know for sure. His reaction has confirmed my thoughts about Tilbury.'

'Henley does not like to accept help as it means he has failed. It is this fact that sharpens his tongue.'

'The reason he has failed,' said Jack, 'is that he has had a spy in his ranks telling the smugglers of their plans. No wonder he has spent the last few years chasing them like a headless chicken and being outwitted.'

'We have no proof it is Tilbury, but I will arrange for him to be moved inland and we will see if this makes a difference.'

'That would be a start.'

'But they will change their communication methods now and you are no further forward to catching the culprit.'

Jenna closed her eyes. Silas was right. Jack was a thief-taker just as he had said. She cared nothing for the smugglers and would have gladly helped Jack. It was the fact that he had used her that turned her stomach.

'If I do find the financier, another will soon fill his boots,' said Jack. 'I do not begrudge ordinary folk making money to help feed their families; it is the gangs I want to stop. They torture and kill farmers and fishermen who will not lend them their horses and boats for the run. They threaten wives and daughters of landlords if they do not buy their goods. However, I have said it before; it is the law that needs to be changed regarding taxes on imports. Only then will the smuggling trade decrease.'

'The law is wrong in many areas. A judge can see fit to have a child hung for stealing a handkerchief, yet lets a smuggler walk free due to lack of evidence. It has been at least twenty years since the last smuggler was convicted in these parts.'

Jack's voice seemed a little further away when he next spoke, as if he was nearer the window. It was a voice she had once loved to hear. Even now it stirred her, which made what he said harder to bear.

'Did you say that my housekeeper's late husband, Henry Kestle, was planning to sell information before he was caught poaching?'

'I did. In other areas I have found that judges understand the hunger that drives a man to poach and are usually more lenient in such cases. They prefer to give a gaol sentence rather than the hangman's noose.'

For a moment there was silence and Jenna strained to hear Jack's reply. Eventually it came.

'Perhaps the situation is not as bleak as you think, Enoch. I have found out that there is a man they call Lambskin who has a penchant for art and china.'

'Who told you this?'

'I would rather not say,' replied Jack.

Jenna felt her legs weaken as she slid slowly to the floor. He had questioned her after their lovemaking and like a lovesick fool she had answered.

'This Lambskin must have plenty of money to waste,' said his friend.

'Yes. He must have wealth at his fingertips but the greed to have more.'

'Lambskin,' Enoch mused. 'It is a strange name.'

'Perhaps it is not his name at all,' replied Jack.

'What do you mean?'

'What if it is a nickname? I have heard the name used as slang for judges on account of their woollen lined robes.'

'You believe he is a judge?'

'Why not? People see a judge as the paragon of the law and all that is good. Such a man wields great power and is feared for the sentences he can hand out. Fear can buy a man's silence, and those who will not hold their tongue can be lawfully disposed of. No one would question the hanging of an informer if he is found guilty of another crime.'

'Even so,' replied Enoch uneasily, 'a judge ...'

'Am I right to assume Henry Kestle approached Henley and Tilbury?' Enoch must have nodded in reply, for Jack said, 'He was caught poaching, and brought before Judge Buller. Yet Buller showed no leniency when it is usual to do so for such a crime. Perhaps it was because Buller had discovered that Kestle was planning to inform on him.'

Jenna felt a wave of nausea sweep over her as she listened. Jack knew more about her late husband than she did. Was Jack at his hanging by design?

'And he learnt about this impending betrayal from his spy,' Enoch added. 'What better place to hide than in plain sight? But ... Judge Buller. Who would believe such an accusation?'

'No one is untouchable,' she heard Jack point out.

'Even so, Jack, although I do not like the man, we need more evidence than our surmising.'

'Everyone has a weakness and perhaps the paintings will be his undoing.'

Jenna heard a drink being poured. 'Why would Buller smuggle paintings into the country when he has enough money to buy them?' asked Enoch.

Jack's voice grew a little louder, and for a fleeting moment Jenna thought he was about to open the door.

'When a collector wants what is not for sale,' said Jack steadily, 'he arranges for them to be stolen to order.'

There was a pause and Jenna tilted her head to listen.

'If it really is Buller,' said Enoch, 'it would explain the lack of sentencing for smugglers in this area. How will we know what paintings have been smuggled? We would need someone to identify them and even then we would have to prove they came from across the water.'

'The trail would have to be followed back to France,' said Jack, 'but first we need to know if the paintings are in his possession.'

Jenna saw Jack's coat hanging on the hook by the door. She slowly stood and reached for the sleeve. It would provide the last piece of evidence she would need. Turning it she found all the buttons intact. Still hopeful that her brother was mistaken, she reached for the other.

'Do you really believe it is Buller?' she heard Jack's friend ask on the other side of the door.

Jenna lifted the sleeve and saw broken threads, sticking out like black spider's legs, where the buttons had once been. She dropped it as if it burned her and returned to the door.

'Does he like to collect art?' asked Jack.

'He does,' came a solemn reply.

'Then, yes, I do. If the paintings are in his collection, it will provide the evidence we need.'

'Fortunately, I still have the invitations to his evening party in my desk drawer, although I am not sure how that will help. We do not know what the paintings look like.'

Jenna had heard all she needed to hear. Silas had spoken the truth and she wanted to make Jack pay for using her and killing her brother. She briskly opened the door. She wanted to meet Lambskin and tell him who Jack was.

'I know what the paintings look like,' she told the surprised men looking back at her. 'Take me to this judge's home and I will identify them.'

# Chapter Sixteen

'Have you taken leave of your senses?' said Jack, escorting her back out of the room. 'Excuse us, Enoch, while I have a word with my housekeeper.'

In the hall, Jenna shook her arm free. 'I thought I could help,' she retorted.

'Well, you can't,' said Jack, shutting the door. 'How much did you hear?'

Uneasily, Jenna stepped away. 'Enough to know that you need my help.'

'I did not want him to know who you were,' Jack said irritably. 'Now he knows it was *you* who told me about Lambskin.'

'You were the one who was happy to share our bedroom talk,' Jenna replied tersely.

'Our conversation was not what I consider bedroom talk.' Jack held Jenna's shoulders and made her face him. 'If I was going to make bedroom talk with you, it would not be about smuggling or your snake of a brother.'

His angry frown framed his dark brown eyes and for a brief moment Jenna faltered, but it did not last long. Those same dark eyes had seen her brother's battered body. It was his strong hands that beat him.

'No matter the subject,' she said coolly, 'you shared it all the same.'

'Enoch can be trusted.'

'But not me. Why did you not tell me that you are a thief-taker and the one to capture my brother?'

He let his hands fall away.

'Being a thief-taker is dangerous work,' he said, looking away. 'It was safer for you not to know my business.'

'You did not trust me to keep your secret?'

He glanced up and saw from her expression she was hurting. He softened towards her. Lifting a hand, he let the back of a single finger graze her cheek. 'It is not a matter of trust. Let us not argue, Jenna,' he soothed.

Jenna closed her eyes to blot him out, but she could still feel his touch upon her skin. He is so convincing and appears so earnest, thought Jenna. It is hard not to be swayed, but I must not be. She moved her cheek away from his touch and heard Jack sigh.

'I see that you are angry with me and I deserve it. It was not gentlemanly to slip away before you woke.'

Jenna's eyes narrowed. Until this morning, she had trusted him completely. She would have done anything for him – all he had to do was ask. Now she knew her trust in him was misplaced. Now she found herself questioning everything he had done or said, or where he went when he did not work on the farm. Melwyn sprung to mind.

'What sort of business was so important that you could not say goodbye?' she asked.

'There was a man I wanted to see and did not want to wake you.' She was not impressed by his answer and he could see it in her face. His patience with her was wearing thin. 'As your employer, it is I who should ask you where you have been all day.'

'Thank you for reminding me of my position in this house.'

'Jenna …'

'I went to the village.'

'Without a basket?' he asked. 'I saw it when I returned. It was not the shops you visited.'

'I have been visiting a man too.'

His frown deepened. 'What man?'

'You see,' Jenna argued, 'you do not trust me.'

'That is not the case.'

'Then prove it. Take me to this judge called Lambskin and I will identify the paintings.'

'I don't want you involved,' he repeated. 'I want you out of harm's way.'

'Those are fine words, Jack,' she said, reaching for the door, 'but I am already involved, whether you like it or not.'

'Can we trust her not to be in cahoots with the smugglers?' asked Enoch, looking at her muddied skirts as Jack finished lighting the fire.

Jack stood and glanced irritably at Jenna. 'Yes,' he answered reluctantly.

Enoch remained seated, looking at her over the steeple of his lightly clasped fingers.

'How will you recognise the paintings?' he asked her. 'Judge Buller has many.'

Jenna stood in front of him, her hands tightly clasped. 'I helped carry them on one of the runs. The cargo was dropped and the landing men wanted to check the goods were undamaged. I was told they were for the boss. They called him Lambskin. I held the lantern while they looked them over. The goods were paintings and vases. The vases would be hard to distinguish amongst others of a similar design, but the paintings are unique. I have a good memory and will recognise them again.'

'Do you know this man called Lambskin?' asked Enoch. His eyes were steely grey and she saw hardness in them as he looked at her. She wondered if Jack ever saw it.

'I do not.'

'And your brother, does he know him?'

'He … does not, but I believe he has heard of him.'

Jack took no part in the questioning, preferring to keep his back to her and look out of the window.

'We will have to school you in upper class etiquette. My wife will take you under her wing. If the reason for your presence is discovered it would be very dangerous.'

Jack turned around. He had heard enough.

'Jenna cannot go. I won't allow it.'

'May I remind you that you will not be paid unless this man is caught,' said Enoch. 'She is our only chance.'

'Then I will not be paid until I find another way.'

'She is not your wife to command, Jack.'

'Even so I do not want her to do this.'

Ignoring his reply, Enoch looked at Jenna's muddied dress. 'I can provide her with suitable clothing. Do you think she can masquerade as a gentlewoman?'

'She has a gift for imitation,' was Jack's terse reply.

Jenna did not like being discussed as if she was not there.

'It is not up to Jack whether I help or not. I can play the role well with a little tuition.'

Enoch raised his brows. 'She has spirit. And she is right: it is not up to you whether she goes.' Enoch pushed himself up to standing. 'I want Buller caught and I think this might work.'

Jack realised he was outnumbered.

'I will not allow her to go alone. I will go with her.'

'Then it is fortunate that Judge Buller mistook you for William Pitt the Younger, as he has given me enough invitations for all four of us.'

'Four?'

'You don't think that my wife would let me go to such a house without her, do you?'

'You do not fear for your wife?'

'I do not. She is not the one who will have to find and identify the paintings without raising suspicions. Jenna is going to do that. And who better to trick a room full of guests than a Cartwright?'

Jenna felt her heart sink. Even this man, who she did not know well, knew about her family's reputation and recognised that she was no better.

'Indeed, sir,' said Jenna, lifting her chin. 'I am a Cartwright and as you have implied, I was born to deceive.'

That evening, much to Jack's frustration, Jenna was whisked away by Enoch and taken to his country home overlooking the peaceful Galva estuary. She arrived in the dark and was shown to one of the smaller bedrooms. Alone, her confidence began to waver. The memory of Jack's stern face as the carriage pulled away stayed with her and she began to wonder what would happen tomorrow evening. That night she slept fitfully and what little sleep she had was plagued with terrifying dreams that saw her running for her life.

In the morning, Jenna's mood lifted a little as she discovered that Galva House was situated on a hill and had one of the finest views in Cornwall. Although it was winter, the tidal waters below were a wonder to see. Large flocks of waders and peregrine falcons frequented the salt marshes of the estuary. Their antics continuously changed the scene before her, providing a strange comfort for her grief. In the summer, Jenna knew that the dark murky waters would turn turquoise blue and its beauty and birds would increase tenfold. It would be hard to leave Galva House, she thought, if one were lucky enough to own it.

Her time doing little but admiring the view did not last

long. As soon as she finished her breakfast, which was thoughtfully brought to her room, Lady Pickering came to find her. For a moment the woman looked at Jenna as if she were an oddity.

'My husband has asked me to teach you how to be a lady, and told me that you will be accompanying us tonight when we dine with Judge Buller.' Her eyes did a sweep of Jenna's dress, still muddy from the night before. 'Take a turn of the room so I may see you properly,' she instructed, with a wave of her hand.

Jenna did as she was asked.

'You have clear skin and healthy hair,' Lady Pickering mused, tilting her head to one side as if she were studying a painting.

'I have been fortunate.'

'Your voice is pleasing to the ear. Are you able to control your vulgarities?'

Jenna kept walking. 'I was not aware I had any.'

Lady Pickering considered her answer. 'My husband told me that you were not uncouth.'

'But you did not believe him,' said Jenna, realising she was coming to the end of the room. She made a wide arc and began to retrace her steps towards Lady Pickering who appeared to be watching her feet.

'I like to form my own opinion,' replied Lady Pickering, without looking up. 'However, you do walk with a certain dignity.'

Jenna stopped in surprise. 'I do?'

Her assessor's face broke into a smile, and she lifted her gaze. For the first time the two women's eyes met.

'Yes.' The older woman studied her for a moment. 'You do not appear nervous. It is not pleasant to be observed and scrutinised, but you seem quite at ease.'

221

'I have attended several Mop Fayres; I am used to being observed and scrutinised.'

'It is a cross we all have to bear.' At Jenna's questioning look, Lady Pickering added, 'Unfortunately, it is a young woman's lot, no matter her circumstances, to be observed and judged before her hand is asked for.' She instructed Jenna to come closer with a modest wave of her hand. Jenna obeyed. Lady Pickering immediately began to walk around her to assess her figure. 'My daughter is married and lives elsewhere, but she has left several gowns here which will fit you well. You have a natural grace to your movement, better than some of my friends. Have you any experience of the aristocracy?'

'Only seeing the possessions my family stole from them.'

Lady Pickering laughed. 'You have wit that will delight the judge. I think today may be quite amusing.' Energised, she beckoned Jenna to follow her.

'You are willing to teach me how to be a lady?' Jenna asked hopefully, following her out of the room.

'I cannot teach you all that you will need to know to pass yourself off as a gentlewoman, so we will concentrate on what you will need for tonight. I hope you are a quick learner, for we do not have much time.'

Lady Pickering took the role as her tutor so seriously it was as if she had spent her life waiting for such an opportunity. Standing stiffly by Jenna's side, her mentor showed Jenna how to be escorted into dinner and accept a chair at a table. She described at great length how the table would be laid with a large selection of dishes but it was deemed good manners only to take from a few. She showed Jenna how to toast her neighbour's health, what topics to discuss and what to avoid. She made her practice leaving the table at the end of the meal to follow the hostess out of the room so the men could converse alone. At the end, when Jenna's head was heavy with it all, Lady Pickering smiled, clapped her hands twice, and made her do it all again.

On the third session, Jenna was made to wear linen hoops stiffened with whalebone under her skirt so she could feel what it was like manoeuvring and sitting in them without, as Lady Pickering said, 'disgracing herself'. Finally, at the end of the fact-filled day, they returned to Jenna's bedroom where they found two maids carefully laying a gown upon the bed. Lady Pickering nodded to them and the maids, instinctively knowing what she wanted, soundlessly retreated and left the room.

'They will be back shortly with some water and to help you dress,' said Lady Pickering, casting a glance over the gown. Satisfied with what she saw, she turned to Jenna. 'Now I must leave you so I can be made ready. If you need anything, just ask one of the maids.' She looked Jenna up and down with a whimsical smile upon her face, before turning with a swish of her dress and leaving a waft of perfume in her wake.

Jenna was finally alone and free of scrutiny. She looked at the gown on the bed and cautiously approached it. Her eyes widened at the silk creation. The ivory gown was exquisite, with narrow pleated robing that fell from the back of the neckline to skim the floor. The skirt, made of the finest handwoven French silk, was delicately patterned with lines of floral and leafy motifs in silk thread. Jenna lifted a single sleeve. They were scalloped, double cuffed and trimmed in pink edging to match the thick padded trim that zigzagged down the front panels of the gown. She lifted the dress up and held it against herself. It felt heavy and luxurious in her hands, and far too expensive for the likes of her. Jenna's mouth turned dry as she laid it back down on the bed. For the first time, she began to doubt her ability to deceive – despite still having the desire to.

Not long ago she would have cared what Jack would think of her in this dress. Jenna remembered his teasing, his kindness and his lovemaking as she followed a trail of flowering motifs with her fingertips. How had she been so blind? He had fooled her and she had been his willing fool. Jenna lifted the other sleeve and imagined Jack's hand brushing the scalloped edge from her arm. She dropped it and stepped back, despising herself for thinking of him.

He had used her and beaten her brother for betraying him. She thought of Silas, lying bloodied in her arms. Now, he was dead and Jack was to blame. She must not waver now, for tonight she would be dining with one of the most powerful men in the county. She must remember all she had been taught and find an opportunity to speak to Judge Buller alone. Only then could she inform him about Jack and grant her brother's dying wish.

Jack arrived early and waited impatiently in the drawing room. Eventually, Enoch came down to greet him and offered him a drink. Jack refused with a curt shake of his head.

'You look quite sour.'

'I did not want Jenna to be involved. If things go wrong ...'

'Nothing will go wrong.'

'It is all right for you, Enoch. If Buller finds out who we are, he will have us punished. You and your wife, on the other hand, are too valuable to him. He still needs your support for his political career.' Jack watched Enoch sip his port. 'But I suspect you will deny that you knew what our intentions were. It would be an easy yarn to believe.

Jenna's family history would be evidence enough that she is a deceiver and that you were tricked by her.'

'You do not trust me, Jack?' said Enoch, looking at him over his glass.

'It is hard to trust anyone when at seventeen you discover that some of your neighbours were responsible for killing your father, while others were too scared to talk.'

Enoch's expression changed to one of concern as he rested his glass in his hand.

'I think it would be prudent for you to have a different name. Your reputation as a thief-taker may have reached the judge's ears and put you at risk. How about the name, Jack Trago? We could introduce Jenna as your cousin.' Jack gave a curt nod of his head in agreement. Enoch toyed with his glass. 'You have never disclosed the full details of your father's death to me. What were the circumstances?'

Jack moved to the fire and warmed his palms against its heat.

'My father refused to loan his horses to the local smuggling gang. Horses that are worked all night are too tired to work on the farm during the day. He knew this, so he stood up to their demands. My father was punished for refusing.' Jack inhaled deeply at the painful memory, before releasing it slowly through pursed lips. 'They did not take kindly to a local farmer objecting. If they allowed one to refuse, many would follow, so they made an example of him.' He paused briefly before continuing on. 'They beat him and tied his legs to the stirrup of his own horse. They hit the horse with a poker and it bolted. He was dragged behind it for almost a mile. He survived long enough for me to find him, but died in my arms shortly afterwards.'

'I'm sorry you have suffered so much.'

'Me? It was my father who suffered.'

'You have suffered and are suffering now. Ever since your father's death you have dedicated your life to purging Cornwall of the smuggling gangs. Revenge consumes you.'

'It is an impossible task I have set myself, but I cannot rest until it is done.'

'I want you to settle and have a good life, but revenge is still too important to you, Jack. Until the day comes when you can walk away, we must continue to try and bring these gangs down one at a time. We are close to closing down the Blake brothers for the first time and Jenna's help is the key to achieving it.'

'She has never socialised with the aristocracy. You ask too much of her,' argued Jack.

'Relax. My wife tells me that Jenna is an extraordinary woman. I believe that my wife is coming now. Perhaps she can reassure you.'

Lady Pickering entered in her finest gown and powdered wig. It was the first time Jack had met her and he greeted her with a bow. He made no attempt at small talk.

'How is your charge?' he asked.

'It has been quite a day. Exhausting, but satisfying all at the same time. You would not know she has not had the benefit of a governess. At first she made many mistakes, such as asking one of the imaginary guests to pass her a dish. I told her that was ill-mannered and it is what we pay servants to do. Curiously she said that doing it oneself encourages conversation around the table. I could not disagree with her, however I told her that understanding the proper etiquette separates the upper class from the lower and she had best remember that. I received no more defiance from her. She has a way of making a point that is unconventional but yet difficult to argue with. I think she will hold an interesting conversation at the table remarkably well.'

'You sound like you have taken a liking to her, my dear,' Enoch teased.

'She is a likeable person, but not someone I would want our son to marry.'

'She is not open to offers,' said Jack.

'Mr Penhale,' replied Lady Pickering. 'Every woman is open to offers, but whether she accepts them is quite a different matter.'

The door opened to reveal Jenna standing in the hall.

'Your housekeeper is ready, Jack,' said Enoch, putting down his glass. 'Now you will see why I am not so concerned that she will be found out. Look, Jack, see what a fine lady she makes.'

Jack did not need to be told to look at Jenna as he had waited for this moment since she left. He had tried to imagine what she would look like, yet seeing her now still took his breath away. He swallowed the thick lump of emotion that rose in his throat, but said nothing. Instead he allowed Enoch and his wife to greet and pay her the compliments that he wanted to give.

Her gown was the finest he had ever seen, but it did not outshine her. The rich silk only complemented the softness of her skin and the colour of ivory only added a contrast to her rich dark hair that begged for his touch. It was as if Jenna were illuminating the darkness that he was not aware had been present.

Jack felt drawn to her and stepped forward, but his way was barred. He had to remain satisfied with catching only glimpses of her between the bodies that fussed around her. He saw the curve of her neck and longed to kiss it, not the diamond necklace that glinted at her throat. He saw the rise and fall of her bosom as it strained against her square neckline, and he longed to feel her softness. He saw the gown's fastenings and imagined being alone with her and ripping them apart.

Enoch and his wife moved aside and Jack could see her fully again. He swallowed, struck dumb at the transformation, yet still hoping to see the old Jenna in the eyes of this new fragile beauty. He waited for her to look at him, ready to offer her a smile of encouragement, but her eyes did not search for his and the moment did not come.

'Our coach is outside. Let us depart,' said Enoch, taking his wife's hand and leading her to the door.

Jack noticed Jenna begin to wring her hands. Her distress helped him find his tongue and he stepped forward again to place his hand on hers to still them. Turning his back on Enoch, he tilted her chin with a single finger so she looked at him.

'I'm afraid for you,' he said softly. 'Don't do it, Jenna.'

Jenna lifted her chin away from his touch and looked down at his hand on hers. His words of concern appeared to catch her off guard. Perhaps this was the reason she chose to echo his own answer on the night of the smuggling run.

'And if I don't do this, what then?' she answered. Before he could reply, Enoch called to them to follow and she pulled her hands away from under his. 'We must not keep them waiting,' she said coolly. 'I have a task to do and I will not change my mind.'

# Chapter Seventeen

The coach that took them to Judge Buller's country estate was claustrophobic and thick with tension. Although it was winter, the cramped conditions soon warmed the interior and the blankets provided for their comfort were quickly set aside. Lady Pickering's and Jenna's dresses took up much of the room, overlapping the men's knees to provide warmth of their own. However, the swathes of material did not cushion its four occupants as, throughout the journey, their knees and hips jarred impolitely against their neighbours' as the unforgiving carriage wheels bumped along the poorly maintained road.

The journey was made no more pleasant by the people inside the coach. Lady Pickering took to grumbling and complained that Enoch should have accepted the offer of rooms to stay for the night. Enoch retorted that they did not have time and it was best to depart quickly once the evening was over.

'In refusing the offer, you have placed us at risk of being held up by highwaymen on our way home,' snapped his wife.

Enoch reflected his wife's nervous tension with a curt reply of his own.

'I'm sure your tongue, dearest, will send them away.'

Jack remained silent, broodily watching Jenna, who sat diagonally to him looking out of the window into the blackness of the night. A slight furrow marked his brow. Her apparent lack of nerves and refusal to meet his eye troubled him, but if Jack thought she was ignoring him he could not have been more wrong. Throughout the journey, while the senior occupants bickered around her, Jenna's

229

eyes never left his face. In his reflection in the window, she saw his concern and every flicker of his cheek muscle as he tightened his jaw. Jenna felt unmoved. His furrowed brow was nothing to the suffering her brother had endured.

Jack remained unaware that he was being observed until the carriage came to a lurching halt and it was time to disembark. Then, without warning, his eyes flicked across to her reflection in the window and locked with hers. She quickly looked away and began to fuss with her dress, but it was too late. He had caught her watching him and it was not a look of love that he saw in her face.

'Sir Enoch Pickering!' shouted the butler.

Smiling broadly, Judge Buller came striding across the hall to greet his newly arrived guests. 'I hope the journey was not too tiresome.'

Enoch returned a brittle smile. 'A journey is rarely as good as the feeling of arrival.'

'Although that depends on where you are going, eh,' said the judge, jovially looking around at his new guests. 'We will be a party of thirteen,' he said, 'and some have already accumulated in the drawing room for drinks.' Jenna saw his attention settle on Jack. 'I am glad that you have decided to accept my invitation,' he told him. 'There is much I would like to discuss with you.'

Jack acknowledged him with a slight bow, but did not reply. Instead Enoch stepped forward.

'May I formally introduce you to my friend, Jack Trago,' he said with a smile.

An awkward silence descended and Jenna watched the judge's own smile fade a little, before he found his tongue and manners again. 'Are you involved in politics, sir?' he asked him.

'No, sir. I leave politics to those who have a thicker skin than I.'

Enoch's laughter was hearty. It was joined belatedly by the judge's, but Jenna thought it sounded forced. It was too hearty, too abrupt and ended too quickly. No wonder, he had expected to meet the former prime minister's son, not a man who was no help to him at all. His initial good mood was dampened by the error and showed in his greeting of Lady Pickering. Jenna was the last to be introduced. A curt bow of his head was the only greeting she received before he solemnly led them to the drawing room, where the other guests were gathered.

Jenna remained on the fringe of the party, watching Judge Buller circulate the room to talk to his guests. Their opulent finery appeared like a sea of colourful silks, linens and braids and in its midst was the host whose duty was to ensure everyone had a good time. Jenna gnawed her bottom lip, as she realised she would have great difficulty getting him alone in order to speak with him. The task she had set herself suddenly appeared insurmountable. She felt someone come to stand beside her and knew that it was Jack.

'Are you afraid?' asked Jack under his breath.

'I have felt true fear in my life, Jack, and it is not fear that I feel right now.'

'What do you feel?' he asked.

She could sense he was looking at her with that same troubled expression that she had seen in the coach.

*I feel angry*, she wanted to shout at him. *I feel betrayed. I feel overwhelmed with painful grief.*

Instead she replied quietly, 'I feel nothing … nothing at all.'

Before he could reply, another guest interrupted them to seek Jack's opinion and after some persuading, Jack reluctantly left her side and followed him. Jenna watched him being led to a small group of men who were voicing their opinions in loud voices. It was a situation she knew he would hate, but the thought of his discomfort did not bring a smile to her lips. Instead, she became aware that her hand was hurting and looked down. To her surprise, her fingertips were blanched and marked from holding the stem of her glass too tightly. She had come close to it shattering and making a spectacle of herself. She must be more careful.

As she waited for dinner to be announced, she cast her eye on the paintings that adorned the walls. There were many, but none like the ones she had seen in the cave.

'You look like you have a secret,' said a man's voice at her side.

A frisson of fear shot up Jenna's spine, heightening her senses and lifting the hairs at the nape of her neck. Had she been discovered? In the pause that followed, Jenna realised that the tone was not one of accusation. *I must remain calm*, Jenna scolded herself, *I must play the game.*

Jenna looked up into a pair of smiling hazel eyes. Quietly she released the breath she had been holding. The man raised an eyebrow; and she could see that he was waiting patiently for a reply. It was the first time someone had spoken to her with the aim of making conversation. Belatedly, she wondered if she was up to the task.

'I have no secret to share.'

The man would not be put off.

'Does that mean you have no secret, or that you have one but you are unwilling to share it?' asked the man, smiling.

Jenna decided to return his smile. 'Can a secret be shared?' she teased. 'Surely if a secret is shared it is no longer a secret.'

The man, who had a strong jawline and straight brows, considered her reply.

'I see that I have met my match tonight. I am content for you to keep your secrets if it means that you continue to share your smile.' He looked about him. 'As there seems to be the lack of someone to introduce us, may I take the liberty of doing it myself?'

Jenna liked his relaxed approach; better she conversed with him than someone who may notice her failings in etiquette.

'If we only spoke to those to whom we were formally introduced, we would miss the opportunity of speaking to many interesting people.' Her reply pleased him.

'My name is Edgar.' He gave a slight bow over her hand. 'Charles Buller is my uncle.'

'I am pleased to make your acquaintance,' she said to his bowed head. 'My name is Jenna. Mr Trago is my ...' She swallowed the lump rising in her throat. '... cousin.'

Edgar slowly straightened. He was as tall as Jack, with a similar build, but where Jack exuded a quiet, earthy strength, Edgar had aristocratic refinement.

'Do you know many people here?' he asked.

Jenna smiled. 'No, I do not.'

Edgar took it upon himself to remedy the situation. 'Then let me tell you about my uncle's guests, for you can be assured that there is a reason for each invitation.'

'Isn't there always a reason to invite someone?'

'Reason, yes. A family member, a friend, a loved one. But not one of these guests falls into any of those categories. I see that I have surprised you. My uncle is efficient; he does not waste good food where there is no chance of receiving a reward.' He raised his glass. 'Twelve guests ... thirteen in total. It is an unlucky number for some, but my uncle has no fear.' He looked across the room. 'See over there, the man with a florid complexion with his little wife by his side.' Jenna followed his gaze. 'That is Edward Grantham. He was a Member of Parliament until an unfortunate scandal forced him to leave. He is now impoverished, but he has much information that will one day be useful to my dear uncle Charles.'

Jenna looked up at Edgar. For the first time she could hear an edge to his voice.

Edgar ignored her questioning look. 'See those men speaking to your cousin – William Morton and Horace Polmean. They both own large estates that have been in their families for generations. Their fortune is more than you could ever imagine. They are the perfect acquaintances to have when it comes to buying a seat in Parliament, don't you think? The two women at their sides are their spouses. One dutiful and meek, the other one is a tyrant.'

'And what about me? Why am I here?' asked Jenna, trying to lighten the mood.

'I'm afraid that you were a delightful error that has cheered me up no end. He thought Mr Trago was the former prime minister's son, William Pitt, who would have contacts that would be useful to him. It has put me in good cheer to see that my uncle is not always as successful as he would like. I believe you already knew this, though.'

'And now it has been confirmed. I am glad that you are in good cheer, even though I am not sure that I should condone the reason for it.'

'You will not tell him that I am rejoicing in his discomfort.'

'I will not.'

'Then we have a secret between us. You see, secrets can be shared.' All heads in the room turned as dinner was announced. 'May I escort you into dinner?' he asked hopefully.

She saw Jack break away from William and Horace to join her. She placed her hand firmly in Edgar's.

'I would be delighted,' she answered, smiling, and allowed him to lead her away.

Judge Buller and his wife sat at opposite ends of the table. Although the guests were at liberty to choose their own seats, the rules of good manners meant that preferred seats were not always the ones secured. Jenna found herself seated near the hostess and away from Enoch, Lady Pickering and Jack. Fortunately, Edgar took a seat opposite her and much to Jack's brooding resentment made it his duty to entertain her.

The first course consisted of soup, vegetables, boiled fish and meat. It was enough food to feed her brother's family for a week and the injustice of it all almost threatened to overwhelm her. She took a deep breath to steady her nerves. Now was not the time to allow her emotions loose rein, she told herself.

Jenna gave the appearance of enjoying the dishes laid before her, but she ate very little. Nerves were beginning to build and although she found it easy to talk to Edgar, she had a growing concern that she would make a mistake and be unmasked. When the first course and tablecloth were removed, and replaced by a new cloth and further dishes, she felt a sense of achievement, which strengthened her nerve. The feeling was heady, until she realised everyone was looking at her waiting for an answer to a question she had not heard.

Edgar came to her rescue. 'I think she did not realise you were speaking to her, Aunt,' he said loudly across the table. He turned to Jenna. 'She asked if you have travelled?'

Jenna blinked. Out of the corner of her eye she saw Enoch move uneasily in his seat.

'I beg your pardon, Mrs Buller. I did not realise you were speaking to me.'

Needlessly the woman raised her voice. 'I said "have you travelled?"'

'No, I have not, although I would like to.'

The questioner persisted. 'And where would you like to go?'

What did she know about the world to enable her to give a good reason to visit another place? She felt her mouth go dry and quickly took a sip from her glass.

'Somewhere quite different from England – perhaps the Fiji Islands.'

Enoch almost choked, but Edgar's face brightened.

'How adventurous,' he remarked, with a whimsical smile.

'Why should male explorers have all the fun of discovering exotic locations?' Jenna added. 'If I could travel anywhere I would like to go to the Fiji Islands where the sea is turquoise blue and the inhabitants and their culture are so very different from our own.'

Jack smiled. She had seen that smile before, when she had read a difficult passage, or proudly shown him her written hand. He was proud of her, and even though she wanted to hate him, she couldn't help feeling glad that he felt it.

For the first time, Judge Buller took an interest in her. 'Surely the islands are filled with uncivilised savages.'

'They have their own rules, hierarchy and laws. Just because we do not recognise them, that does not mean they are savages. They are a proud people, who love and care for their families as we do. If they come to this country and learn of the law we live under, they may consider us to be uncivilised.'

'It is true,' said Enoch. 'I wonder what the inhabitants of Fiji would think of us when they hear that we have over two hundred crimes that are punishable by hanging, including the cutting down of a young tree.'

'They would think we are the savages!' said Edgar, laughing.

'I will leave the Fiji islands to you, my dear,' replied Mrs Buller. 'I would rather stick to the tried and tested. Two years ago Charles and I undertook the grand tour of Europe. Charles has a weakness for art and we spent much of the time visiting the museums along the way.'

'Did you follow the route that so many young gentlemen favour?' asked Horace.

Mrs Buller nodded. 'We did. Charles missed out on the opportunity when he was younger.'

'My father was a tyrant,' interrupted the judge, 'and refused to support me in the experience. When a man has little support, he either falls by the wayside or it makes him tough. I think we can see,' he said, waving at the laden table, 'that I did not fall by the wayside.' There was a ripple of laughter.

'I would rather see the country than the museums, though,' William replied, 'and I hear the conversation of a French woman is particularly interesting.'

'I hope you are not suggesting that English women are not interesting?' said his wife.

'You always interest me, but the younger ones have their heads filled with art, music and nothing more.' He looked across to Jenna. 'Although you are an exception. You are quite divine.' Jenna felt ridiculously pleased with the compliment. 'Tell us a little about your family.'

She heard Jack's voice. 'Your wife will grow concerned at the interest you are showing in Jenna,' he teased William, hoping to divert his attention away. It was kindly meant, but Jenna was in no mood to accept his help.

She arched a brow at him then turned to William. 'My ancestors made their money trading fine jewellery.'

Enoch fingered his collar uncomfortably.

'And have you inherited their expertise?' asked Horace.

'I can tell the difference between a gem and glass.'

There was a short silence. 'I believe you have now worried all the husbands in the room, Jenna,' Jack said evenly. 'They are concerned that their wives will ask for your expert opinion after dinner.'

If Jack was hoping to break the tension in the room that had suddenly reared its head, it worked. All the guests burst into laughter to prove there were no concerns for the gifts given and received. The gentlemen's wine was changed to port and the ladies' to sweet wine as the laughter slowly died away. Enoch seamlessly steered the conversation back to the museums the judge and his wife had visited on their last grand tour. They were content to speak at length until Charles Buller suddenly looked at Jenna.

'Do you have an interest in art?' he asked her suddenly as the second course was removed and dishes of dried fruit, nuts and sweetmeats were brought in to replace them. 'I only ask as I saw you looking at my art collection in the drawing room earlier.'

'My husband has a great art collection which he is very proud of,' interrupted his wife fondly.

Jenna saw a chance of being alone with him. 'I do. You have a fine collection, sir. Do you have any more?'

'I do. I will show them to you if you like.'

'It is not something I would find an interest in,' said Edgar under his breath.

'Mind your manners,' said Buller. Laughter and

conversation hushed and Edgar reddened. 'My nephew does not appreciate the skill of the artist or the intelligence of the message it portrays, Miss Trago.'

Jenna felt for Edgar as all eyes turned to him. He examined a dried piece of fruit in his fingers as his neck developed red blotches of heat. She heard him take a deep breath.

'I am to be transferred inland, Uncle,' he said, popping the fruit into his mouth and meeting his uncle's gaze. 'I will no longer be stationed near the coast to watch for smugglers.'

Jack and Enoch exchanged glances across the table.

The judge's eyes narrowed. 'Transferred? I will put a stop to this. It will not do.'

William watched his glass being refilled. 'Why should the transfer concern you, Charles?'

'Yes, Uncle,' Edgar sneered. 'Why should it concern you? It is I who is being transferred.'

Judge Buller pursed his lips, but did not answer.

Lifting a single hand, Enoch refused the manservant who approached to refill his glass. 'I hope this transfer is not inconvenient for you, Edgar. I did not catch your surname earlier. What is it?'

'My name is Tilbury,' replied Edgar. 'I was informed of my transfer this morning and no, it is not inconvenient for me as I welcome it, but there are others who will not be so pleased.'

After dinner the hostess led the ladies into another room. Lady Pickering remained by her side, and Jenna began to suspect that she had been given orders to keep an eye on her. When Horace's wife presented Jenna with her necklace to inspect, Lady Pickering paled quite significantly. Jenna, however, was not in the least concerned as she had spent much of her childhood watching her parents examine stolen jewellery. As Lady Pickering fanned herself anxiously, Jenna's examination, and final verdict, spurred others to offer their jewellery too. Out of the five pieces, only one was made of glass. Thankfully, the owner already knew this, as the original was at home in her safe.

Raucous laughter at Jenna's unusual skills replaced the usual sedate after dinner conversation that might be expected from gentlewomen. Jenna's entertainment was a success and some of the women sighed reluctantly when it was time to join the gentlemen.

Jack approached her immediately and took her aside. 'Be careful of Tilbury. He is connected with Buller in more ways than by blood.'

She felt his hand support her elbow and heard his words of warning, but he did not really care for her. All he cared about was foiling the smuggling gang.

'Leave me alone,' she said, attempting to move away. His hand tightened on her elbow.

'What is the matter with you? Are you still angry that I left your bed?'

'No.'

'Then your pride has been hurt and it is this that makes you angry.'

'What do you mean?'

'You thought that I smuggled for you but in reality I had reasons of my own to go. Discovering this has hurt your pride and now you flirt with Tilbury to wound me.' He lowered his head. 'The truth is,' he whispered against her ear, 'I would still have gone if the only reason was for you.'

His words brushed her sensitive ear and sent shivers down her back. She pulled her elbow away.

'I felt guilty that you had been injured for me. You let me think that there was something between us. Now I know that words mean nothing – especially if a man speaks them when he is in his cups. I would never have lain with you if I thought ...'

Jenna could not bear to think how freely, and foolishly, she had given herself to him. Desperate to put some distance between them, she walked away, only to be halted abruptly by his hand in the crook of her arm. She tried to shake it away but his fingers only tightened further. Jack's eyes darkened and she could see his mounting anger in their hidden depths.

'I have only been drunk once in recent times,' he said solemnly, 'and I remember and meant every word that I spoke.'

Jenna faltered. He had said such nice things to her and he was telling her he meant them all.

'Tell me what is bothering you,' he said more kindly. 'Something has come between us and I am determined to find out what it is.'

'I saw my brother yesterday,' she said under her breath. 'He was badly beaten.'

'So that is where you spent your day. His beating does not surprise me and I doubt it surprised him.'

'Why do you say that?'

'Because I told him to expect it. A man cannot lie with snakes and not expect to get bitten.'

Jenna's stomach lurched. Jack *had* killed her brother. She wanted to be sick.

'You feel he deserved it? Perhaps he is not the only one who deserves to be punished.' Jenna left him and began to cross the room. Jack followed.

'Where are you going?' he asked under his breath.

241

'I have a task to achieve.'

'The paintings can wait until you are calmer.'

'The paintings are not the only reason I am here. You see,' she said, arching a brow, 'you are not the only one who is capable of duplicity.'

Jack's eyes narrowed. 'What do you mean?' he asked, but it was too late. They had already arrived at her target audience and he would receive no answer from her now.

'Sir,' Jenna said to the judge's back, 'you promised me a private tour of your paintings.'

The judge, glad to have his conversation with Horace's wife interrupted, turned immediately. 'I did,' he said, looking down his long thin nose at her. 'Do you mind, Mr Trago, if I steal your pretty companion away from you?'

'I mind very much,' he answered. 'But I believe I have little choice in the matter. If I have learnt anything from my cousin, it is that she has a mind of her own.' As he turned to leave, he looked down upon her. 'I just hope she remembers that,' he said solemnly as he walked away.

Judge Buller took great pride in showing Jenna the paintings in his collection. Every room in his large house was adorned with expensive works of art that varied from collections of mythology and portraits, to landscapes and still life. Although Judge Buller's enthusiasm did not waver, Jenna's appreciation dwindled the further away from Enoch and Jack she was taken. There was a sinister strength in the judge that unnerved her, born from her growing isolation from the other guests. While he appeared content, she grew quieter.

Alone, they entered yet another large room, where she pretended to study a painting of the sea. Judge Buller looked down at her with interest, ignoring his art collection for the first time.

'Something has been troubling me since dinner,' he said ominously. 'I have the strangest feeling we have met before.'

Jenna was confident that they had not. Perhaps it was this mistaken identity that was adding to the tension.

'You are mistaken. We have not met before.'

'You certainly look familiar, but if you say we have not met, then I must concede to the fact.'

Despite his answer, he did not look convinced. Jenna began to feel uncomfortable under his lingering gaze. It was as if he was waiting for her to say something more. The air of expectation was palpable. It was the time for the charade to end, but now that the moment had arrived, she felt sick to her stomach.

'I have something to tell you,' she said quietly.

Judge Buller met her gaze with watery eyes and a wet smile. His guests believed him to be the perfect host, taking an interested guest on a tour of his home. How little they knew about this man dressed in finest linen and silk, thought Jenna. Who would have thought he was the head of a smuggling gang and had such dubious morals? And he did have dubious morals, perhaps even no morals at all. She knew by telling him that Jack was on his trail, he would make him suffer. She wanted Jack to suffer – didn't she?

Jenna looked away and moved to another painting. He followed her, watched her tilt her head as if to study the painting, but in reality she saw none of it. She was thinking of Silas, his face unrecognisable, his body contorted in pain, his blood spattered on the floor and walls. He had not looked like her brother, but then he had spoken and she knew it was him. The voice she knew as well as her own told her Jack had done it and the nightmare she had found herself in grew worse.

She tried to imagine Jack beating him until he was a

broken mess, yet no matter how she tried she couldn't. Can such a man kill another? Jenna felt aware of the judge waiting for her to say more. She focused on the painting in front of her.

'Such a beautiful dark sea,' she murmured absently, hoping to delay the confession for a moment. Reservation had set in, as once the words were spoken there would be no going back. Jack had shown only concern for her welfare and a desire for her to have a better life. He had offered to pay Silas's debts. He had saved her life from a musket shot.

The judge had stepped closer to the painting and was speaking, pulling her from her thoughts. 'I agree, but dark seas also have power and hide great danger,' he replied.

She looked at his back. What evidence did she have of Jack's involvement, but for Silas's dying words? Silas had no affection for Jack, only mounting jealousy. The judge took a step back again which brought him to her side.

'What confession do you have to make?' the judge reminded her. She glanced sideways at him and noticed his grey eyes grow hard as granite.

Jenna opened her mouth, her mind still whirring at what she was about to do. She was not only going to betray Jack, but also those who were trying to uphold the law and stop the smuggling in Cornwall. When did right and wrong become so blurred? When did her morals become as twisted as her own family's? If she truly thought Jack had hurt her brother, why did she not report him? Why take revenge in this sordid manner? She knew why. Loving a man and discovering he could hurt you in this way is enough to turn anyone's mind for a while. She was strong once and knew right from wrong. Revenge is for the weak.

'Miss Trago, what confession do you have to make to me?' she heard him ask again.

Jenna turned doe like eyes to him. 'I confess that I find landscapes rather boring. Do you have any paintings of horses?'

A short silence followed as he studied her face, but then his manner brightened. 'Indeed. I have recently acquired two that may interest you. I felt your interest in my collection was waning. Now I know why. Eh?'

Jenna felt a flood of relief sweep through her body and the tension between them appeared to lift. Moments later, he led her to an ill lit room where further paintings were stored wrapped in cloth. Jenna held the candle as the judge carefully exposed the paintings so she could view them. She knew what she would see long before the last piece of cloth was flicked aside to fully expose the canvases beneath – the two distinctive equine paintings she had seen on the beach all those weeks ago.

# Chapter Eighteen

The carriage ride home was a time to reflect. Sir Enoch's and Lady Pickering's mood was greatly improved from their nervous bickering only four hours before. Jenna and Jack listened in silence as they recounted the evening and its final successful conclusion.

'I feared my heart would burst from its chest,' Lady Pickering confided to her husband, 'when Jenna examined their jewellery.' She tapped Jenna on the knee with her fan. 'Where did you learn such a skill?'

Jenna reluctantly turned away from the window. 'My parents spent their evenings looking at what they had stolen throughout the day. They had an instinct for what was valuable and what was not. It is hard not to pick up the tricks of the trade when it forms a large part of your childhood.'

Lady Pickering was horrified. 'Your parents were thieves? I thought you were jesting.'

Enoch patted his wife's hand. 'I thought it best not to tell you Jenna's background as you were reluctant to tutor her in the first place.' He nudged Jack, who had also spent much of the journey looking out of the opposing window. 'We can be certain it is Buller now that Jenna has seen the paintings in his possession. I did not suspect that Tilbury was his nephew. We are building a case that will eventually lead to Buller's downfall. We have seen progress and there is much to rejoice in.'

Jack returned his gaze to the window. His reluctance to celebrate threatened to dampen Enoch's spirits.

'Come, Jack, we are finally getting somewhere. It is a

felicitous discovery that Tilbury has such a connection. Don't you think?'

'I feel Edgar is a reluctant partner,' Jenna interrupted. 'He showed a dislike for his uncle and seemed pleased to tell him, in front of all the guests, that he was being transferred. It was as if he enjoyed seeing his displeasure.'

'You feel he has been coerced into informing his uncle of the dragoons' plans?' Enoch considered the suggestion. 'It's a possibility. What do you think Jack?'

Jack wiped the condensation from the window with a single stroke of his hand. 'If anyone got to know Edgar this evening, it is Jenna,' he said quietly, with an edge to his tone. He did not speak again for the rest of the journey, preferring to stare through the window at the shadows of the night, than converse with the occupants inside.

'Open the door.'

Jenna slipped the nightgown, loaned by Lady Pickering, over her head and let it fall down around her to cover her naked body. After refusing the servant's help to undress, she had struggled to rid herself of the elaborate silk dress. Now, finally free to relax and get some sleep, Jack was at her door and he did not sound pleased.

'I'm in bed,' she replied curtly, gathering her clothes from the floor.

'Open it,' he commanded with the same edge to his voice he had earlier. 'We need to talk.'

'We have nothing to say to one another,' she replied, knowing he would not go away. She picked up a blanket and wrapped it around her shoulders in readiness for him to ask again.

Jack, however, was done asking. 'If you don't open the door now, I will break it down.'

Jenna hesitated. Having received no immediate reply, Jack shouldered the door and broke its lock. The door burst open to ricochet against the wall as a splinter of wood flew across the floor. Jack ignored the damage and stepped into the room.

Where Jenna was not prepared for this meeting, Jack had planned it since they left Judge Buller's home. His body, taut with frustration and anger, slammed the door behind him, closing her only route of escape.

'The servants will hear.'

'I don't give a curse what they hear.'

'They will come.'

'And I will send them away.'

He took a step nearer and looked at her through heavy lids.

'Did you betray me?'

Jenna pulled her blanket tighter around her. How could she pretend she did not plan to, when her behaviour towards him had been so cold?

'No,' she said confidently as she attempted to meet his gaze. She failed and began to fuss with her blanket instead. 'How did you know?'

'I didn't know for sure … until now.' She saw a flash of disappointment in his eyes before he turned away and began to pace the room. 'Why would you want to betray me?' he asked, bewildered. 'Was it because you were angry I did not tell you of my profession? Did you want to hurt me because I had not been truthful to you? I did not tell you because I wanted you to be no part of it. It was your safety I wanted to ensure.' He paused in his pacing and faced her. 'I told you this! When someone hurts you, you must consider the intention, not the deed itself. My intention was good.' Anger and confusion was etched on his face as he struggled to understand her. Finding no satisfactory answer, he began to pace again. 'Was it to have me punished or to have me killed?'

'Never killed!'

'Then you trust Buller too much. He would not have forgiven and forgotten that I intended to find him out. Within four and twenty hours I would have been at the bottom of the sea.' Jenna watched him struggle to contain all the pent up anger inside him.

A servant arrived to enquire if all was well.

'Leave us!' barked Jack. His order, and the angry look upon his face, was enough to send the servant scurrying away. He turned back to Jenna. 'I thought I knew you, but to consider changing sides at such a late hour,' he looked at her suspiciously. 'Unless you were working with them all along.'

'I have never worked for them.'

'Did he offer to pay you for information? Did Tilbury's flirting change your mind so easily?'

'It had nothing to do with Edgar.'

'You were cosy enough together. To watch you simper at all his jokes made me want to retch.'

'It is because I remained truthful to who I am that I did not betray you in the end.'

'And not because you cared for me?' The new revelation stopped his pacing. Each new hurt showed in his eyes and pained her. It forced her to realise the truth.

*I lie. I lie. It was my love for you that stopped me, despite what you have done. I should hate you. I want to hate you.* Jenna turned away, but Jack's hand caught her arm and spun her around to face him.

'Why did you want to betray me?' He shook her arm roughly. 'Answer me!' he demanded.

249

'The day before I held Silas's badly beaten body in my arms! That is reason enough!'

'You were in shock – is that what you are telling me?' She turned her back on him. 'I know distress can send one mad. Seeing a loved one suffering is enough to turn one's mind.' He touched her arms and turned her to face him. 'I experienced the same with my father. I watched my father being dragged along the ground behind a horse because he dared to stand up to the smugglers. I watched him die in my arms. I listened as he drew his last painful breath. His untimely, brutal death stayed with me, and still does to this day. When it happened I had so much anger inside me at the injustice of it all that I wanted to hurt anyone who came near.' It was a valiant attempt to convince himself that it was distress that turned her against him, but the more he remembered, the less he felt it was possible. He let her arm go. 'In the end I channelled it into revenge and became a thief-taker. I did not, however, take revenge on those that I cared for. It makes no sense that you would want to hurt me. Was it because I arrested him?'

'No. You were doing your job and he was in debt. I hold no grudge for that.'

'But you hold a grudge for something.'

'I saw his body. I saw his suffering,' said Jenna, turning away from him again. Jack followed her.

'He ran the risk when he sold information on the smugglers. I warned him. I told him he should leave before something bad happened to him.'

Jenna swung around to face him. 'You warned him and when he didn't leave, you punished him!'

'Punished him for what?'

'For selling information knowing that you would be on

the beach that night. If it had not been for Silas you would not have been shot.'

Jack dismissed her accusation with a wave of his arm. 'That is not true. When I visited him it was to warn him. He was well when I left.'

'Why would you warn him? Why would you visit him at all? You did not care for him.'

'But I cared and loved you.'

'Cared and loved?'

'Yes, cared and loved – not care and love, for the woman I thought I knew is someone very different.'

'You warned him for me?'

'The fool that I am. I should not have bothered. He is not worth it and now I wonder if you are.'

His barb hurt. She shouldn't care, yet to have lost his affection felt more painful than she anticipated. Wanting to validate her actions to herself, as much as him, she retorted.

'Silas is dead.'

His tone softened. 'I'm sorry to hear it. I know you cared for him far more than he deserved.'

'His dying wish was for me to tell the judge about you.'

Jack looked at her incredulously. 'And you considered it?'

'Of course, I considered it. I hate you for what you did!'

'What did I do?' he said, taking her by the shoulders again. 'What did I do?'

Deep furrows marked his brows and the hurt and confusion remained in the depths of his eyes. He does not know that his beating was the cause of his death, thought Jenna.

'Your beating killed him. He told me it was you.'

Jack did not answer straight away. She felt his fingers loosen slightly, before they fell away.

'And you believed him?'

His shock did not seem the same as the shock of a guilty man being found out.

'Not at first ... but then ...'

'You believed him enough to consider betraying me.' She did not need to answer; her silence said it all. 'And even when you thought better of it, you still believe I am responsible for killing your brother.' He stepped back from her. 'You think I am capable of murder.'

'Who would tell a falsehood when he is about to meet his maker?'

'Your brother would,' said Jack, resting his hand on the dressing table, as if for support. 'Your brother was no better than the rats in the sewer that spread their diseases to the good people in this world. It was only in your eyes he held some importance.' Jenna opened her mouth to say something but Jack was not ready to listen. He raised his hand to stop her from speaking. Voicing his thoughts, Jack said, 'It must have come as a shock to hear that you were building a new life with me – a life that did not include him.' He looked down at the polished wood of the table and saw his reflection looking back at him. 'He had no affection for me as I had none for him.' He gave a short hollow laugh, marking the wood with his finger to obliterate his face within. 'What better way to destroy his sister's affection for his enemy than to accuse me of his murder.' He looked up at her. 'I credit him with a touch of genius to leave a dying wish that would not only destroy me but any love between us.'

Jenna moved towards him. Although each thought he expressed made sense, Silas was her brother.

'Why would he not tell me the truth?'

'If he told you who the real culprits were, and you reported it, they would come after you. It stands to reason it would be the Blake brothers taking their revenge for Silas selling information to Henley.'

'Silas would not lie to me.'

'Your brother has spent his entire life lying. People like that convince themselves that their own lies are true.' Jack held out his fists. 'Look at my knuckles, no bruising, no grazes. Do I look like a man who has been in a fight?'

Jenna looked at them before he snatched them back again. He was right, there was nothing.

'Silas has no moral compass. Even after I warned him to leave for his own safety, he picked my pocket as I left. Lord knows how he managed to survive as a pickpocket. He was so clumsy that I caught him red-handed.'

Jenna's stomach dropped as she felt her face drain of its colour.

'My brother has never been caught before.'

'Well, I caught him. I gave him the money anyway, emptying my purse onto him so the coins fell onto the floor.' Jenna remembered the landlord's eager hands collecting coins at her feet. 'I hoped your brother would reconsider and leave, but it now appears that he didn't and he has paid with his life.'

'My brother has never been caught,' she muttered to herself, 'unless he intended it as a distraction.' Jenna felt as if her eyes were opened for the first time. Silas *had* lied and Jack was innocent of the charges he laid at his door. She stepped towards him. Her relief that Jack was innocent almost overwhelmed her. Excitement bubbled up inside her. 'You did not do it!' she said, reaching for him.

As she touched his arm, he parried her away. 'Don't touch me, Jenna,' he said menacingly.

'I'm sorry. Silas told me you had done it.'

'And you believed your viper of a brother over me.'

'He was my brother.'

'Who thought nothing of dragging you down to his level!'

'He cared for me.'

'He asked you to break the law for him!'

Jenna reached for him again, but this time he did not move away.

'I'm sorry, Jack,' she pleaded. 'Forgive me. I did not believe he would lie on his death bed.'

He looked down at her hand and took it in his. 'I was afraid he would corrupt you one day. When I woke and saw you in my bed, sleeping soundly with your legs tangled in the sheets, I wanted to protect you from him.' He reached out and touched her cheek, brushing away a stray hair so it lay with the rest behind her shoulders. 'I could not wait and left before you woke so that I could speak to him. I asked him to leave so he would be safe, but I knew his leaving would also mean that you would be away from his influence.' He wrapped her hair around his fist like a rope. 'I wanted to protect you,' he said, pulling her gently towards him. 'I loved you.'

Jenna willingly came towards him. 'And now?' she asked, through shallow breaths. She wanted the hurt between them to end. She wanted to be held in his arms and be forgiven for not believing in him.

'Now,' he said, letting her hair fall from his hand, 'I don't know any more. You thought I was capable of killing your brother and that is a bitter pill to swallow.'

# Chapter Nineteen

'So we know he has the paintings,' said Enoch, offering Jack a glass of port as he entered the drawing room.

Jack, taking a seat by the fire, declined. 'The hour is late, I do not want a drink. I have broken one of your doors. Send me the bill when you have it repaired.'

Enoch raised an eyebrow, but seeing Jack's expression he thought better of pursuing the matter.

'What is the next step that we should take?'

Jack sat back in the chair and stared into the fire, as he massaged his right temple with two of his fingers.

'His wife mentioned that they visited museums during their grand tour of Europe. Perhaps enquiries should be made as to whether they have had any thefts or orders.'

'You could get a ship from Dover to Calais and follow the grand tour route. I understand Paris, Rome, Naples and Venice are the main stops. I could arrange a letter of credit from my London bank so you could present it in the major cities. It is too risky to carry too much money on your journey.'

'Me? I have no wish to leave at this moment. Our agreement was to find the person who finances the gang. My work here is ended. It is time for me to move on.'

'We know who it is, but we do not have the proof to have him convicted. Our contract ends with his conviction. I need you, Jack. My son used an interpreter when he travelled in Europe. Julien, I think his name was. I can provide you with his details.'

'I am sick with it all.'

'You are lovesick, that is all.'

Jack pushed himself to standing and stood in front of the

fire. The warmth from its flames gave him the comfort he craved.

'I don't know what you have fallen out about, but she played her part well and provided us with the information we need. It will be foolish to not pursue what we have discovered. If Judge Buller is convicted of possessing or soliciting stolen art, we can be rid of him.'

'And you will be rid of a man you detest.'

'True, I have never liked the fellow, but we cannot have a judge who breaks the law himself. Smuggling is not a victimless crime. The Indian Tea Company wants the free trading to end. They will pay handsomely for any help they receive.'

'There is nothing that can tempt me to cross the water. Do I have to remind you that France has taken the side of America in the Revolutionary War? The French may not take too kindly to a British man crossing their land.'

'The French have troubles of their own. They will not concern themselves with you.'

'Troubles?'

'There is frustration brewing against their own aristocracy. Some years back there were bread riots. The peasants have had a taste for making themselves heard and they will do it again if their lives do not improve.'

'Even so, I have things to sort out here.'

'Sometimes time apart can help put matters into perspective.'

'I know what you are doing, Enoch. Nothing will persuade me.'

'Name your price and I will arrange it.'

Jack looked up. 'Your determination is making you loose with your tongue.'

'I mean it, Jack. Name your price and I will agree. I want Buller to fall.'

'Buller's involvement has turned it into a personal vendetta for you, Enoch.'

'He is a dangerous man to have in power. If his political ambitions are realised, it won't be just a poacher suffering at the end of a rope, it may be all of us.'

Jack thought for a moment. 'Perhaps time away is what I need.'

'It can do a man good.'

'There are two things that will persuade me to leave.'

'What are they?'

'I do not know if there is a future together for Jenna and myself. Too much has been said, too many lies and betrayals. However, the first thing is that I want her to be cared for while I am gone. I want her to be able to stay in the Captain's Cottage if she should choose.'

Enoch did not need to consider his terms for long. He wanted Jack in France and he wanted him there soon.

'I agree. She will be taken care of until your return. Of course she may choose to refuse my help. She is a woman with her own mind and I cannot help her if she does not want it. What is the second?'

'What I will receive in payment.'

'What do you want?'

'Something that was taken away from me when my father died.'

Enoch emptied his glass with a backward tilt of his head. 'What is that?'

Jack told him.

'I will arrange it. When can you leave?'

'Tomorrow,' Jack said, looking into the depths of the amber flames in the fire. 'I can leave tomorrow.'

Jenna sat on the bed, hugging her knees and staring fixedly at the open door. She did not see it. Her mind's eye was elsewhere, remembering the look of disappointment on Jack's face before he left. The painful memory sapped her motivation to move from the bed and close it and brought tears to her eyes. She was losing him, she realised, and in the worst possible way.

The thought of living a life without him now filled her with dread. How could she have ever contemplated such a future before? How could her mind have become so distorted in thought? She must do something – anything, to gain his forgiveness. After Henry's beatings, she swore she would never beg a man again, but for Jack she would. She would crawl over burning embers to have his love again if she had to. There would be many women who would despise her for such thoughts, but she did not care. To be judged so harshly meant they had never experienced a love comparable to her feelings for Jack. A love she had denied in her hours of madness. A love she may never experience again, for she knew that no other man would do.

Jack climbed the stairs to his room, his mind brooding over the events of the day. Discovering that Jenna planned to betray him shocked and confused him. Discovering that she believed he killed her brother almost felled him. He still felt wounded, as surely as if she had fired a musket ball into his chest. Any man in his right mind would have nothing more to do with her, but loving someone as he loved her made the sensible thing to do impossible.

He stepped on to the wooden landing and looked at the colourful rugs dotted over the oak boards to add extra warmth. He looked down the row of doors, knowing he would have to pass Jenna's bedroom on the way to his. As he approached it he could tell, from the light cascading onto the rug at her door, that she had not closed it since he left.

She was still awake. This fact alone made him decide that it was only right to tell her he was leaving.

He approached quietly and looked into her room. Her small figure sat on the bed, her face hidden in cradled arms that rested on bent knees. He wondered if she had been crying. When she looked up, he knew that she had.

Stripped of her finery, she still retained a fragile beauty, made all the more poignant by her tearstained cheeks and wet lashes. He almost weakened. Almost ...

'I am leaving for France in the morning. I have arranged for you to remain in the cottage until you choose to go. You may leave when you want, you do not have to stay for my return.'

'Do you want me to stay?'

'I do not know.'

He made to leave, but she slipped from the bed and came towards him.

'Go back to bed, Jenna,' he said gruffly, halting her steps. 'The night has turned cold and you will catch a chill.'

'I don't care,' she said, stopping and wringing her hands.

He looked at her.

'Don't cry. It will do us both good to have distance between us.'

'It will do me no good. I will worry until you are home. When will you be back?'

'I don't know. I will travel through Europe and hope to discover where the paintings came from and if they were stolen. It will take time – two, maybe three months.'

She was trembling, he realised, as she tried to hide her hands in her oversized nightgown. It covered most of her curves, except for the top swell of her breasts. He swallowed and dragged his eyes away. He knew from experience what lay beneath the shapeless sack, and the knowledge made it hard to turn away, but he did all the same.

'I will send word when I plan to return,' he told her curtly. 'There is no more to say.'

'I'm sorry,' she cried. He heard her bare footsteps run towards him. He halted, but still refused to look at her. Her slight frame slipped between him and the door so he had no choice but to see her. 'I was wrong to believe Silas's lies. It was four and twenty hours of madness. Please, Jack, do not go away.' She shut the door. 'Stay, do not leave me. Let us forget what has happened.'

He shook his head and Jenna became more desperate. She reached up to touch his chest and he felt her warm body press against his. 'I have never met anyone who was as good and kind to me as you. It was easier to believe the worst, than to think I was worthy of your attention.'

He held her arms to ease them away. 'Don't,' he whispered hoarsely.

Jenna reached up to lay small kisses upon his cheek. 'Please stay, Jack,' she breathed. 'Please forgive me. Hear me beg … you see, I have no pride left if it means I can persuade you to stay.'

Jack closed his eyes, hoping to shut her out, but all it did was heighten the sensations of her kisses. Her body pressed still further against him.

'When will you cease playing these games?' he said into her hair.

'I play no game at all.'

Jack's hands left her arms and followed the arch of her back to the curve of her hips.

'You will not persuade me to stay,' he said, burying his face into the crook of her neck to smell and taste her soft skin beneath his lips. He had wanted this woman since the first day she smiled at him. After tonight he may not see her again.

'Then let me persuade you to stay for tonight,' she coaxed.

He felt the firmness of her bottom in his hands and roughly pulled her up towards him and off the floor. 'You are using your charms to change my mind. You will not change it, even if I do take what you are offering.'

Her legs wrapped around him. 'I know you will not change your mind,' she whispered. 'I do this for myself as well as you.'

He felt her lips against his skin; angrily he claimed them with his mouth wanting to taste their sweetness and make her feel the passion and anger he held inside him.

Their kissing was the undoing of him and any resistance he thought he had crumbled into nothing. The urge she was coaxing rose up inside him and he cared nothing for what had happened between them. All he could think of was the present and that he wanted her.

He slipped his hand beneath her gown to feel the thigh that wrapped around his waist. It felt how he imagined it and he wanted more of her. He carried her to the bed and laid her down, then he began a trail of hungry kisses towards her breasts. He could feel Jenna's fingers raking his hair and hear her soft moans beneath him. Both only fed his desire for more ... and his resentment that he could not resist her.

I will make you remember me, he thought angrily, I will make this night a night you will cherish for the rest of your life, for if I find I cannot forgive you, I want no other man to fill the void I leave.

'Please stay,' Jenna whispered as she arched to his touch.

'I will not stay.'

A tear fell from her eye as she sighed at his touch.

'Then promise me, Jack,' she whispered into the night air. 'Promise me that you will leave before I wake, so I won't have the pain of saying goodbye.'

261

# Chapter Twenty

A silent covering of grey clouds hung harmlessly over Goverek town for most of the day. Eventually they darkened, churning up inky black seas in the sky, which drained the colour from the day and brought a sense of foreboding to the inhabitants below. The growing tension finally broke when sheets of rain fell onto the warren of cobbled streets. The downpour helped cleanse the narrow alleyways of loiterers and stray dogs, and flushed animal and chamber pot excrement into the rudimentary gutters.

Only one woman, slight in frame, remained outside in the rain. Occasionally the woman stopped to look about her, holding her shawl like a tent above her head to ward off the rain. Eventually she found the door she was looking for. She ran across the road, sidestepped a puddle and sheltered under an overhang as she banged against its wooden surface with a rain soaked knuckle.

The woman tilted her head to listen to the unwelcoming mumbling voices inside. Silence fell and no one came to the door, so she knocked again. More voices, a child talking and eventually footsteps. Finally the door opened a little. A thin-faced young woman looked through the crack.

'Hello, Nell,' said Jenna, letting her shawl drop onto her shoulders to expose her face.

'Tell them you don't know where he is!' shouted an older woman who remained hidden from view.

'It's true. I cannot help you or him,' Nell said, attempting to shut the door again. Jenna blocked it with her foot.

'I have not come to ask anything of you, Nell.'

The door opened a little to expose her narrow face again.

'I won't go back to him.'

'I have not come to ask you to return to him.'

Nell frowned. 'Then why are you here?'

'I have grave news to tell you.'

Nell rested her head against the door. 'Is it about Silas?' she asked reluctantly. Jenna nodded solemnly. 'Then you better come in.'

Nell opened the door and stepped aside, revealing the dark and cluttered interior. Her mother sat in the far corner, surrounded by laundry in various states of wash. Jenna recognised her instantly, although she had only met her once. Despite Jenna's polite greeting, the older woman refused to look at her, grunting in reply as she continued to sort the neighbours' washing.

A warmer greeting came from Silas's two children, Talek and Grace, who raced towards her with outstretched arms screaming her name. Jenna fell to her knees and cradled them against her, tightly encasing their small waists with each of her arms. She inhaled deeply into their hair to savour the smell of them. It had been too long since she last saw them and enjoyed their joy filled hugs.

'I have missed seeing you both. It has been far too long.' She held them at arm's length to look them over. 'You have both grown so tall! Talek, you are going to be as tall as your father when you grow up.' She looked at Grace, her image blurring before her eyes. 'And your smile is as cheeky as his, too.'

Nell noticed Jenna's trembling lips and took the children from her.

'Mother, take Talek and Grace next door to see Meg. I'm sure she will be glad to see them. Jenna has some news of Silas and I think it's best if we are left alone.'

Nell's mother began to grumble loudly again as she

heaved herself to standing and fetched a coat and cloak for her grandchildren.

'Don't go back to that man, Nell,' she warned her daughter. 'He is no good for you.' She looked angrily at Jenna. 'And don't you go and try to talk her round.' Without saying anything more, Nell's mother ushered the children out of the door and into the rain. Needing no further direction from their grandmother, the children ran ahead to the house next door, eager to see their friend. Nell's mother gave Jenna a sidelong glance, before following them out into the dark.

The room fell silent. Nell turned to look at her sister-in-law.

'You looked like you were about to cry. I have never seen you cry before.'

'I have cried a river these past few days,' said Jenna, arranging her shawl on a chair by the fire to dry.

'Is he dead?'

Unable to speak, Jenna resorted to a slight nod of the head. The movement caused the colour to drain from Nell's face. She looked blankly at the floor as her mind absorbed what Jenna was telling her. The fire crackled between them and mocked them in their silence, before Nell broke it by stiffly walking to her mother's vacant chair. She held it for support, her knuckles pinching white, before carefully lowering herself down upon it as if her bones ached with age.

She took a deep breath and rolled up her sleeves. 'I knew he would not live to be an old man,' said Nell calmly as she neatened the fold of her sleeves. 'It was not his way to lead a peaceful life.' She picked up a shirt from the tub of water and began to scrub the cloth together. 'How did he die?' she asked bravely. She did not fool Jenna. The news was a shock and Jenna must tread softly with the details, yet she could not lie.

'He died from a beating, Nell,' Jenna said quietly. 'I'm so sorry.'

'Revenge?' Jenna nodded again. 'I am not surprised. What was it about? No, don't tell me. It is better that I do not know the details. It is best I keep my distance.' Her scrubbing became more vigorous. 'I knew the fool was up to something.' She gave a curt laugh to herself. 'He was always up to something. Did you know he visited me a week ago? Dressed like a dandy and showing off his money. He wanted me to go back to him. I said no and then he left.' Water sloshed over the side, but she ignored it. 'Give him his due; he did give me some money to buy Talek and Grace something.'

'I noticed their coat and cloak looked new.'

'What good is a new coat when their father lies cold in the ground? Better they had a father who took care of them than a man who chose trouble over them.' Angrily she slammed the shirt back into the tub making more water slosh over the side. She reached for another. 'You think me a hard woman.'

'No,' Jenna replied, coming over to crouch beside her. She placed her hand on Nell's, just as Jack used to do with her. Nell's hands stilled beneath hers, but she could still feel them trembling. 'It is all right to feel angry towards Silas. I am angry with him, too.'

'A sister can feel anger towards her brother, but a wife should not leave her husband. I know that is what you are thinking, but I could not bring up our children fearing who may knock on our door. It is no way to live.'

'No, it is no way to live.'

Their eyes met. 'You do not blame me?'

'Of course, I do not. I came here to tell you about Silas, not to lay fault at your door.'

'I thought you were angry with me and sided with Silas. You have not visited since I moved in with my parents.'

Jenna took her hand away and fetched a chair so she could sit next to Nell.

'I thought you were in the prison with Silas. Now I feel foolish for believing Silas's tale. He wanted me to help pay his creditors and knew that I was more likely to help him if I knew Talek and Grace were there with him.'

'I thought he kept his tales for me.'

Jenna rolled up her sleeves. 'Silas had enough tales for everyone he met.' Together, the women reached into the water and began to scrub the shirts.

'Mother and I take in washing. Father does the odd job as a labourer but there is not much money coming in. I don't know how we are going to pay for a funeral.'

'I have spoken to the vicar of Lanros. He has a poor hole due to be covered this week. There is room for one more and he is willing to take Silas's coffin.'

'Did Silas have much money left?'

'The landlord of Lanros Inn took most of it to cover his boarding bills and for keeping his body until burial. There were a few coins left, just enough to buy a cheap coffin, but not enough for a service. Silas was not a God-fearing man so I do not think he will mind. The vicar is willing to say a few words over his grave for us.' They both squeezed out the water from the shirts and placed them in another tub full of washed clothing.

'That is kind of him,' said Nell, drying her hands and passing the cloth to Jenna.

'The funeral will be at noon tomorrow if you are in agreement.' Jenna dried her hands. 'Will you bring the children?'

Nell got up and pushed away a stray hair with her hand. 'I don't think I will go,' she said, trying to look busy sorting through more clothes in a basket. 'I left him. It would look odd if I played the grieving widow now.'

'You loved him once. You are his wife and the mother of his children. Besides, if you do not go, there will be no one in attendance.'

Nell looked up, surprised. 'You do not intend going?'

Jenna joined her and began to fold some clothes. 'I am too angry with Silas,' she confided. 'Silas told me a falsehood about a man I loved and I believed him. In revenge I almost betrayed Jack and in doing so probably ruined any chance of a future with him.' Jenna paused in her folding. 'I find it hard to understand why Silas would do such a thing. I thought he cared for me.'

'He did care about you. I often thought he cared more for you than me. He loved you. Perhaps he felt this man was not right for you. I know he carried a lot of guilt about how Henry treated you. The day he discovered the truth of it, he came home and sobbed like a child. He felt he let you down and that he should have known earlier. He thought you were going to die that night.'

Silas had cried? Silas never cried. Jenna felt her heart begin to ache with all the sadness that filled it as she laid a neatly folded shirt aside and picked up another.

'I thought I was going to die, too. I even prayed that I would.' Seeing Nell's expression, Jenna added, 'I could see no end to it, Nell. I was too scared to leave.'

'It was a terrible time for us all,' her sister-in-law agreed. 'I am glad Silas put a stop to him.'

'You knew that Silas arranged for Henry to be caught?' asked Jenna, wide-eyed.

'Knew?' said Nell, folding the clothes with renewed

vigour. 'It was my idea.' She gave Jenna a sidelong glance. 'Don't look at me like that. Henry broke the law as many times as Silas did. It was Henry's idea to go out poaching that night. It was only a matter of time before he was caught. I'm just glad it was before he killed you.'

Jenna was about to reply when they heard her mother's voice outside.

'Mother is coming,' Nell whispered abandoning the clothes. 'That is all I need right now. She will spend the rest of the evening rejoicing when she hears about Silas's death. I don't have the strength to face her right now.' She showed Jenna the back door. 'Go out this way,' she urged, 'and I will take myself up to my room. You see,' she said, her eyes misting slightly, 'I am not as hard as I pretend to be. I knew this day would come and I thought I would feel nothing. I was wrong, and feel grief for his passing more than I care to admit. I can moan to you about him, but I could not bear hearing my mother gloating just now.'

'Will you go to his burial?' Jenna asked as she covered her head with her shawl.

'Father says forgiveness brings freedom. I just don't know if I am ready to forgive. I think you should go.'

Jenna looked up at the night sky. 'I think I should, too. Even though I hate what he did, I don't think I can abandon him now, even though I wish I could. Perhaps, if I try to understand him, I will be able to forgive him and find my own freedom.' She clutched Nell's hand in hers. 'Mark, my brother who ran away to sea, once said that saying goodbye is a good way of starting afresh. Come and say your goodbyes with me tomorrow.'

'I don't know, Jenna. I really don't know if I can.'

Silas's final resting place was in the shadow of the trees,

where moss choked the growth of lush grass and flowers failed to flourish. Above, seven rooks gathered in the trees' leafless branches and looked down on the mound of earth that lay beside the hole. A gravedigger, leaning on a shovel, greeted Jenna's arrival.

'It is fortunate that your kin is the last to be buried,' said the scruffy man. 'I dug this poor hole several weeks ago and it has taken until now for it to be filled. A neighbour has written a letter reporting that a stray dog has been seen sniffing around. It is time the bodies were covered before more dogs are tempted here. Are you the only mourner?'

Jenna had waited by the gate of the graveyard hoping Nell would change her mind, but when the church bell chimed, she knew she could wait no longer.

'I am a mourner for Silas Cartwright. I do not know if there will be any more.'

The gravedigger scratched his head. 'We don't usually get many mourners for these types of burials. Ah, here comes the vicar now,' he said. 'It looks like he has found some more.'

Jenna turned to see a young woman walking with the vicar. Two young children walked beside her, holding her hands.

'Do you know her?' he asked.

Jenna smiled. 'Yes, it is my brother's widow. She has come to say her goodbyes.'

The graveside service was short and soon over. Jenna suspected he used the same reading for all the paupers' burials he attended, but she did not mind. They were well chosen and brought a finality and dignity that gave a comfort all of its own. Jenna and Nell stood side by side at the grave's edge, their arms linked to support one another. Grace and Talek copied their mother and aunt, and remained silent and well behaved until it was time for the earth to fall. Curious faces looked down at the earth on the coffin and Nell had to pull them back before they fell in.

'I'm glad you decided to come,' said Jenna, linking her arm in hers again to follow the children away from the grave.

'So am I.' Nell watched them begin to chase one another around the gravestones. 'They do not understand. It is an adventure. It is too much to grasp.' She shouted to the children to be quieter, but they ignored her. 'I did not expect to be a widow at my age.'

'I did not expect it either.'

'They look so happy, but this is not a place for laughter. I must make them be quiet.'

Jenna gave her arm a squeeze. 'No, don't stop them being happy. Their laughter is a reminder that life goes on. Let us go to Lanros beach, Nell. The children can play and the fresh air will do us both good.'

A rook called out above them, making the women look up. They watched it take flight, abandoning the others as it flew away.

'Yes,' said Nell. 'Let us leave this place. It is no place for the living. We have said our goodbyes. It is time for us both to start afresh.'

The beach of Lanros was wide and exposed. No good for smuggling, thought Jenna, as she enjoyed the view from her rocky perch. Shielding her eyes against the sun, she watched the children shrieking and laughing, as they chased one another in a chaotic game. In the distance, a woman and her children walked the water's edge collecting driftwood for burning at a later date.

'I am learning my letters. If you like, I could teach Talek and Grace.'

Nell shook her head. 'What use will they have for penmanship? Talek needs to learn a trade and Grace needs to marry a man who has a trade. Knowing their letters will not help them.'

Jenna felt she was wrong, but now was not the time to persuade her. Nell was a simple woman with simple needs, she would never understand the benefits of being able to read and write.

'I did love him once,' said Nell suddenly.

Jenna dropped her hand and looked at her sister-in-law sitting on the rock beside her.

'I know you did.'

'I thought when the children came along he would be more responsible and get an honest job. Only Silas did not want to change.' Nell looked at Jenna. 'Rearing children needs regular money coming into the house, not a bit stolen here and there. Every time there was a knock on the door, I thought someone was coming for him. I had to leave. Next time I marry it will be to a good man, who will care for me and the children. Your brother had a cheeky smile and a twinkle in his eye, but he could not be relied upon.'

Jenna swallowed down the thick emotion in her throat. I will never see Silas's smile again, she thought, and it hurt.

She cleared her throat. 'Love can make you do silly things.'

'My parents warned me against him, but it only made him look even more attractive to me. Did you love Henry?'

Jenna shook her head. 'No. I was attracted to him in the beginning, but I know what love feels like now and it was not love. I married Henry so I would no longer be a Cartwright. It made no difference. I am no better than my family. Sharing the same blood brings an inevitability that bad things will happen. Blood will out.'

'That is nonsense. You are nothing like Silas and the rest of your family. You are too good.'

'I was a smuggler for a night ...'

Nell's mouth fell open at her confession.

'... and I almost betrayed the man I loved for Silas. It was easier to think the worst of Jack and, for a short while, I wanted to make Jack suffer. I fear I have lost him.'

'Women do silly things in the name of love. I married Silas despite my parents being against it and you believed Silas despite knowing he is a rogue. Women do not always think straight when they love someone.' Nell took Jenna's hand. 'You did not take revenge in the end, did you?'

Jenna shook her head. 'No, I didn't.'

'Then you are different from your family, Jenna. You are not like them.' Nell let her hand go and rested back onto the rock to feel the sun on her face. 'Where is this Jack now?'

'His work has taken him away. I have disappointed him and he is taking the time away to consider what to do next.'

'Do you think he will come back to you?'

'I don't know.'

'If he loves you enough he will want to try again.'

'I am willing to try. I thought I would never want to marry again, but I would marry Jack if he asked me.'

Nell opened an eye. 'How long will you wait for him?'

'As long as he needs me to.'

'And if that means you are waiting for years with no answer?'

'As you said, Nell, love can make a woman do the strangest of things. I will wait, for no other man will do.'

# Chapter Twenty-One

'Good morning, Jack, I trust you slept well.'

'As well as one can in a busy trading port,' said Jack, offering the chair opposite him with a push of his boot. 'And you?'

'I did not sleep well at all so I rose early and arranged your papers.' The Frenchman sat down and poured himself a drink. 'The *Fortitude* is waiting offshore for high tide. I suspect it will be another hour before it can enter the harbour,' he said, taking a drink.

Jack took the papers that were passed across the table. He was pleased to see that they were his passage home.

'These past two months have not been easy. I could not have managed without you as my interpreter. Should you decide to come to England, my door will always be open to you.'

Julien smiled. 'I was born in Brittany. I hear Cornwall is not so very different.'

'If Brittany has beaches, cliffs and green rolling hills then, yes, they are not so different. I think you will like it.' Jack turned his attention to the window. He could see a number of ships waiting out at sea, their sails tied up and their masts no more than fragile sticks. One of them was the *Fortitude*, he thought, and it would take him home. He wondered if Jenna waited for him on the other side of the Channel.

Julien interrupted his thoughts, by nudging his arm.

'Did you hear what I said? The art gallery curators will follow in a week or so. I wish I could be there to see the results of our hard work, but I have a wife and children eager for me to return home, so I will leave the last part to you.'

'I will write and let you know how it unfolds. You are fortunate to have a family waiting for you.'

'It is times like these I can see my good fortune. Time apart can make the bonds stronger when it's time to return. What will you do when this is over for you?'

'I want different things out of life from what I did only a few months ago. When I return, I will make some changes, but first I need to get back to England.'

The two men sat in companionable silence watching the bustle of Calais port play out before them. They were happy to not speak and had sat many times like this since Jack's arrival, as they mulled over their plans or thought of home. Fortunately, they were well matched as spending so much time in the company of a man one disliked would have made the trip far more difficult.

Julien eventually leaned back in his chair, content that his part was now at an end.

'I trust you are glad to return home.'

'I cannot pretend otherwise,' said Jack, toying with his tankard.

'You are more relaxed than when you first stepped on French soil,' Julien observed.

'Is that surprising?' asked Jack. 'I have found the evidence I need and the trip has been a success.'

'You arrived in France an angry young man with a short temper. I told myself I would give you a week. If your character did not improve I promised myself I would leave.'

'But you didn't.'

'No, because I discovered that was not the real you. The real you I am proud to call my friend.'

Jack looked up at his kind words. 'I am sorry I did not give you a good impression.'

'It was understandable, given the circumstances. I wish

you well in whatever you decide, for I think you have made a decision about this woman.'

'I have,' said Jack, pushing his tankard away. 'I think I made it when I first set foot in France, I just did not want to acknowledge it.'

'Then I wish you good luck for the future,' Julien said, finishing his drink. He stood up. 'It is time for me to leave and go home to my wife.'

Jack stood and the two men shook hands.

'Thank you for your help, Julien. Our countries may be on opposite sides in America, but I mean it when I say that you are welcome in my home.'

'And I will look forward to seeing it, when I step on British soil.'

Jack solemnly watched his friend leave. They had become as close as brothers during his time in France, yet he had the strangest feeling that he would not see the man again.

Jack stood at the harbour's edge and watched the *Fortitude* being loaded. The wind had died away and there was concern that if it did not pick up, the departure may be delayed. Jack was aware it was not uncommon for passengers to wait up to a week for the direction of the wind to change. He wanted to be back in England, and the thought of a delay did not cheer him.

To make matters worse, the noise of the port resonated around him and made his head ache. Port labourers shouting directions as they transported the cargo, passengers talking as they waited to embark, children running, stray dogs whining, wheels turning ... the noise reflected the anticipation, excitement and danger of the sea journey ahead.

A shout went up that the wind was changing. A man

waved to the waiting crowd, signalling it was time for them to board. Eager to be on his way, Jack reached for his bag.

'Cartwright!'

Jack straightened and turned in the direction of the call, lengthening his neck in order to search the sea of faces behind him. None of the workers on the dock took ownership of it, preferring to keep working with bent backs and sweating foreheads. The throng of passengers were no better and Jack began to doubt what he had heard. He waited for the name to be called again, but it did not come. Jenna had plagued his thoughts too much of late, he concluded, and was now spilling forth to play tricks on him in the day. It would not do.

Even keener to leave France behind him, he stepped onto the sloping, narrow gangplank which provided a path to board the ship. Others followed, bustling and forcing his momentum forward to the deck above, as the wooden bridge bounced and strained under their combined weight. Despite his earlier doubt, Jack was unable to quell his curiosity and his gaze was drawn back to the group of French labourers. They remained busy, muscles straining in the sunshine as they loaded a stack of wooden boxes onto a waiting cart. He was about to look away when one of them shouted again.

'Cartwright!'

Jack quickly stepped onto the deck and nudged his way through the crowd to the edge of the ship. He looked down on the busy quayside to see who had acknowledged it. A man, in his late twenties and with dark, almond shaped eyes, had stopped working and was answering in fluent French. Jack frowned as he watched an animated conversation take place, where orders were given and questions were asked in frustrated tones, until it ended amicably with a joke and a laugh. Leaving his current task, the young man picked up a trunk belonging to two young gentlemen travellers and reluctantly followed them on board.

Jack waited impatiently for the labourer to step on deck with the trunk. He immediately approached him when he arrived.

'Monsieur Cartwright,' he said as the dark-eyed man put down the trunk. Jack saw him hesitate, before straightening his back and turning to go.

'I know your name is Cartwright,' Jack insisted. 'I heard one of the other workers call to you.'

The man ignored him, but Jack caught his arm. 'I am not here to cause trouble,' he reassured him under his breath.

The man shook him off and rebuffed him in French. It was clear that the man denied his English connections and that Jack was to leave him alone.

Jack attempted to reassure him, but the man grew angry.

'You cannot have a decent conversation with any of these foreigners,' said one of the young gentlemen who owned the trunk.

Jack, unamused by the interruption, snapped, 'We are the foreigners, sir, as we are on their soil.'

'Nevertheless, they lack the manners of our country so there is no wisdom in trying to engage with them.'

'I see you have learnt little from your European excursions,' retorted Jack, his gaze remaining on the labourer. 'I thought the purpose of your travels was to gain education, not to become bigoted.' He saw the French labourer smile as he turned away. 'Or perhaps,' continued Jack, 'being a bigot comes naturally to you?'

'You have no manners, sir.'

Jack turned his attention to the young gentleman for the first time. The labourer seized the opportunity and slipped away.

'What do you intend to do about it, sir?' Jack challenged the traveller.

Realising he was no match for Jack's retorts and bad humour, the gentleman uneasily moved away.

Jack, noticing the labourer was gone, searched the crowd and eventually saw him making his way down the gangplank and onto dry land. The labourer looked up at the ship and their eyes locked briefly, before he disappeared into the sea of bodies that lined the quay.

Jack was now convinced that he could speak English, as he had seen the man smile at his well-chosen words before he left. To find a labourer speaking two languages was a rarity indeed.

He turned away and sat down to wait, eager for the ship to leave as men gathered in preparation to remove the gangplank and break all links with the land. Jack thought of Jenna and what would happen at their next meeting. There was much to say to one another and it could not be put off any longer. It was best he did not tell her of the incident that had just occurred. It would raise her hopes and she would spend the rest of her days wondering if the man he had seen was one of her brothers. He may have misheard or it may have been a fanciful thought on his part. Perhaps he was trying to replace the brother she lost by hearing the Cartwright name in his head. It was best if she knew nothing, he concluded, it was best if he did not speak of it at all.

# Chapter Twenty-Two

Jenna placed the book she was reading on her lap and let her head fall back to rest against the wall of the window alcove. She loved sitting on the window seat and gazing out at the dark blue sea in the distance. She spent far too much time watching the colours of the sea change – from dawn's silvery shimmering white light, to the blood red sunset as the sun sunk below its flat horizon. As she watched, she waited for Jack to come home, just as the wife of the sea captain waited for him many years before.

She thought back to her last day at Galva House. After a passionate night she would never forget, she had woken alone. She had thought it would be less painful that way, not to see his face or hear his goodbye, but she was wrong. Even now, two months later, she ached at losing him. Everything she said, saw and did brought home to her that he was not there to share it with her. It was as though he were dead, yet somehow worse, as he had chosen to leave her and put an ocean between them. She often wondered if he had fallen in love with a French or Italian beauty and if he ever thought of the woman who waited for him in Cornwall – the woman who had almost betrayed him.

Sir Enoch and Lady Pickering had been kind to her, offering her the option to stay with them for a few more days. Jenna politely refused. Galva House, for all its beauty and fine views, was not a place where she felt comfortable. She wanted to go home to the Captain's Cottage.

She was able to play the fine lady for a night, but in reality she was no one special, just a woman brought up in a family of thieves, but striving to be better. At times she failed, but, she told herself, failure does not have to be final. Each decision and each action is a chance at a new beginning. She could only hope that Jack would find it in his heart to forgive her when he returned. No, she scolded herself, Jack's absence was not as if he were dead, for she still hoped that he would return to her one day. With death, there was no hope at all.

In the distance a competent rider followed the cliff edge from the direction of Lanros. Jenna lifted her head and narrowed her eyes as the visitor approached. Her heart skipped a beat, as it often did whenever she saw someone that resembled Jack, but as the figure came nearer, she recognised the older frame of Enoch and went to greet him.

This was his third visit since Jack's departure and she knew it was out of an obligation to his friend rather than any affection he held for her. His visits were short and his conversation stilted. She suspected he was a man who preferred to converse with men than women, having spent most of his life in their company. Now, he had the unfortunate task of having her in his care until Jack returned or the tenancy came to an end, and she felt sorry that she was now a burden to him.

He greeted her with a curt nod of his head and took off his hat as he entered. Jenna grew concerned. His face was unusually grave, with dark shadows beneath his eyes that she had not noticed before. She gave him a brittle smile, despite feeling fearful of what was to come.

'Good day, Sir Enoch. It is a fine day for taking a ride.' She poured him his usual drink and managed to place it on the table without spilling it. 'Spring is on the horizon,' she wittered on, 'and I will be glad to see the back of winter.'

Enoch sat down and placed his hat carefully on his knee. She watched him smooth the black felt with his fingers.

Poor man, she thought, he would rather be anywhere but here.

'I am concerned for Jack,' he said finally. His sombre tone did not bode well and sucked the sunshine from the room.

Jenna felt her knees weaken. With a trembling hand, she reached for a chair and sat down opposite him.

'When will he be home?' she asked hopefully, ignoring the growing feeling of dread in her chest.

He rubbed his face with his hand. 'I wish my wife were here, she would know the right words to say.'

Enoch had come with bad news, just as she feared. The shadows under his eyes told a tale of their own.

'I find it best to speak plainly,' Jenna replied bravely. 'I have waited to hear from him since the day he left. Please do not delay now.'

Enoch put his hat on the table and pushed it away. 'Two weeks ago I received word that he planned to return.'

'You did not say.'

'I saw no reason to. I thought he would soon be on our shores and you would see him yourself.'

'And that was two weeks ago, you say.'

Enoch nodded. 'I knew that the journey from Calais to Dover would take less than a day, certainly no more than three should the wind die away, so when he did not arrive I made enquiries.' Enoch looked at her with a pitying look.

'Tell me, sir, for what I imagine may be far worse than what you may have to say.'

'I'm afraid my news is grave. I can find no evidence that Jack has returned to England.'

'You believe he has stayed in France?'

'I know of no reason why he should stay longer but, apparently, there was a storm and many ships were forced to seek shelter. One ship, the *Fortitude*, was too far from either coast and could not hide. Wreckage was spotted the following morning. I am afraid all hands were lost.'

Jenna felt tears spring to her eyes but fought hard to control them. Finally she said, 'You believe Jack was on board?'

Enoch sighed. 'I do.'

Jenna fell silent, trying to understand what he was telling her. She shook her head.

'He cannot be dead. I would know ...' She touched her chest with her fist. '... in here. I would feel it.' She looked for a lifeline to raise her hopes. 'You say that the Channel was busy with ships, one of them may have picked Jack up.'

'There were no survivors, Jenna.'

A crushing wave of despair hit her and she felt unable to breathe. Gasping for air, she rushed to the window. *He would not have gone if I had not driven him away*, a voice mocked in her head, as she fumbled for the latch. She flung the window open to allow the strong sea breeze to enter. Closing her eyes, she let her face bathe in it, savouring its salty smell as she breathed deeply to calm her nerves.

'If anyone is responsible it is I. My obsession with bringing Buller down put Jack in jeopardy and now he has paid the price.' Enoch stood, leaving his drink untouched. 'There is a further six months to run on this cottage. You do not need to leave before it is up. Jack arranged for you to stay before he left.'

Jenna ignored him. She did not care about the roof over her head. Enoch put on his hat, eager to go.

'Jack was a good man. Had he been a son of mine, I would have been enormously proud of him.'

'Don't speak of him as if he were lying at the bottom of the sea,' Jenna snapped.

'I wish I brought you better news than this. I delayed it for as long as I could until I could verify my fears.'

'There is no proof he was on board.'

'Your reaction is understandable. It will take time to come to terms with losing him. I will ask my wife to visit. She will be more helpful than I.'

Jenna shut the window and turned stiffly. 'There is no need, sir. She has known me for just one day and I do not want her to feel such a heavy obligation. I can look after myself. Jack left me some money to care for his home until his return, but now ... this news ...' Jenna braced herself. 'You need not concern yourself with my welfare. I will find employment elsewhere.'

Enoch straightened his shoulders and looked at her. 'I admire your strength, Jenna. You have made the task of sharing my grave concerns far easier than I deserve.'

Jenna gave a rigid nod of acceptance at his compliment. She would say no more. She wanted him gone and the sooner the better.

He turned and opened the door, eager to leave as much as she was eager to be alone.

'Good day, Jenna. I know he cared a great deal for you.'

'Please,' she said, closing her eyes tightly, 'don't say any more. I cannot bear to hear about the affection he had for me once, as I have lost it and there is a chance I may never have the opportunity of gaining it back.'

Closing the door behind him, she rested her head against its knotted wood and listened until she heard the sounds of him riding away. She felt a sob rise up into her throat and made a valiant attempt to stifle it with her fist. She was too late. Hearing her own cry of anguish made the news that he had failed to return when planned all the more real to her. It sapped her resolve and any further control of her pain was lost to her. Her weakened knees buckled and she slid to the floor in a crumpled pile. Closing her eyes, she allowed her sobs to come unhindered. As her body heaved with their burning pain, she thought of Jack and the future she may have lost.

Time refused to stand still, mocking her despair and ignoring her pain. The sunlight through the windows cast shadows at her feet. Their movement across the floor marked the passage of time and told her how much of the day was left to endure. She had nothing to fill it and no energy to care.

Once, a bird pecked frantically at a mark on the window until it finally gave up and flew away to find a more tasty morsel. A spider dedicated another day to spinning its web under the table near where she sat. Time and time again, it circled the centre, falling occasionally to climb up and continue on. Jenna watched them both intently but felt no sense of wonder or enjoyment at watching nature try, fail and try again. What was the point of it all, she thought to herself, when death was the final outcome?

Time stretched on and she barely moved, but to use the chamber pot and drink some water. Each time, like a wounded animal seeking shelter, she crawled back to the spot by the door. The weakness she felt made no sense, yet living with such loss felt impossible.

On the fourth day the bird came back and began to peck again. This time Jenna went to the window, intending to shoo it away, but instead she found herself stopping to watch it peck at some ants on the window frame. Its beady eyes and bright smooth feathers glistened in the morning sun as it tilted its head and took cheeky sidelong glances at her. It flew to the ground and picked up a twig in its beak, looking at her again with each eye in turn.

Suddenly it left, flying high into the sky with its precious load until she could see it no more. Such a little bird, she thought, with greater stamina and determination to prepare for spring than I. This type of grief has no body, no ending and no closure. This type of grief will not go away. If I am to survive, I must live in hope that he did not die and try to live through it. That he chose not to return to me and lives a better life elsewhere. Only then, perhaps one day, the pain I feel now will leave.

Lanros remained the same as always, bursting at the seams with transient visitors waiting to leave. Jenna was glad to leave it behind. She had spent the morning visiting her brother's grave before buying a few things for the larder on her way home. Her appetite remained poor, but breaking the day up with small meals helped her to pass the time and get through the day.

As she approached the cottage, she saw three unfamiliar horses tethered outside and two burly men standing in the garden. Her steps slowed as they turned to look at her. She recognised them instantly by their long, black beards and solid frames. It was too late to turn and run as Amos and Job Blake were waiting for her. She noticed they had already gained access to the Captain's Cottage as her door was open. She had no choice but to meet them and act innocent of whatever they wanted to know. Clutching her basket tighter, in order to use it as a weapon should she need to, she approached and demanded to know what they wanted. Amos spat on the floor at her feet.

'I have come to see you,' a familiar voice called from inside. Jenna glared at the two men as she walked past and entered the cottage. Sitting by the dying embers of her fire, with a smile on his face, was Judge Charles Buller. He looked at the book he held in his hand. 'So this is where you got your knowledge of the Fiji Islands,' he said, looking at the back and front cover as if it were a strange object. 'How very ... resourceful of you.'

Jenna put her basket down on the table. She was in no mood for games.

'What do you want?'

'That is not a nice way to greet an old friend,' he retorted as he heaved his great bulk to standing.

'You are no friend of mine.'

Buller dropped the book on the table. 'Perhaps not now, but maybe in the future.' He looked her up and down. 'You are not as finely dressed as when we last met. You had us all fooled, although I knew you looked familiar to me.'

'We had never met before your dinner party.'

'So I later discovered, but even so, the thought that I knew you would not leave my mind and plagued me for many weeks. Then, quite suddenly, during one night, it came to me.'

Jenna raised an eyebrow as if to say she did not care to hear, but Buller would not be put off.

'I think it was your skill at examining jewellery that finally helped me make the connection.'

His confidence began to unnerve her.

'Connection to whom?' asked Jenna uneasily.

Buller looked at her over his spectacles. 'Several years ago, a married couple came before me in court. The man I do not remember, but the woman was pretty, despite having a hard life and being in her middle years.' He looked at her mantelpiece and tested it for dust with a swipe of his finger. 'They were caught stealing jewellery, but they pleaded for leniency, as they did not want to be hanged. I felt generous at the time, so sentenced them both to gaol.' He dropped his hand and returned to his seat, flipping his coat tails out of the way as he sat down again. With an effort, he crossed his legs and clasped his hands across his large belly.

'It was a long time ago, but I can still recall her face, and it was this face that you reminded me of. I was keen to discover if she was related to you so I began to investigate. It was not something I wished to entrust to someone else, so I made my enquiries alone.

'I did not remember their surnames,' he continued, 'but the woman had an unusual first name that I had not come across before, or since. I can see from your face that you know where I am going with this.'

Jenna pressed her lips together, determined to not show how much his words interested her.

'Marguerite. French, I believe. Probably named after her slut of a mother who worked the ports of France.'

Jenna bit the inside of her cheek to stop herself from crying out. She had not heard her mother's name for a long time. Since the day of her parents' disappearance, Silas had taken care of her. Now, after all these years, she would learn what became of her parents and if they were still alive.

'I see you recognise the name, too. It is not an easy name to forget, but having the first name of a thief did not help me find a connection to you – so I went to Launceston Gaol and looked through their records. Marguerite Cartwright was her name, so it was only natural that I should search the baptism records.' He unclasped his hands and began to examine his nails. 'I found many boys' names, most of which have appeared before me at one time, but only one daughter, named Jenna. It is quite a coincidence, don't you think, that this child who has the same name as you would also share the same age?'

He took a greater interest in one of his nails. 'My interest was piqued so I continued my searching and in the same records was Jenna's marriage to a man named Henry Kestle. It always surprises me how the Cornish are so closely linked. I knew his name, of course. It was a pleasure to sentence him to hang for poaching.' He looked at her over his spectacles again. 'You may be interested to learn that both your parents died of the sweating fever which ravaged the gaol in 1776.'

So they were dead. And as shocking as the truth was, it brought her comfort to learn that they did not abandon her willingly. She hoped they did not suffer too long.

He began to tap the table with his long nail. 'Learning of your background, I began to wonder how a woman with thievery in her veins came to be supping at my table.'

Jenna edged towards the door.

'Watch her!' shouted Buller. Job appeared in the doorway to block her exit. Eyes black as coal stared down at her and forced her to back away. 'I feel your manners are lacking these days, Jenna. You have not even offered me a drink, which is customary when a guest is welcomed.'

'I see no guest I wish to welcome,' she retorted.

Buller stopped his tapping and Jenna saw him clench his teeth before taking a deep breath and exhaling slowly. 'You try my patience with your rudeness,' he said, looking at his nail and testing its length with a finger. 'You have a pretty face, it would be a shame to see it scarred.'

'Your threats do not scare me.'

'Is that because you have nothing to live for now that your lover has left you? I see from your face that you are surprised how far I have investigated you. As I said, I was intrigued to know how you came to be supping at my table.' He sat back and looked at her. 'You have quite a gift.'

'Gift?'

'A gift to impersonate. You were able to convince Sir Enoch Pickering that you are an aristocrat. What was your intention – to steal my guests' jewellery?'

Jenna began to unpack her basket as calmly as she could. It appeared that he did not know the real intention of her presence at the dinner. It was best that he did not learn the truth.

'Someone once said I have a gift for imitation. Why shouldn't I put it to good use and get as much as I can out of life?'

To her surprise, Buller laughed. 'I thought it must be so. Leave us and shut the door,' he ordered the man at the door. Jenna stopped her unpacking and looked up uncertainly, as Job followed Buller's instructions.

'Scaring you is not my intention,' he reassured her after his henchman had left.

'Then what is it you want from me? I have nothing to offer you.'

'On the contrary, you have much to offer.'

'Such as?'

'I intend to run for Parliament. There is a borough in Callington that has had the same landowner acting as their representative for many years. I intend to gain his support. The borough has few voters, all who are beholden to him for their tenancy. Out of fear for losing their homes, they will vote as he suggests. My way to Parliament will be unhindered.'

'I do not see how I can help.'

'If you play your role well, a scandalous incident involving the landowner can be orchestrated and witnessed. Afterwards he will be in my pocket, unless he wants his wife to find out and the sordid affair to become public.'

'You want me to play the whore?'

'Only if you wish to, but it is not necessary. All I need is for you to be found in an uncompromising position with him. I will pay you.'

Jenna picked up her empty basket and put it away. Her family would have revelled in the proposition, she thought.

'How much?'

Buller smiled. 'Enough. You will be well paid.'

Jenna did not reply, choosing to take some bread out of the pantry and set about slicing it.

'This will not be your only job. Someone like you, with your background, will help me greatly. I will be able to manoeuvre the pawns in Parliament to my liking with the use of persuasion and blackmail.'

'How much are you willing to pay for this alliance?' she asked as she set the knife down.

'I will set you up in a house, with fine clothes and a monthly allowance. I think we will work well together.'

Jenna thought of her mother. She would have taken him up on the offer for the money and the life it promised.

'You want me to tease and flirt with the men of your choosing?'

'Yes. I think you have the skill and the beauty to find out a great deal of information that would prove useful to me. You had my nephew eating out of your hand.'

'And in return I will live a pampered life.'

'Indeed. You will live the life of a gentlewoman rather than a poorly paid housekeeper that sleeps with her employer to ensure she keeps her job.'

'I loved him,' she snapped.

'We all know that a woman like you always has her own agenda.'

Jenna smiled as she lifted the knife and pointed it at him. 'You have offered me a life that some would consider,

Judge Buller, but I would rather rot in hell than help you to power.'

Noticing the knife in her hand, Buller stood up. 'You will regret your decision.'

'I will never regret my decision.'

'What do you have to lose? You have nothing here.'

'I have my dignity.'

'You are a thief's spawn.'

'My past does not define me. My family does not define me. I am my own person and I will not be tempted away from the path that I think is right. Leave my home. We have nothing more to say.'

Judge Buller's arrogance did not falter. 'You are too intelligent to use that knife against me. If I am hurt or killed, you will be brought before the court. You know what people will think. They will say that a poacher's widow took her revenge on the judge who sentenced her husband. You will hang for your crime in front of a cheering crowd.'

Jenna's hand began to shake. She knew he spoke the truth and that no one would believe her defence.

'Put it down,' he ordered.

Reluctantly, Jenna did as she was told.

'I did not expect this,' said Buller, looking at her with renewed curiosity. 'I am intrigued by your moral stance. If you hold such high morals, why were you masquerading as a gentlewoman at my table?'

Jenna's lips narrowed.

'I see from your face that you are unwilling to tell me. Perhaps I was wrong to investigate you. Perhaps I should have shown more interest in your cousin.' He began to circle her as he studied her. 'I made a few enquiries about him, but they came to nothing.' His eyes turned to slits. 'Who is this man, Trago?' he asked.

Jenna ignored him. Buller grabbed her wrist and shook her, forcing her to look at him. 'Why were you so interested in my art collection?' he demanded.

Jenna's tone was measured. 'You will learn nothing from me.'

He shook her wrist again. 'Why are you protecting him?'

He would not let her leave unharmed now, she thought, she knew too much. Let him do his worst, she would rather die than betray Jack.

'Tell me,' he ordered.

Defiantly, she looked him in the eye. 'I have nothing to say.'

'Let us see how long your bravery lasts,' shouted Buller as he pulled her arm across the table. He pinned it to the wooden surface and picked up her knife in his hand. He placed the blade onto the pale skin of her wrist.

'Tell me who Trago is!'

'Never!' she screamed back at him.

Buller, his eyes bulging with menace, his jowls quivering with anger, pulled her arm closer, forcing her further across the table. 'Tell me or, as God is my witness, I will cut your hand off!'

Jenna looked him in the eye. 'Do your worst,' she replied calmly. 'You will learn nothing from me.'

Something moved in the corner of her eye. A hand, holding a musket, appeared from behind the pantry door. Buller saw her eyes widen and sensed they had company. He froze.

'You heard the lady,' said a man's voice. 'She does not want to answer your questions.' Jack exited the smuggler's tunnel and stepped into the room. 'Your smuggling days have come to an end, Buller.'

Buller's grip loosened slightly and Jenna pulled her arm

free, but her eyes were on Jack. He was here and standing before her. His skin tanned from his travels, his face shadowed with stubble, his body so close she could almost reach out and touch him.

'Jack!' she whispered.

'I am back, although this was not the welcome I envisaged,' he replied, not taking his eyes from his intended target. 'Drop the knife, Buller.'

Aware that Jack's musket was poised to shoot him, Buller reluctantly did as he was told and slowly straightened. Jack glanced at Jenna and she wondered what he saw. Was it someone he cared for, or someone he was still disappointed in? His expression told her nothing.

Buller licked his dry lips. 'There are men waiting for me outside. All I have to do is shout.'

'They are involved in the smuggling too, Jack,' Jenna warned. 'I saw them both on the beach the night I took part.'

'I know they are,' replied Jack. 'Don't worry. Captain Henley will be arriving shortly with some dragoons. You should make such visits more clandestine and find better company to keep. Coming home to find the Blake brothers in my garden was enough to make me realise that Jenna may be in trouble.'

Jack lifted his musket higher and aimed it firmly at Buller's chest.

Buller dared not move. 'I am just visiting a grieving woman. There is no law against that.'

'A woman whose hand you were trying to cut off.'

'That is only your word against the word of a judge.'

'A woman whose brother you arranged to have killed.'

'You can't prove anything. My word holds more weight than any witnesses you can muster.'

'You may be right where Silas's death is concerned. Luck was on your side the day he was beaten, as there are no witnesses willing to condemn you. However, I do have enough evidence to prove that you are no better than the poachers and thieves you sentence to hang.'

Buller glanced uneasily at the musket in his hand. Jack lifted it higher to the same level as Buller's head.

'At this very moment your house is being searched. Ten stolen paintings have already been identified by three museum curators who have accompanied me from France and Italy. Your wife is most distressed with all the upheaval, although, despite her tears, she was happy to tell us where you were. "He is visiting a grieving parishioner," she said, "who lives in the Captain's Cottage up on the hill." Your wife was most helpful.'

'Perhaps we can come to some sort of an arrangement.'

'I make no deals with men like you.'

'Everyone can be tempted.'

'Not everyone,' retorted Jenna.

Buller lurched towards her. His great bulk knocked her to the floor and he quickly trapped her neck with his arm. He held her against him like a shield, tightening his hold and draining the breath from her.

'Let me go, or I will strangle the life out of her!' he warned.

Jenna frantically pulled at his arm to be able to breathe, but like a snake around her neck it only constricted further.

Jack lowered the musket. 'Let her go.'

Buller loosened his hold slightly, allowing Jenna to gasp for air. 'When I am able to leave, I will let her go,' he promised.

Jack was unimpressed. 'The dragoons are coming and you have nowhere to run.' He was right. Jenna also heard the rhythmic thunder of horses' hooves and soldiers' boots as they approached.

Buller stood up and edged towards the door, dragging Jenna with him.

'Get me out of here. Now!' Buller snarled. Shouts and musket fire outside signalled the dragoons' arrival. A skirmish ensued as Job and Amos attempted to fight back. Growing increasingly desperate, Buller tightened his grip around Jenna's neck again, forcing her to claw, wide-eyed at his arm for breath. She saw Jack's concern and it scared her even more than anything that had gone before.

'Let her breathe and I will show you a means of escape,' said Jack. Buller's arm loosened slightly. 'The tunnel is your only route and will take you to the beach. Let her go now and you will be able to escape faster.'

Buller considered the offer, his eyes locked with Jack's. Outside, they could hear Amos shouting profanities as he fought the dragoons. He sounded as if he was doing well, until a single musket fire silenced him. Job Blake burst into the room, shattering the silence within, and immediately set about blocking the door with a sideboard.

'You are losing the battle and time is running out,' taunted Jack. 'Let her go, Buller.'

Buller slipped a pig-sticking knife from his boot and held it against Jenna's throat. 'Follow me and I'll slit her like a pig,' he said, before pulling Jenna with him into the tunnel below.

They half fell, half stumbled down the ladder, landing in a painful heap at the bottom. Above Jenna heard Job charging Jack and Jack's musket firing, but the fight continued telling her the shot must have missed. Buller pulled her to standing and prodded her neck with the cold steel of his knife.

'Remember what I said. I have no qualms about killing

you,' warned Buller, before lowering it, grabbing her hand and dragging her into the darkness of the tunnel ahead.

Cold, damp rock scraped their elbows and banged their heads as they felt their way towards the beach. Several times Jenna tried to hang back in the hope that Jack was following, but the sound of fighting above still continued as the dragoons tried to knock down the door. The further they travelled, the quieter the sounds of life above ground grew, until only the drip, drip of distant water threading its way through the rock provided the backdrop to the sound of their laboured breaths.

With no candle to light their way, the tunnel was pitch-black. Jenna would have felt totally alone, as if buried alive, if it was not for the painful grasp she felt on her hand. The solid rock seemed to press down upon them. The air was stale for want of a breeze and the temperature seemed unnaturally warm. Buller paused. He was breathless and his hand had grown wet with perspiration.

'Which way?' he asked with a tremor in his voice. Jenna could hear his fear and decided to use it to her advantage.

'Let me go first,' she offered, 'but I will need both hands to feel my way.'

'I am not a fool. If I let you go you will leave me in this coffin alone.'

'Then hold on to my skirt. I cannot help you if you do not let me go first.'

She felt him grab the back of her dress before reluctantly releasing her hand.

'Be quick. I want to get out of here,' he muttered.

Jenna turned and slowly felt her way. From memory the tunnel would become narrower before it got wider again. She glanced behind her, but the tunnel remained so black she could not even see Buller's great bulk following her. She moved on slowly, careful not to trip on the uneven ground or catch her forehead on the overhanging rock above.

A single step in the ground jolted her. It was enough for her to recognise in which part of the tunnel she was in. She recalled that she was only a few steps away from the narrow part of the tunnel, just before the chiselled steps that led down to the sea. Now was the time to make her escape. She took hold of her dress and yanked it hard, ripping it from his hand.

She followed the tunnel as fast as she could, blindly feeling her way towards the narrow opening. Jenna climbed through and pressed her body into an alcove in the hope he would pass her by. Buller followed her, cursing and shouting, until he banged his head with a sickening thud. His cursing stopped and silence descended. She knew he was out there somewhere in the dark. She could hear his groaning as he tried to rock away the pain.

Jenna's sharp hearing pinpointed the sound of Buller's knife dropping and bouncing on the rock at his feet. His groaning ceased and changed to laboured breathing, which grew more rapid with his mounting panic. He called her name, but she did not answer.

A minute or two passed, both listening out for each other's breathing, trying to work out where the other one was. A sound from far away echoed towards them. Jenna lifted her gaze and saw a soft glow of light approaching. Buller saw it too. Someone was following them, but who? Jack or Job Blake? A man's dark silhouette appeared, his head slightly bowed, his tricorn hat protecting him from the jutting rocks above. The light he carried grew in intensity, almost blinding them.

Jenna was forced to shield her eyes. She could see Buller clearly now as he straightened to meet the newcomer. Relief swept over her when she saw that it was Jack. Without uttering a word, Jack put down the lantern and lunged for Buller, dragging him towards him by his neck cloth. Buller resisted and they fell against the wall, punching and rolling to gain the advantage, before standing and punching again.

The tunnel was so narrow that at times their blended silhouettes blocked out all the light from the lantern. Fearing Buller would find his knife and use it on Jack, Jenna retraced her steps. She knelt down and frantically searched the ground. At times their feet came perilously close to treading on her outstretched fingers, whilst their punches flew through the air above her head. Finally she found it in the shadows and stood up, holding it tightly in her hand. She pressed the unforgiving tip in the small of Buller's back and warned him she had a knife. Buller turned to grab it, but his hand never reached hers. Jack's fist caught him on the jaw and knocked him to the ground.

Jack dropped to his knees, tore off Buller's cravat and began to tie his wrists.

'Are you hurt?' he asked her as he pulled roughly at the cloth to knot it.

Jenna shook her head.

'Then grab a candle from my pocket and go to the beach. I will meet you there later.'

'I want to go with you,' said Jenna, reluctant to leave him.

'Leave,' he commanded. 'We will talk later, I promise.'

She hesitated, afraid that Buller would attempt to fight back when he came round.

Jack saw her hesitation. 'The Blake brothers are dead and it is not a pretty sight. I don't want you to see them.' Jenna still did not move. 'Besides, if you do not go for your own safety, then go for mine. Buller knows that you are my weakness and he could use you against me. I need to take him back to the Captain's Cottage and hand him over to Henley. Then this business will finally be over.'

Jenna needed no further persuasion. Taking a candle from his pocket, she shared the light from his lantern. Their eyes met above the new flame. His as black as his hair, with a glint of gold reflected in their depths. His beautiful eyes were unreadable.

'Take this knife,' she said passing it to him. Their fingers briefly touched sending a thrill though her veins. She saw his eyes flicker. What was he thinking? She wished she could read his mind as well as he could read hers. Buller groaned as he began to wake.

'We will talk later,' he told her. Reluctantly, she turned away and followed the tunnel towards the roar of the sea.

Enoch entered the small cottage and surveyed the room.

'I see Buller put up quite a struggle before they took him away,' he remarked, noticing the upturned furniture littering the room.

'Cornered animals usually do,' replied Jack, righting a chair and preparing to leave.

'I have just come from Buller's home. It has provided us with more evidence than we could possibly have hoped for.'

'Such as?' asked Jack.

Enoch smiled. 'Buller was fastidious at keeping records. We found a large book where he has logged every aspect of his free trading. He has documented every purchase, every smuggler involved, every payment made. It is a work of art in its own right. If he is not found guilty on the paintings as evidence, he will be found guilty by his own penmanship. It is over, Jack. Your reason for being here has come to an end.'

'It is not over for me, Enoch,' said Jack, making for the door. 'I have someone I still need to see.'

# Chapter Twenty-Three

Jenna walked impatiently along the water's edge where the tide stroked the golden sands of Tudor Cove. When she reached the far end of the beach, she turned and retraced her footprints that were already fast disappearing under the incoming tide. Waiting for Jack to arrive was intolerable and did not become any easier even when the commotion coming from the Captain's Cottage finally quietened and most of the dragoons had left.

She couldn't quite believe that Jack was alive and that he was home. She was desperate to see him again even if it was only to prove that he was not a figment of her imagination.

She heard the sound of a horse galloping in the distance. Shielding her eyes against the sun, Jenna searched the cliff edge. She expected to see a dragoon departing, but instead a lone rider was heading her way. She guessed from its tack that it was a dragoon's horse, but she knew with certainty that the rider was Jack.

Clouds of dry sand rose up behind his horse, until he neared the water's edge where the sand became firmer. Turning his horse, she watched him gallop towards her, allowing his horse a loose rein so it could stretch its head. He looked in a hurry and Jenna began to fear that someone may have been hurt and needed her help. As they approached he reined it in and the horse slowed. Jack, unwilling to wait until it had halted, jumped from his saddle and ran towards her. Jenna found herself laughing as he scooped her up into his embrace and held her tightly against his body. She wrapped her arms around him and buried her face into the curve of his neck. She savoured the heat of his skin against her own, a sensation she had been afraid she would never experience again. Slowly he lowered her body, until she felt the sand beneath her feet again. They stood in a silent embrace, their hearts beating in unison within their chests, their breaths shallow and hurried, the warmth of their bodies shared to ward off the chill from the exposed beach. Jenna did not want it to end.

'Have they taken Buller away?' she asked, fearful Jack would have to leave again.

'They have. And the bodies of the Blake brothers.'

Jenna shivered in his arms.

Jack released her and looked at her intently. 'And you? Are you well?'

'Better now that you are home again. Enoch thought you were dead,' she added lamely.

Jack's horse snorted beside them, demanding attention. He took the reins and held them leisurely in his hand. They retraced her steps along the water's edge.

'I did not know that until this morning. I told Enoch I planned to return on the *Fortitude* as it made regular crossings across the Channel. I did not give a date and was unaware that it had sunk. I did not know that he thought I was on board.'

She glanced at him and found he was watching her. She wanted to still be in his embrace. She had waited long enough for it.

Instead she said, 'Your death weighed heavy on him.'

'So I have learned. And you?' he asked, his face serious.

'What do you think?' she grumbled. 'You delayed coming home. How were your travels? England must seem rather dull compared to the sights you have seen.'

'You are upset with me.'

She stared at the wet sand in her path, wary about how much to say.

'I was distraught when he told me he thought you would not be returning. I still feel it now.'

'You were very brave at the cottage.'

She did not want his praise. 'It is easier to be brave when you feel you have nothing left. I believed I would never see you again.'

'I did plan to leave earlier but I met someone at the port and it delayed my parting.'

Jenna's steps slowed. So he had met a Frenchwoman, she thought. He was back, but suddenly it felt as if he were still on the other side of the water.

She dared not look at him. 'This "someone", do you plan to bring them to England?'

'I think they would prefer to stay in France.'

'Do you plan to go back there to be with her?'

'The person I met was a man, not a woman.'

Jenna stopped again and looked at him. He looked amused. She, on the other hand, was not.

'Who was so important that they stopped you from coming home?'

'Your brother, Jenna. I found your brother.'

Jenna felt her world tilt. 'You found Mark?' she asked in astonishment.

'Yes. There was a man called Cartwright working in Calais. I was on board and about to leave, but disembarked to talk to him. At first he was wary of my interest but when I mentioned you he invited me to his home. He told me he worked on an English ship for many years, but met a girl whilst in a French port and never returned to sea. He is married, with three children. He is happy, Jenna, and he is well. He wanted me to tell you that he has often thought of you.'

*Mark is alive and he is well.*

Jenna found herself smiling. 'I am an aunt again.'

'An aunt to two boys and a girl.'

Jenna's voice almost broke with joy. 'Two boys and a girl,' she echoed. 'You delayed your parting to bring me this news?'

Jack nodded and smiled.

It was a kind thing for him to do and her hopes rose a little.

'Thank you,' she said as she began walking again. This time her steps felt a little lighter. 'What now, Jack? What are your plans?' She had to ask this. His future was her future.

'My work here is done. We have enough evidence to convict Buller and the Blake brothers' hold is broken. I have no reason to stay now.'

Jenna's heart sank. He had said it. He was leaving.

'When will you leave?'

'Soon, I hope.'

'Where will you go?'

'I'm going back to Zennor. I no longer have the heart to be a thief-taker. When I started I wanted to bring an end to the free traders, but at the moment it is an impossible task. Laws need to change and I am not a man who wants to spend his life in politics.' Jack looked at her. 'I know now that I want to settle. Enoch wanted me to go to France and Italy, and asked me to name my price, so I did.'

'What was your price?'

'A house and enough land to support it near Zennor.'

She tilted her chin and smiled bravely. 'You will be in need of a housekeeper.'

'I will not.'

Jenna turned away to look out to sea so he could not see the tears welling up in her eyes. She knew it might come to this, but his decisive answer still surprised her.

'Do you want to know why?' asked Jack, stepping in front of her.

'Why?' she asked reluctantly, refusing to look at him.

He lifted a stray lock of her hair. 'I have plans to get me a wife,' he said, watching it curl around his fingers.

'A wife?' whispered Jenna as he stepped closer. She dared to look at him. The corner of his lips curved into a gentle smile. She felt something pool and melt deep inside her as she watched his mouth form the word, 'Yes.'

The incoming tide rolled over her feet, but she did not care.

'Do you have someone in mind?' she asked breathlessly.

'Yes,' he replied, releasing her hair. 'Would you like me to tell you about her?'

Jenna slowly nodded and closed her eyes. His husky voice was filling her thoughts as he gently traced the curve of her cheek with his touch.

'She has big doe-like eyes the colour of rosewood,' he mused quietly. Jenna opened her eyes to find him gazing at her mouth. 'And she has a gentle smile which makes me feel ten feet tall when I am the one responsible for putting it there.' His fingers traced a path down her neck to her breast. Jenna shivered with the thrill of his touch. 'She has a courageous, kind heart which I want no other man to claim.'

Drunk on his words, Jenna swayed towards him. She felt his embrace wrap around her. He pressed a kiss on the top of her head. 'And she has a sharp wit,' he breathed into her hair, 'and she is trusting ...' He tilted her chin so she would look at him. 'Although she needs to learn to trust me a little more than she does.'

'What is this woman called?' asked Jenna as he began to kiss the curve of her neck. 'I don't know if you are asking me to marry you, or just being cruel,' said Jenna, smiling.

'If you think I am being cruel,' he murmured between kisses, 'then I assume that means you might like the idea of being my wife.'

She tilted her head to expose the other side of her neck to him. 'Are you sure it is what you want? I believed Silas over you.'

Jack moved to her lips to kiss away her last remark and then cupped her face in his hands to look at her. 'How can I not forgive a woman who is willing to have her hand chopped off for me? Although I had already forgiven you before the ship had even set sail for France. I am not a man who can speak words of love easily, but it does not mean I do not feel the emotion deeply. I love you, Jenna. And although I tried to resist falling in love with you, I failed miserably very soon after meeting you.'

'You have spoken words of love very well.'

'You have brought them out of me. Will you be my wife? You have not answered me yet. Should I be concerned?'

Jenna smiled. How could this handsome, good man ever doubt she would accept? 'I was once warned that if I did not mind my ways a thief-taker would come to get me. I did not know then that I would want to go willingly. Yes, Jack, I want nothing more than to be your wife.'

He took both her hands in his. They stood for a moment, their fingers caressing, the horse forgotten by their side. Another wave rolled in and soaked their feet making them laugh.

'Come, your feet are wet,' said Jack. 'You will catch a chill.'

He brought his horse closer and stooped, cradling his hands so she could place her foot in them to mount. Jenna lifted her hem and placed her foot in the makeshift stirrup. They looked at each other and smiled, an unspoken memory passing between them of the time they had first met. Moments later, he was sitting behind her on the horse with his arm about her waist. He held her close and caressed her cheek with his own.

'I love you, Jenna,' he whispered against the corner of her lips. 'I have missed you these past months.'

Jenna leant against him, letting her head fall back onto his shoulder. 'I have missed you, Jack. You will never know how much I love you. It is too deep and too powerful to put into words.'

His eyes darkened. 'Perhaps you can show me tonight, for tomorrow we will leave for Zennor.'

'Zennor,' Jenna murmured, enjoying the sound of the place they would make their home together. 'What is it like there?'

'It is south-west from here. It is small and beautiful, although isolated.'

Jenna's smile broadened. 'Isolation is good,' she said quietly, enjoying his warmth about her.

Jack kissed her hair again and held her tight.

'When did you realise you had failed to resist me?' asked Jenna, warm with happiness and content to bask in the moment.

Jack did not answer straight away, as their bodies swayed together in tune with the horse beneath them. Eventually his soft husky tone voiced his thoughts. 'When you first smiled at me from the top of the wall. I thought then we were two sides of the same soul. Now I know it to be true. Let us go home. I have a burning need to have you.'

'And I you.'

'I am glad. We have been apart for far too long.'

# Author's Note

*English smuggling in the 18th century*

As a result of ever increasing punitive taxation on luxury goods, the archaic collection system of taxes and successive costly wars, opportunists in southern England expanded their smuggling activities to almost industrial proportions. During the 17th and 18th centuries, smuggling of highly taxed items became part of everyday life and at one period the amount of tea, tobacco, silks, spices and spirits smuggled into the southern counties of England exceeded the amount brought in through legitimate routes. Cornwall was an ideal county for the trade, as its coastline, which stretches for more than 400 miles, provided ideal coves and beaches to land the contraband.

At the age of 21, William Pitt, the younger, became an MP. At the age of 24, he became the youngest Prime Minister in British history. Acting on a committee's recommendations, Pitt reduced the high duties that encouraged smuggling and simplified the customs and excise duties. It was the start of the decline in smuggling, but it would not be until after the Napoleonic wars were over, and a more effective coastal prevention service was in place, that smuggling became less viable and declined further. The heyday of smuggling silks, tea, tobacco and spirits was over by 1840, and although smuggling continues to this day, the clandestine trade, which in the past involved large numbers of the local community, was never the same again.

# Thank you

Thank you for reading *The Thief's Daughter*. I feel honoured that you chose to read it when there are so many other books available to you. I really hope you enjoyed following Jenna and Jack's journey, the challenges they faced and the love that blossomed between them.

Two years ago, while walking the coastal path, I came across Pepper Cove. Its peculiar name came from the smuggled spices brought into Cornwall under the cover of darkness. The narrow, rocky inlet became the inspiration for this novel.

It has taken over two years, from conception to publication, for *The Thief's Daughter* to be out in the big wide world. From being its creator and caretaker, it is now out of my control and I must admit it feels similar to the day I sent my children to school for the first time. Familiar anxieties have resurfaced. Will it be accepted? Will it be liked? So it is always wonderful to receive feedback from the people the novel was created for.

However, a reader's feedback has so much more value than soothing my neurotic anxieties. Readers' positive comments and recommendations, or lack of them, will help determine the success or failure of a novel by influencing how the fiction distributors promote a book and what other readers choose to purchase. Decisions to publish more novels by the same author will be based on past successes or failures.

With this in mind, if you enjoyed *The Thief's Daughter*, I would be so grateful if you could take a moment to write a review on any, or all, of the following websites: Amazon, Apple iBooks, Kobo or Goodreads. A review can be as short as two words or much longer if you are so inclined.

The present and future readers of *The Thief's Daughter* are its new custodians as your opinion really does matter.

Thank you again for taking the time to read it. I do hope you enjoyed the story, because I enjoyed writing it for you to read.

Love,

Victoria Cornwall

# About the Author

Victoria Cornwall grew up on a dairy farm in Cornwall. As a child, she had a dog, an albino rabbit and a disabled hen as her pets. Add an adopted lamb and fifty yellow, fluffy chicks which arrived at the farm each year and you have an idea of her childhood. Victoria can trace her Cornish roots as far back as the 18th century and it is this background and heritage which is the inspiration for her Cornish based novels.

Victoria is married and has two grown up children. She likes to read and write historical fiction with a strong background story, but at its heart is the unmistakable emotion, even pain, of loving someone.

Following a fulfilling twenty-five year career as a nurse, a change in profession finally allowed her the time to write. She is a member of the Romantic Novelists' Association and the Historical Novel Society.

*The Thief's Daughter* is her debut novel and the first in her series of Cornish based novels. The second book in the series, *The Captain's Daughter*, will be released soon.

Follow Victoria on:
www.victoriacornwall.com
www.twitter.com/VickieCornwall
www.facebook.com/victoria.cornwall.75

# More Choc Lit

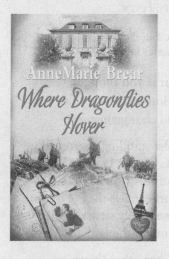

## Where Dragonflies Hover
*AnneMarie Brear*

**Sometimes a glimpse into the past can help make sense of the future ...**

Everyone thinks Lexi is crazy when she falls in love with Hollingsworth House – a crumbling old Georgian mansion in Yorkshire – and nobody more so than her husband, Dylan. But there's something very special about the place, and Lexi can sense it.

Whilst exploring the grounds she stumbles across an old diary and, within its pages, she meets Allie – an Australian nurse working in France during the First World War.

Lexi finally realises her dream of buying Hollingsworth but her obsession with the house leaves her marriage in tatters. In the lonely nights that follow, Allie's diary becomes Lexi's companion, comforting her in moments of darkness and pain. And as Lexi reads, the nurse's scandalous connection to the house is revealed ...

Available in paperback from all good bookshops and online stores. Visit www.choc-lit.com for details.

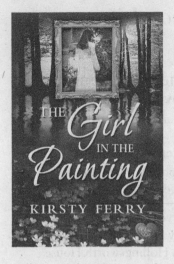

# The Girl in the Painting

*Kirsty Ferry*

Book 2 in the Rossetti
Mysteries series

**What if you thought
you knew a secret that
could change history?**

Whilst standing engrossed in
her favourite Pre-Raphaelite
painting – Millais's Ophelia
– Cori catches the eye of Tate
gallery worker, Simon, who is immediately struck by her
resemblance to the red-haired beauty in the famous artwork.

The attraction is mutual, but Cori has other things on
her mind. She has recently acquired the diary of Daisy, a
Victorian woman with a shocking secret. As Cori reads, it
soon becomes apparent that Daisy will stop at nothing to be
heard, even outside of the pages of her diary …

Will Simon stick around when life becomes increasingly
spooky for Cori, as she moves ever closer to uncovering the
truth about Daisy's connection to the girl in her favourite
painting?

Available in paperback from all good
bookshops and online stores. Visit
www.choc-lit.com for details.